MARKED MAN

MARKED MAN

A Joe Gunther Novel

ARCHER MAYOR

MINOTAUR
BOOKS
NEW YORK

First published in the United States by Minotaur Books, an imprint of St. Martin's Publishing Group

MARKED MAN. Copyright © 2021 by Archer Mayor. All rights reserved. Printed in the United States of America. For information, address St. Martin's Publishing Group, 120 Broadway, New York, NY 10271.

www.minotaurbooks.com

Library of Congress Cataloging-in-Publication Data

Names: Mayor, Archer, author.
Title: Marked man / Archer Mayor.
Description: First edition. | New York : Minotaur Books, 2021. |
    Series: Joe Gunther series ; 32
Identifiers: LCCN 2021015938 | ISBN 9781250224163 (hardcover) |
    ISBN 9781250224170 (ebook)
Subjects: GSAFD: Mystery fiction. | Suspense fiction.
Classification: LCC PS3563.A965 M39 2021 | DDC 813/.54—dc23
LC record available at https://lccn.loc.gov/2021015938

Our books may be purchased in bulk for promotional, educational, or business use. Please contact your local bookseller or the Macmillan Corporate and Premium Sales Department at 1-800-221-7945, extension 5442, or by e-mail at MacmillanSpecialMarkets@macmillan.com.

First Edition: 2021

10 9 8 7 6 5 4 3 2 1

ACKNOWLEDGMENTS

This is a book bursting with characters, covering two New England states, and spanning several decades—a lot of moving parts, as a mechanic might put it, all of which I hope you will find move smoothly as one. Given my lifelong interest in human nature, and with the ongoing and stalwart encouragement of my supportive readers, I have therefore plunged ahead, but not without the help, advice, and insight of those below, all of whom were invaluable with their counsel. My most profound thanks.

Steve Shapiro

Wayne Gallagher

Ray Walker

Castle Freeman

Corin Rogers

Erik Johnson

Daveq Anderson

BDCC

Keith Kahla

Wally Mangel

Margot Zalkind Mayor

John Martin

Scout Mayor

Jeff Trombly

Bliss Dayton

Robert McKenna

Adam Grinold

Ledyard Bank

Terri Walton

MARKED MAN

CHAPTER ONE

Warren Kitzmiller looked around the large, almost empty morgue, tugging at the sleeve of his starched white lab coat and painfully aware he should be presenting a more detached demeanor. He was standing alone beside a flayed, cold, gray corpse, spread out in a grotesque parody of a post-Thanksgiving feast. It was supine on a waist-high steel table, tempting the young medical student with an unacceptable choice of either dissecting more of its anatomy as assigned, or upending the table and consigning the gristle to the nearest hazmat receptacle.

Unacceptable, given that this was medical school, where people took note of your visceral reactions to such scenarios.

Fortunately, the only other live person in the room right now was a female fellow student, far off and too absorbed with her own cadaver to notice him. They were coincidentally there at night, after dinner, each logging extra solo time with their so-called patients—although Warren hoped any future patients of his would look a lot livelier than this one. Right now, his ambitions lay in family medicine, not forensic pathology.

It was late in his two-month anatomy block, and he was having trouble processing the avalanche of details. Every day began with a lecture concerning a certain body section, followed by his group of six repairing to this room and "their" specimen—or what was left of it—to slice and prod and fiddle and talk about the inner workings of that section, guided by various illustrated anatomy atlases and the roving instructor. Thankfully, they'd all started with the body's back. That was pretty easy, with the big muscles, minimal nerves and vessels. Also, the cadaver had to be prone, thereby eliminating surreptitious glances at the man's face or penis. It lessened the impression of settling down to a meal on a fellow human being. As it was, the smell of preservative in the room was cloying, memorable, and stuck in one's nostrils, ironically including during meals later at the cafeteria.

Kitzmiller's study group had been forging ahead dutifully. By now, the body was faceup. More personal, no doubt, but also more complex. More daunting. Overriding most initial squeamishness. Almost.

The initial assignments had been straightforward: lower extremities, upper extremities. Warren had managed those well enough, even with the inherent jostling of six aspiring doctors, equipped with scalpels and trying to get in on the action while juggling those anatomy atlases.

Things had ramped up afterward, moving from the axilla to the thorax, abdomen, and pelvis. That's when Warren had started coming in after hours—the lab was open 24-7—revisiting the ground they'd been fumbling with earlier.

He bent at the waist and peered at "his" corpse's neck area. Given what flesh they'd whittled away so far, even considering the growing familiarity, the entire process had entered into another realm of weird.

"Goddamn traffic," Eddie growled, even now—so many months after regaining his freedom—haunted by the absence of gray walls, steel bars, an endless orchestra of lock buzzers, and the jarring clash of slamming metal doors. He wondered if this is what aquarium fish felt like when they were finally released back into the ocean—part free; part bait.

"Oh, Dad. This is nothing. You just refuse to get used to it."

"Can't get used to a lot of things."

The older man craned his neck to see more of the skyscrapers they were passing, many completely unknown to him. His daughter, Marie, was driving by three of the taller buildings in Providence— One Financial Plaza, Fifty Kennedy Plaza, and his favorite, the Industrial National Bank, universally called the Superman Building for its resemblance to Clark Kent's *Daily Planet* jobsite. Eddie Moscone didn't comment about having also seen the building housing the FBI office down a side street. Those kinds of references, she didn't need. Marie had a new and gentler image of him, and he didn't want to disabuse her of it.

"It's a new world, Dad," she continued, easily negotiating the traffic on her way toward the Federal Hill district, where he was headed for lunch. It had snowed earlier, but minimally, and typical of a seaport town's warmer air, none of it had stuck except in a few well-shaded crannies. "Not like it used to be. I mean, things've changed like nobody's business. You ask Fredo about it when you meet up. He'll tell you, if he hasn't already."

Fredo Sindaco was Eddie's lunch date, and his second cousin, not to mention a fellow soldier from back in the day. Back in the life. Their conversation wasn't going to be about the onslaught of modernity. Eddie had better things to discuss. He'd been out of the joint for ten months. He was getting restless.

But again, need to know, need to know. And Marie just needed to know her old man was back home and minding his manners.

Earlier, the anatomy study group had come up with Wilbur as a nickname—in violation of hospital policy to never name your bodies. It had felt innocent enough, but by now, Warren was grasping the thinking behind the anonymity policy.

Wilbur, whose neck and face only remained to be exposed, seemed downright discomfited by what he'd endured, as if someone had stripped him naked and pinned him down in his sleep. With his neck on a metal block, his head extended back to expose his throat, and his eyes partially open, Wilbur was looking betrayed by people he'd once trusted.

The school had tried to forestall this moment of truth. Whether because this was the University of Vermont, located in a city with socialist leanings, no less, or because a heightened sensitivity was trending across the profession, Warren didn't know. But his first-day introduction to this anatomy block had rivaled the formalities preceding a debutante ball, minus the need for a corsage. In a formal ceremony at the semester's dawn, the students had been introduced to their subjects, lectured about how these patients had given themselves to science, and otherwise been told that any comparisons between cadaveric volunteers and, say, an oversized Christmas goose—or any other juvenile allusion—would be considered grounds for reprimand.

Warren, heeding the company line, had nodded solemnly, keeping all world-weary cynicism to himself.

Now that no one was watching him, however, bent over his subject as if whispering into his ear, Warren could acknowledge Wilbur's commitment, and Warren's own embarrassment for being cavalier. Wilbur had been generous, uncomplaining, intriguing, and even surprising at times, more than fulfilling his end of trying to make Warren a better doctor. As with a stranger opening up in conversation, this older man had revealed things about himself that transcended the intimate.

It was therefore with genuine and newfound respect that Warren mouthed almost soundlessly into Wilbur's alabaster ear, "Thank you, sir. You've been really great about this."

It wasn't over yet. They'd exposed the neck hours before, as a group. The face and brain were scheduled for last, the brain in its own teaching segment, for obvious reasons. But Warren had found the neck challenging enough, which explained his presence here now, to retrace what they'd done earlier.

The human anatomy has some inordinately well-designed bells and whistles in the area of self-preservation. There are bones to protect vital organs, redundancies to ensure survival after amputation or destruction, and even regeneration to replace parts whose functions are irreplaceable. But in the neck, it all comes to naught. Yes, the spinal cord is tucked into the bony spine, and the esophagus is as tough as an elephant's hide, and all those surrounding strap muscles do people like Arnold Schwarzenegger proud. But, as Warren could not resist thinking, scalpel in hand, none of it stood much chance against the single sweep of a well-handled sword.

He took a deep breath, his small blade not quite resting against Wilbur's flesh, high up and under the old man's slightly stubbly chin. It might have been in imitation only—Warren wasn't actually cutting what had already been opened—but he wanted to act out the real incision as closely as possible.

The neck's challenge was that it resembled a sausage stuffed with cables. Fine that everything ran top to bottom. Granted. But blood vessels, lymph nodes, glands, tubules, musculature, cartilage, ligaments? All of it packed into an area you could wrap in both hands.

If one needed a single, very compact example of the human body's miraculous ability to combine form and function, this was a good place to start. The neck was a thick, bulging, hypercritical power cord, literally linking heart and mind, but lying perilously exposed between two armor-clad factory buildings.

No wonder the school put it off until late in the anatomy block.

Letting out a small puff of air, Warren gingerly applied the pad of his index finger to the back of the blade and pantomimed his first cut.

Fredo looked up as the restaurant door opened, his attention caught as much by the cold draft as by his cousin's recognizable body shape, even bundled as it was in a bulky, calf-length, black leather coat.

Old-school, he thought, touching his coffee mug and looking down briefly. That was Eddie, through and through. For that matter, it spoke of Fredo himself, whose own black leather coat was draped over the back of his chair. Just a couple of swaybacked warhorses, almost ready for the glue factory.

That was okay with him. It was as much part of the tradition as the dead wiseguys on barbershop floors, or the dandy bosses being hustled off to jail, their cuff links sparkling in the flashbulbs as grim-faced cops held open the doors. People like Eddie and Fredo weren't those. They were the underlings. Not made men, foot soldiers, or even *cugines*. They were connected, but no more than regular grunts working off the books—reliable, trustworthy, unambitious, always available, never curious.

People who knew their place, understood the natural order, and were disposable.

Fredo saw that more clearly than his second cousin and best friend, Eddie. That had always been a difference between them, as they'd worked the jobs they'd been assigned through the decades—watching, driving, moving things around without question. Fredo alone had known it would eventually peter out, that the loyalty demanded ran in one direction only and would result in no benefits. Not for men like him and Eddie.

As the ironfisted influence of organized crime atrophied from corruption, competition, and better federal laws, its structural integrity began flying apart like a spinning sphere's through centrifugal force. The smallest, lightest, most peripheral parts of that, like Fredo and Eddie, had been the first to be cast away.

Nevertheless, despite the hard-hearted logic of such inevitability, Eddie had stubbornly expected *something*, to use his word, especially after getting out of the can. Maybe the Outfit wasn't what it used to be, he'd argued, but he'd given it his entire life.

Fredo looked up as Eddie shrugged off his coat and got ready to sit. Maybe the higher-ups could still call in markers, he thought. But not nobodies like them. They were cosmic dust, floating in space. Fredo had planned ahead and now lived in a small apartment on the edge of Pawtucket, north of Providence. Eddie lived with his daughter and her family, in a crowded high-rise.

"Hey, cuz," he addressed the newcomer. "How ya doin'?"

"Doin'," Eddie answered shortly, looking around for a waiter so he could order coffee.

"How's Marie?"

Eddie eyed him briefly before responding sarcastically, "Really?"

Fredo let him sort himself out in silence, balancing his frustration against attracting a waiter's attention, and finally placing an order—none too graciously. Fortunately, they were not merely in Providence, but Federal Hill, a neighborhood the Mob had once utterly controlled. Here, abruptness was taken as a regional norm, even if those days were but a memory today.

He and Eddie may have been related, known each other all their lives, and pursued the same line of work—if what they'd done could be called a profession. But they had distinctly different karmic DNAs.

Eddie adhered to ancient codes of loyalty, trust, righteousness, and caste. Fredo was more of a practical fatalist. As a result, where life's surprises usually caused him to only raise a weary eyebrow, they brought outrage and fury to his cousin.

"Been burning up Marie's computer?" Fredo asked, aiming Eddie toward the only topic he'd be discussing anyhow—what Fredo had come to see as his life-support obsession.

"Damn thing's too slow. I keep askin' her to increase its download speed."

Fredo laughed. "Listen to you. You're gonna have to pierce your nose, you keep talkin' like that. Cool dude."

Eddie's coffee arrived. He took a swig and cupped his hands around the mug. "Whatever."

"It's gotta be better than schlepping to the library every day," Fredo suggested, hoping to lighten his mood. "Or the senior center to check out the babes."

Eddie was barely listening. "I guess."

"How 'bout your pet project?" Fredo asked. "Ya getting anywhere, or is he still a mystery?"

"He" was Vittorio "Vito" Alfano, the man Eddie had been convicted of dumping into the Providence River, despite barely knowing him. Fredo had never voiced his opinion on the subject, but Alfano was nevertheless dead, Eddie had copped to the crime, and the rest of the world had happily closed the books. Except that Eddie's current version was that he hadn't killed anyone, but had been requested to lie down by the bosses in exchange for a handsome life pension upon his release.

Sadly, the bosses who mattered had since died of drink and fatty foods, while everybody else had been afflicted with amnesia.

According to Eddie.

"Nah," was the response.

Eddie was staring into his mug, as if wishing a solution to miraculously surface from its inky depths. Fredo glanced around at the lively clusters at other tables, the activity at the bar, the comings and goings. This was life in one of New England's biggest cities, a place renowned for crime and corruption in its past, and more recently for the schools, food, urban renovation, and cultural diversity that had always been there in the background, overshadowed by a few decades of misdeeds and mobsters. It made him sad to see his cousin—a good man, if stuck in his ways—so fixated on events and people that were becoming increasingly difficult to remember.

"Maybe you been barking up the wrong tree," Fredo suggested, wanting to tell him to drop the whole thing and get on with his life. "Instead of worrying about who really iced him, ask yourself who ordered him dead in the first place. Vito musta pissed off somebody."

Eddie hitched a shoulder, not looking up. "He was an asshole. That's probably a small army."

But not only was Fredo probably right, Eddie had already made it his life's work to find and confront whoever had orchestrated his downfall.

Fredo continued studying him as he began his usual muttering about combing over old newspaper files. The point of it all eluded Fredo. The two cousins had roughed up a few mopes back when. But nothing beyond that. What was Eddie hoping to do, if and when he finally located a target of his bitterness? Talk him to death?

Fredo therefore waited for Eddie to take another swig of coffee before asking, "You never told me what you were planning for these guys if you ever got one."

Eddie stopped in mid-sentence. "What d'ya think, Fredo? I'm gonna give 'em a kiss?"

"I don't know."

"They'll get what they deserve."

Fredo spoke kindly. "Eddie, we're old men. You're gonna have to shoot 'em. That's messy. Noisy. You even got a piece?"

An odd smile creased Eddie's worn features. "There're other ways. I been boning up. That internet can be a wonderful thing, if you know the right questions," he answered enigmatically, adding, as if echoing an overheard advertisement, "There's a whole world of people who know your pain."

Warren Kitzmiller had gotten into the swing of it by now. It was like any other set of misgivings, usually worse from afar than closer up. Fortunately for him, he'd begun with several advantages. Wilbur had not been fat, nor had he suffered from any last-minute medical interventions, like a direct line into his jugular or an ET tube down his throat, which might have complicated Warren's so-called field. Instead, old Wilbur had just died of a recipe now common among the elderly: dementia, arteriosclerotic cardiovascular disease, hypertension, atrial fibrillation, general deconditioning. Pretty standard stuff.

And, as Warren proceeded, straightforward.

Indeed, this mimed dissection had followed the book, and Warren had become increasingly self-confident, one layer after another. Additionally, since he was now without his fellow students, he could take his time and even gingerly progress beyond simply mimicking, making original incisions of his own, exposing more of Wilbur's inner workings than required by the class.

Which explained his bafflement upon reaching the hyoid bone.

The hyoid, thanks mostly to TV and a few modern, scientifically geeky murder mysteries, had recently emerged into prominence. Small, fragile, unconnected to any other proximate bone, making it unique in the human body, it lives tucked up in the neck's anterior between the larynx and the tongue. It's U-shaped, made of a short straight piece across the front, and two flimsy wings projecting back, called the greater cornua, which are attached by fibrous joints that calcify through the years, eventually making of the U a single rigid whole.

The purpose of this seemingly random piece of the neck's otherwise logically laid-out armor is a little vague, but its popularity in forensics has grown because it breaks easily when brutalized. Wrap your hands or a rope around another person's neck, and you are quite likely to fracture the unoffending hyoid in the process.

A broken hyoid is therefore often cited as evidence of strangulation.

It ain't always so, of course. Hyoids, like karaoke singers, can be of unreliable quality. Some are undeveloped, others asymmetrical, a few become damaged earlier for unrelated reasons.

And, not surprisingly, they don't always break under pressure.

If you do find a fractured hyoid, however, you better explain its cause, which is exactly what Warren suddenly needed to do, because one end of Wilbur's right greater cornua, just where it hovered over the man's deep-lying carotid artery, was clearly broken.

Warren stood back and surveyed the room, discovering that his fellow late-night student had been fortuitously joined by a member of the teaching staff. He caught this woman's attention with a raised hand and beckoned her over, revealing what he'd found.

"What did you observe before making your incision?" she asked, a little more severely than he thought necessary, as if he'd been the one to strangle his patient.

"Nothing." He quickly thought to add, "No contusions, discolorations, lacerations, or other abnormalities. It was just a neck."

She didn't berate him, leaning forward to expose the guilty hyoid more expertly than he had.

"Nevertheless, you see the hemorrhaging here, don't you? Along the underlying strap muscles?"

"Yes."

"That finding is equally relevant. A fractured cornua may not be telling in and of itself. Accompanied by hemorrhaging like this, however, whether external or internal—or both—you're looking at a different creature entirely."

Warren was momentarily stumped. "Like what?"

"A homicide. You've just lost your patient to the medical examiner."

CHAPTER TWO

Joe Gunther studied his thumb under the gooseneck lamp, appraising it carefully. He then opened his desk drawer, extracted a small green tin of Bag Balm ointment, and smeared a bit of the yellow goo onto the small fissure next to the tip of his fingernail. For a lifelong, gently aging Vermonter, winter-related split dry skin was a regional commonplace, as ubiquitous as it could be painful if not addressed in time.

The jury was out on his timing with this one.

The phone rang as he was easing the lid back onto the tin.

"Special Agent Gunther, Vermont Bureau of Investigation. How may I help you?"

There was a playful feminine chuckle at the other end. "Ooh. Just how special are you, Agent Gunther?"

Smiling, he explained, "Memo from on high. Director Allard just got back from a training at Quantico. We're now supposed to amp up the professionalism. We have a small pool running on how long it'll last."

The caller was Beverly Hillstrom, the state medical examiner and Joe's significant other. "What are you betting?" she asked.

"Two weeks. Willy said his time was over as soon as his money went down, so it's probably a self-fulfilling prophecy."

Willy Kunkle was one of three other agents Gunther led in the Brattleboro office, in Vermont's southeast corner. He was their mascot renegade—a PTSD-afflicted cynic, inspired investigator, and not someone Beverly had ever warmed to, despite his talents.

"I'm not surprised," she commented shortly, knowing of Joe's fondness for him.

A New England legend herself, having headed the Office of the Chief Medical Examiner, or OCME, for decades, Beverly was as reputed for her high standards and expectations as Kunkle was for sometimes behaving like the people he arrested.

Joe swiveled in his chair and propped his feet up on the windowsill, admiring the gentle snowfall drifting by outside.

It had been a fluky winter so far, marked by blizzards at one moment and springlike rain at another. A prime example of climate change, for those who believed in it.

"Are you calling on a wild and crazy impulse?" he asked her. "Or is there an ulterior motive lurking?"

"Both," she admitted. "I was missing your voice, so I'm bending protocol to let you in on a small discovery of a professional nature."

Their jobs kept them in separate corners of the state, two and a half hours apart. Beverly had a second house partway in between, in Windsor, where she spent at best three nights a week closer to another job as a visiting professor at Dartmouth's medical school in Hanover, New Hampshire. But that didn't mean Joe's own timetable would necessarily cooperate. On top of being the Brattleboro squad leader of this VBI unit—one of five across the state—he was also the agency's field force commander, further guaranteeing his enslavement to additional pager calls.

He and Beverly were seasoned professionals, however, and took most near-chaotic schedule changes in stride.

"Speaking of the first, then," he said, "are you still hoping to be on this side of the state on Thursday?"

"I am," she replied happily. "Does your evening have any openings?"

"Unless you're about to close them up," he said. "Choose your next words carefully."

He could hear the relief in her voice. "I don't think so," she told him. "We just received a case from the cadaver class up here that appears to have changed its spots from a natural to a suspicious death."

He frowned at the image. "The cadaver class? What shape's this guy in?"

"Predictable," was her response. "They'd worked him up to and including his neck."

Joe imagined what she hadn't described. "Ouch."

"Precisely," she continued. "A medical student working outside of class hours discovered a fractured hyoid, with attending hemorrhaging, consistent with a strangulation. The gentleman's name was Nathan Lyon, from your town." She gave him Lyon's date of birth and street address.

Joe did the math in his head. "Eighty-two? Damn. Somebody didn't like him. All they had to do was wait awhile. What were they thinking he died of?"

"The usual," she said. "Bad heart, diabetes, essentially old age."

"Except it wasn't," he interjected. "When did he die? Recently?"

"No," she said, giving him the date. "Nine months ago."

He reflected a moment before asking, "How sure are you of this?"

"I have an eager beaver intern who wants to do an in-house tox screen on Mr. Lyon, just to see what else might have been missed.

I'll be changing the death certificate to pending until the results of that come back."

"You can still do a tox? I thought they were embalmed before being handed over to the school."

"They are. We can exclude those specific chemicals from the screen. They may not be the purest end results, but they might be worth waiting for."

"Huh," Joe grunted. "Well, I guess you were right about none of this messing up my schedule for a while. You looking at the usual four to six weeks for the tox to come back?"

"Oh no," she countered. "A couple of days, more likely. As I said, this is a special project for credit. In a sense, it's off the books. I'm not even paying for it. The school is. I should be letting you know before we see each other."

"More's the pity," he said softly.

She matched his tone. "I know, sweetheart. I miss you, too."

Monica Tardy stood at the penthouse bay window overlooking the parking lot of her 150,000-square-foot converted mill building and watched grimly as an older, winter-stained SUV rolled to a stop far below. Two people got out.

"Who do you think they are?" the tall man next to her asked.

"Cops," she said, her voice carrying a faint nasal twang hinting of southern New England, despite her decades of living in Vermont.

"Really?"

She eyed him wearily. "Trust me."

He was Rob Lyon, her late husband's son, a blond, bland, unimposing man whose height helped disguise a soft, protuberant belly. Rob was "part of the package," as Nathan Lyon had put it when he and Monica had married. She'd taken it in stride, which one learned to do with Nathan. Rob was Monica's age—sixty—twenty-two years younger than father and husband. Monica had never been told about Rob's real mother. Nor had Rob, as far as she knew.

Welcome to the Lyon clan, or the Lyons' Den, per Nathan.

Rob returned the gaze. In fact, he did trust her, which was a little unexpected, given how little they discussed personal matters. But he'd always known of a fundamental depth to her, a reliability he imagined his father had also appreciated.

She'd entered the union with a child, too, if in a roundabout way, unacknowledged until a few years ago. Given up for adoption, Gene Russell, complete with a replacement set of parents, a wife, a stepsister, and even a kid, had been located by Nathan and folded into the larger family—Rob always thought over Monica's puzzled and silent misgivings. It had certainly come as a surprise to Rob and his half brother, Mike, even as familiar as they were with their father's often eccentric behavior.

Still, Rob concluded, not for the first time, what was the downside of adding a whole other branch to this already offbeat tribe? It's not like Nathan hadn't planned ahead by buying an abandoned factory building for a home.

He turned away from the enormous window to take in their surroundings. The so-called penthouse, where Monica now lived alone under twenty-foot ceilings, covered a third of this brick monstrosity's fifth floor, and at some ten thousand square feet all by itself, was larger than many freestanding mansions.

God knows, the behemoth below them had room for a lot of people. They didn't even need to see much of one another.

"Well," Rob said, starting the journey toward the refurbished freight elevator in the far corner of the cavernous room, wending his way around and between oversized furniture, ornate shelf units, freestanding sculptures, and a large table festooned with knick-knacks. "Whoever they are, might as well greet them properly,"

Lester Spinney and Samantha Martens—Sam or Sammie to all who knew her—paused halfway between their car and the towering, red-brick façade confronting them, framed against a snow-laden sky.

"You ever hear about this place?" she asked her colleague, squinting up against the falling snow at the vastness of wall space opposite, which was punctured by a row of several imposing entrances, some marked by tastefully demure business signs.

They were the two other members of Gunther's squad, Sam sharing a home and a child with the infamous Willy Kunkle. Once members, respectively, of the state police and the Brattleboro police, Les and Sam had both come to the VBI to work with Joe and enjoy the focused mandate of an agency that pursued major crimes only.

Lester shook his head. "Never had a reason to. No more than we hear about most high-end residences." He let out a low whistle, adding, "Is this really a single-family home?"

"That's what I was told," she replied. "It's even got a swimming pool somewhere."

"Well, sure," he said. "Why not? Heliport on the roof?"

She resumed their walk toward a centrally located pair of large, wooden double doors, so big one of them had a smaller entrance cut into it for conventional access. This appeared to be the front door, if such a term even applied. "Not that I know."

"So what third-world country do you overthrow to buy a pile like this?" Lester persisted.

Stamping their feet, they entered a broad, high, industrially sized corridor with heavy pipes and massive cable conduits overhead and rows of large sliding freight doors along one wall facing windows lining the other. The accents were heavy on old wrought iron and wood, but not just as survivors of a long-gone industrial era. Looking around, both cops could appreciate how carefully and expensively all aspects of their once purely utilitarian surroundings had been enhanced with modern amenities. Sunken lighting, radiant floor heating, sound-absorbent glass, and power-assisted doors had been blended into the preexisting, seemingly crude environment to somehow, and with great subtlety, transform it into something exotic, rarified, and palpably upper-class.

Opposite them, mounted beside a freight elevator door, was an office building–like plaque listing names of individuals and businesses inhabiting the building, along with numbers indicating the floors they occupied. Included were references to PENTHOUSE, HEALTH CLUB, and, more pompous still, NATORIUM.

"Hot damn," Lester said, distracted by the scenery.

Sam couldn't fault him. It felt as if they'd walked into a proletarian factory version of a buffed-up Louis XIV castle—a complete and utter paradox of form over function.

They both paused as a small child—fitting the otherworldly aura— came soundlessly twirling out of the distant shadows, barefoot and wearing a ballerina's tutu, and continued past with only a distracted, high-pitched hello to mark her passage. The word seemed to hang in the air following her disappearance.

"All right, then," Lester murmured.

He looked questioningly at Sam after crossing the corridor and letting his finger hover over a separate lighted button on the elevator's jamb, above the conventional two, labeled PENTHOUSE.

"Sure," she assented.

A male voice addressed them over a speaker. "May we help you?"

"Police," Sammie said. "We'd like to speak with Mrs. Lyon."

"I'm Rob Lyon," the voice responded. "Mrs. Lyon's stepson. Would that do?"

"Whatever works for you," Sam told him.

"Please ride the elevator to the fifth floor, unless you'd like me to come down, of course."

"No. That's fine. We'll come to you."

"Thank you. Welcome."

The enormous door facing them silently slid open like a silk curtain. Lester stood aside for Sam.

The interior, similar to the lobby, combined a perfect mixture of old and new, handcrafted and high-tech.

"I have no idea what it's all about," Lester ventured as they smoothly began their journey, "but so far, I think these people spend more on door fixtures than I did to buy my house."

When the ten-foot-tall doors swept open on the top floor, they found themselves staring at a well-preserved man in slacks, button-down shirt, cardigan, and loafers, a welcoming smile on his face and a hand extended. He was close to Lester's height, which was saying something. "Come in, come in. I'm Rob Lyon."

He gestured across the room to a woman who reminded Sam of an older Lauren Bacall—the version that sold cat food—and whose glamorous outer shell looked even more endangered.

"This is Monica Tardy, my stepmother," he said, immediately creating a disconnect between the stated relationship of the two and their visible similarity in age.

It made Sam study Monica's expression, watching if she might betray irritation with the introduction. She did not.

However, befitting the setting and Monica's quasi-regal stance by the light of the window beside her, the two cops were obliged to cover the distance to her like supplicants in order to delicately exchange handshakes, which the matron of the mansion did with fingertips only.

"What can we do for you?" she asked, her accent, to Lester's ear, betraying origins at odds with the opulence around them. He sensed a woman whose roots had found life in considerably poorer soil than this.

"Are you the widow of Nathan Lyon?" Sam asked her.

She seemed to ponder that before responding, "I am. You may call me Monica Lyon, if that's easier. Why do you ask?"

"He was my dad," Rob contributed, unasked.

Sam indicated the cluster of overstuffed leather seats nearby, positioned to alternatively enjoy the view of Brattleboro's distant skyline out the window, or a large, wall-mounted TV screen that currently resembled a hole as black as a tar pit.

"Why don't we sit down so I can explain?" she proposed.

Rob was amenable, moving accordingly. Monica was less eager and seemed to fight her initial instinct by nodding slowly. "If you'd like."

Lester was under the impression that their news was not going to be a surprise.

Monica covered her hesitation by asking, "I'm sorry. That was rude of me. I should have offered you coffee or something."

"No, thanks," Sam replied. "We're all set."

Speak for yourself, Lester thought, eager to find out what the upper crust drank. He'd recently read about some coffee made from exotic cat turds and costing a fortune. He resisted asking and sat on the edge of an armchair that threatened to swallow him.

The two Lyons chose the couch, side by side, but a distance apart.

Sam continued, "What I'm about to say is going to be a little difficult to absorb, I'm afraid."

"All right," Monica said archly.

"Your husband, as you know, donated his remains to UVM for use in the education of medical students. I think you were told that the turnaround time from donation to his ashes being returned could run to a couple of years, just because of how they do things up there."

"Go on."

"Well, they got to him a lot quicker than that. Mr. Lyon was being studied in an anatomy lab this week, and they found something that'll probably come as a shock."

Studying Monica's face, Lester renewed his doubts about that last comment. Although, to cut her a little leeway, she did present as distant by nature.

"What?" Rob asked.

"It's looking like Mr. Lyon was murdered."

Monica Tardy, or Lyon, stared at Sam, unblinking.

"Murdered?" Rob echoed. "Why?"

"Somebody didn't like him," Monica said evenly, still watching Sam. "Tell me more."

"We think he was strangled," Sam said, suspecting along with her partner that this woman could handle bad news.

Rob was more spontaneous. "*Strangled?* What the hell?"

"Control yourself," Monica said in a flat voice, before asking, "You catch who did it?"

"Not yet," Sam told her, thinking Rob's loss of self-control was perfectly reasonable.

"We'd like to ask you about that," Lester weighed in, now that the impact of their news had been absorbed.

"You think *we* know anything?" Rob asked incredulously.

Monica finally stared at him, but it was Sam who told him, "We're just asking for help here."

Rob took that at face value. "Of course."

"When your husband died," Sam resumed, "it was deemed an attended death. He'd been in declining health; his doctor had seen him recently. He died here and not at the hospital, according to the death certificate, but hospice had been called in and the doc was comfortable signing off, so neither we nor the medical examiner's office were ever contacted. Is that correct?"

"Yes," Monica agreed. "Something arteriosclerotic."

Sam quoted the paperwork she'd pulled from her pocket, "Arteriosclerotic hypertensive heart disease, atrial fibrillation, and general deconditioning. Were any of you surprised by any of that at the time?"

Monica's face expressed resignation while Rob answered more calmly, "Of course not."

"It was only a matter of time," she volunteered. "I didn't expect it to happen so fast, but he and I had talked about life not being what it used to be. He was ready for it to end." She smiled thinly and tacked on, "Although not through murder."

"Who would want to kill a sick old man?" Rob asked no one in particular.

"Our question exactly," Lester encouraged them. "Who?"

The two cops were looking at Monica.

"No one I know," she said.

"What did Nathan do for a living?" Sam asked.

"He managed his assets," Monica answered. "Investments, both on Wall Street and tangible." She waved her hand around slightly. "This building, for one thing. But he had other properties, mostly around Brattleboro."

"I'm guessing that was later," Sam suggested. "How did he make that money?"

"Nathan was in the food supply business," Monica replied. "Between producers and consumers. He mostly dealt with restaurants and hospitality companies. Not in Vermont, though, and more than two decades ago."

"Is this building *just* your home?" Lester asked, his voice neutral.

"That and more," she said. "Nathan was very big on having as many members of his family under the same roof as he could fit. But he recognized people need their space, not to mention room to express themselves, entertain, and perhaps make a living. This building supplies all of that."

"How so?"

Here, unexpectedly, Rob spoke up. "I can tell you that. I'm kind of the building manager."

"He's paid to be," Monica clarified. "That's his job."

Rob ignored the condescension. "There are five stories," he explained. "Each measuring roughly thirty thousand square feet, skipping the fact that any room—like this one—can accommodate a second-floor loft insert just because of its height. You take away some of the overall footage because of the swimming pool, the utilities—which are big enough to power a ship—the elevators, the gym, and other stuff, and you still have enough to fit six distinct and separate living quarters of varying size, plus three areas given over to the businesses that some family members own and run."

"All under the same roof," Lester confirmed.

For a moment, Rob seemed to have forgotten the reason they were here. "Yup. A roof in need of constant attention. Which also brings up the staff needed to keep things running and maintained. Some of them have stay-over quarters here, too, though most of them live off campus."

"We'll be needing a complete list. Who are the family members, exactly?"

Monica took back the reins. "Nathan and I bought the building and had it converted decades ago. Rob's lived here all that time. So have Mike, my natural son with Nathan, Gene Russell, my son from earlier, and Gene's family: son, Mark, and wife, Peggy."

"You left out Michelle," Rob added.

Monica cast him a baleful look before saying, "I'd never leave out Michelle. She's married to Mike. Their child is Debbie."

"She's six," Rob added.

"Fond of ballet?" Lester asked. "I think we saw her downstairs."

"Yes," Monica said dryly. "Very precocious."

"Some family members come and go," Rob filled in. "Gene was adopted by Betsy Russell and her husband, Ned, and they drop by. Their daughter, Penny Trick, actually lives here in her own apartment." He looked at the ceiling, as if watching the *Hindenburg* coming in to dock, and concluded, "In a way, the building's like a village, where you can wander around and visit people, or just keep to yourself when you want. You can even go shopping, after a fashion."

Sam pursued that point. "So you said. What kind of things are made here?"

"There's a woodworking and design shop, a pottery, and a specialty food products manufacturer, all owned and run by family," Rob replied.

"And employees?" Lester asked.

"Yes. Those, too. Sure."

"Okay," Sam spoke up. "Again, we'll need a full list, with contact information."

"Would tomorrow do for that?" Rob asked her.

"Sure." Sam shifted in her seat and changed topics. She glanced back down at the death certificate in her hand and read the date aloud, along with the recorded time of pronouncement, adding, "Does that correspond to your memory of when he died?"

"Yes," Monica said shortly.

"Tell us about that day."

The recent widow's expression remained cool as she paused. Lester imagined her weighing her options, including asking for a lawyer. When she spoke, however, it was only to comment blandly, "Not much to tell. Nathan and I slept apart. Had for years. I came in and found him dead. Cold and stiff. I called his doctor, who told me it qualified as an attended death, because of the hospice contract and his awareness of the situation, and that he would therefore sign that," She gestured to the document Sam was holding.

"When was this?" Sam wanted to know.

"Right before the time you just read off. I didn't wait around or have breakfast. This may have been expected, but I did love the man. It was still a shock, attended death or not."

"Where was hospice in all this?" Sam asked. "Aren't they supposed to be there?"

"Within reason, and sometimes according to the patient's needs. Nathan was stable, just slowly going downhill. He didn't need anyone except maybe three times a day, and I was also helping out."

"When did you last see him alive?" Lester asked.

"The night before. I checked on him before I went to bed. He was fine. Watching TV as usual."

"Might he have had a guest? Do people here visit each other much?"

"Sure we do," Rob answered. "We're family."

Precisely the people we suspect first in a homicide, Sam thought.

Out loud, she said, "This may not be what you want to hear, especially given the passage of time since Nathan's passing, but we're going to have to either remove or preserve certain areas and items relating to Nathan until we complete our investigation. It's going to be a little intrusive. There'll be people coming and going."

"Whatever on earth for?" Monica demanded.

"Someone killed your husband. We're already late finding that out. With any luck, there's still enough left to help us find who did it."

Fredo eyed his cousin, not for the first time wondering why he was aiding and abetting this old man to tilt at windmills, especially when he knew of the futility involved. They were in Cranston, a down-at-the-heels, mostly white bedroom community below Providence, facing a small brick apartment building wedged against the junction of an expressway and a ninety-degree overpass—the home of John Neri, like them an anonymous floor-worker in a long-gone gray underworld. The air was thrumming with the sounds of endlessly passing traffic.

Fredo faulted himself for their being here. At the coffee shop, after listening to Eddie ramble on about having been wronged and needing to set things right—yet again—he'd begun to interact, at first in monosyllables, and then, whether from boredom or growing engagement, he'd conceded Eddie's point, that he had acted according to code and been left with a record and nothing more to show for it.

That's when Fredo had mentioned Johnny Neri. Another Mob gofer, Johnny had kept his eyes open over the years, noting how the true players got things done, who was in, out, or didn't matter. Where Fredo had made it through by keeping his head down and his mouth shut, Johnny had survived because of what he'd seen and understood.

And so here they were, crossing a threadbare patch of crusty, soiled snow, unique to urban centers for its complete lack of appeal, about to meet a man who, like them, was a fragment of the behemoth that had once been organized crime in the United States.

It was Eddie's first sure-footed step on his journey of discovery.

CHAPTER THREE

Willy entered the squad room, brushing snow from his coat.

Joe looked up, surprised, and swiveled to look out the window behind him. "I thought it had stopped snowing."

"It has," Willy confirmed. He displayed his chest by spreading his right arm out, the other one permanently hanging limp by his side—an ancient, bullet-caused disability. "Snowball fight with my daughter. That's what I get for picking her up from the one preschool in town that didn't call a snow day."

"You are clearly losing your fighting edge," Joe commented.

It was a pointed reference. Willy was a veteran combat sniper, with multiple confirmed kills. Combining that background, the damaged arm—incurred later as a cop—and his being a recovering alcoholic, those who knew Willy the best, mostly the people who worked in this office, understood these moments of happy fatherhood to be near miracles.

Willy Kunkle was a singularly intricate piece of work.

"Where is everybody?" he asked, hanging the coat near the exit. Their office was impressively small, on the second floor of Brattleboro's municipal building, whose first floor had once housed the police department where they'd all, except Lester, once worked together as detectives under Joe's supervision.

Jamming the space were four desks, extra chairs, filing cabinets, a small counter for a coffee machine, a large whiteboard, and an absurdly dominant monitor covering most of one wall, sized for an auditorium, and hooked up to their computers. It had been supplied by the VBI's director in Waterbury, after years of nagging, but appeared to have been purchased at a sports stadium's fire sale.

"The medical examiner sent us an interesting one," Joe explained, handing him a printout, complete with a full-body photograph.

"Holy shit," Willy said, settling behind his desk. "What the hell happened? Your girlfriend have a bad day and put him through the shredder? I thought she had a more delicate touch."

The girlfriend reference was a nod toward Beverly Hillstrom, whose antipathy for him Willy happily acknowledged, while in turn holding her in high regard. Nevertheless, he could never resist poking fun at her and his boss for being romantically linked.

"Anatomy 101," Joe explained. "Some student thought he was working on a natural-causes old-timer, until he found a busted hyoid. Beverly confirmed it was a homicide."

"Far out," Willy said, studying the report. "It says there was no external bruising on the throat, only hemorrhaging in the strap muscles. What's that about?"

"I asked her," Joe told him. "One hypothesis is gradual, fairly long-term pressure on the arteries with both thumbs. Slow and easy."

"While the victim was watching TV?" Willy asked incredulously.

"Or was knocked out chemically. Beverly's doing a tox screen in-house. We should be hearing back pretty soon on that."

Willy tossed the sheet onto his desk and sat back. "Huh. So, what're our two missing colleagues doing?"

"Interviewing the widow and family members and securing what's left of any evidence," Joe said. "You ever hear of Nathan Lyon?"

Willy looked surprised and double-checked the paperwork. "The guy who owns the mill? You're kidding."

"What do you know?"

"Nothing personal, but nothing good. The politest thing I ever heard was that he was a very rich, grade-A asshole. Everybody who ever dealt with him thought he was an ego-driven narcissist."

"What's the story with the mill? Rumor is it's the state's largest single residence."

Willy tilted his head to one side. "You know as much as I do. Les and Sam'll have to give us what they got. Did your better half have anything besides cause of death? Like some DNA left on the guy's throat?"

Joe frowned. "Nope. He'd been on the shelf too long. Washed, embalmed, moved around like a slab of beef . . ."

"Not to mention sliced and diced," Willy finished for him. "I get it. So we hold our breath and hope the money trail reveals all. A guy that rich gets snuffed, chances are somebody benefited who wasn't supposed to. That'll most likely be our bad boy. He leave a will?"

Joe reached for the ringing phone, answered, and almost immediately switched on the speaker, saying, "You're being broadcast to everyone now, so brace yourself, Dr. Hillstrom. I have Willy in the room with me."

Beverly's voice was precise and authoritative, despite the tinny acoustics. "Agent Kunkle," she greeted him.

"Dr. Hillstrom," he responded with false formality.

"You said you found something more on Mr. Lyon," Joe suggested.

"A through-and-through bullet wound," she told them. "Old, clean, and with no obvious signs of medical intervention."

"How old?" Willy wanted to know.

"Many years," she answered. "Beyond that, I cannot say. It took me this long to find it because of the cadaver's presentation. I and my staff had a lot of reconstruction to do."

"Did the bullet cause any damage on its way through?" Joe asked.

"No," she said. "Quite remarkable. I'm not surprised the medical students missed it. It was literally what they call a flesh wound in our westerns, and so old it resembled an ancient skin defect."

Willy snorted audibly. "You two watch westerns? I love it."

Beverly's voice darkened slightly, even while she ignored him. "From the damage presenting at both entry and exit sites, I'd say the bullet was fully jacketed and non-expanding. It also didn't encounter much resistance since it traversed just above the ilium and to the left of the small intestine, ergo the lack of serious trauma."

"His left flank, just above the belt line?" Joe asked.

"Essentially, yes. It would have been painful, and could have caused problems had it become infected, but there are no signs of that, so he either was lucky or he paid it the care it deserved, shy of any suturing."

"You're saying no doc was involved," Willy rephrased.

"No," she corrected him. "I said there were no obvious signs of medical intervention. A physician might have administered antibiotics or dressed the wound, but no stitching occurred. That would strike me as unusual in any hospital setting."

"So you think he was cared for elsewhere," Joe guessed.

"It's a credible hypothesis," she answered.

Willy rolled his eyes.

"Another item, since I have you on the line," Beverly said.

"Go ahead."

"My medical student has already found something unexpected in his tox analysis. It's preliminary, and I give you this with that understanding. But it might be relevant to your investigation."

Joe was intrigued. "What did he find?"

"Elevated levels of diphenhydramine," she said.

"Benadryl?" Willy countered.

"I wouldn't know the brand, but yes."

"What do you make of it?" Joe asked, knowing her well. "You've got something up your sleeve."

At last, she relaxed enough to react more playfully. "It's another hypothesis, so most likely right up Agent Kunkle's alley, but a finding like this dovetails neatly with the lack of external bruising in the area of the offended hyoid."

To his credit, Willy kept his mouth shut, impatience stamped on his face.

To Joe, however, she was making sense. "The Benadryl stepped on Lyon's ability to fight off his attacker."

"It's a possibility," she stressed.

"Huh," Willy conceded. "Sounds good. If he was doped up enough, the killer could've taken his time shutting down the arteries."

"And reducing the chances of external evidence," Beverly said.

"How much Benadryl would've been needed?" Joe asked her.

"A fair amount, but it could have been disguised in something like a milkshake, or where the flavor and possibly the color wouldn't stand out."

The two men exchanged glances. "There's something to add to the next interview," Willy said. "What kind of crap did Nathan enjoy as a nightcap?"

"Any other rabbits?" Joe asked her.

"Not a one. Hope those two help. Goodbye, Agent Kunkle."

"Back at ya, Doc."

The line went dead.

Three bachelors, Fredo Sindaco thought, sitting in a circle, in the worst of the three home settings they each had available to them. Fredo was not a compulsively neat man, but John Neri? The guy was a pig. Looking around the one-room apartment on the second floor of Neri's stained, aging, cracked brick building, Fredo again rued having mentioned him to Eddie as a possible source of information.

Not to mention, of course, that Neri's attitude matched his décor.

"For fuck's sake, Eddie," he was saying, settled like Jabba the Hutt in an extra-large, overstuffed, suspiciously stained BarcaLounger. "What d'you expect? Coming at me all these years later, asking, 'Who set me up?' How the fuck'm I supposed to know? You, me, your prissy cousin Fredo over there, we were mutts, mopes, nobodies. We didn't count for nuthin', and we still don't."

He pointed a fat, cigarette-stained finger at Eddie. "*You* were the one with delusions of grandeur, Mouse. Sucking up to the brass, pretending you could catch the up escalator. You saw what it got ya. You were never Mob. None of us were. But you bought into the omertà shit, and agreed to cop to the crime, do the time, and get a pension for life. Nice job, Mouse. Now you can't even figure out who screwed you." He tapped the side of his round head. "Smart."

Eddie hated being called Mouse. Always had. But he kept quiet. He needed this fat slob. He also couldn't entirely deny Neri's claim. He had been an idiot, dealing wholly with a go-between instead of consulting with the higher-ups.

Reluctantly, he also couldn't argue with Neri's appraisal of his motives for agreeing to the deal. He'd always feared ending his years like this, living in a hovel, a dung beetle in a sty. Like a man whose retirement plan was winning the Lotto, Eddie had figured a few years in stir for a crime he hadn't committed would set him up for life. John Neri was right. Eddie had ignored that the Mob's aura of honor among thieves had been good PR and Hollywood romanticism, but in fact had disguised a cynical means to an end at the best of times.

He therefore said, "I just want to figure out what happened, Johnny."

"What happened?" Neri echoed back, pausing to light the third cigarette since they'd arrived twenty minutes ago. "You're so late catching the train, the goddamn station's been taken down, Mouse. You were living in a movie. *The Godfather*, starring Mouse as the stand-up guy."

"Enough," Eddie said quietly, staring at him, his hands unconsciously balled into fists.

Neri conceded his excessiveness, waving a hand and sprinkling ashes. "Okay, okay. I get it. More to the point, *you* get it. It was pathetic, when I heard what you done. I said then you were gonna get chewed up and spat out. But we were never friends, you and me."

He pointed at the almost forgotten Fredo. "Sindaco? God knows why, but we got along. You, Mouse? You were just a train wreck waiting to happen."

"What're you sayin', Johnny?" Eddie asked, his patience surprising even him; a testament to how much he'd learned in prison about watching and waiting, reading the land ahead.

"I'm sayin' that even if the old ways had been alive and well when you did your deal, you were talkin' to the wrong people."

The cousins waited for him to explain. Neri took a long drag on his cigarette, killing half of it before continuing. "You did time for offing Vito Alfano, right? Definitely a connected guy. Son of Knuckles Alfano, who worked for Al Zucco. Born to the life. But did you think that maybe Vito was like tits on a bull to the Outfit? Not even Knuckles liked him. He was greedy, disrespectful, lazy, you name it. But everybody was stuck with him. Blood tie, you know? They had to park him somewhere, preferably where he'd do the least damage, so Zucco made a deal with his protégé, Nick Bianchi, an outsider but at least an Italian. If Bianchi would take Vito as a lieutenant and keep him occupied, that would make Knuckles and Zucco both happy. A definite good move by Bianchi."

Eddie didn't respond, sitting, waiting.

Johnny got the message. "Well, this whole story is full of weird shit like that. For instance, that loser Vito was the best thing that ever happened to Nick Bianchi. He ripped off Nick every chance he got, figuring he could do what he wanted 'cause he was real family, where Nick wasn't. But he stepped on too many toes, especially Zucco's, who reached the conclusion that—family or not—Vito had to go. Nick made out good. He not only hired Vito without whining, but what Vito didn't know was that Nick had been bankrolled by Zucco, which means Vito stole from Zucco every time he dipped into Nick's till. All that was left was to find somebody to take the fall for killing Vito, and who couldn't be tied to Zucco."

Johnny made a theatrical flourish in Eddie's direction. "Enter the Mouse, a stand-up guy, eager and disposable."

The fat man clapped his hands, asking, "Tell me something, Eddie: Did you know anything about all this? You shoulda done your homework. It was all about money, not honor, meaning nobody was gonna pay for upkeep after."

"Where's Zucco now?" Eddie asked, stung by the impact of this. It had seemed such a sure thing. The pitch had come from some smooth-talking made man, Manny De Luca, whose word Eddie had accepted without question.

Neri was having a good time. "So you can hunt him down and do him in, Charlie Bronson–style? Zucco and Bianchi and Knuckles and everybody else're all gone, Mouse. History. Shoot yourself if you want revenge. You're the one you should be mad at."

Eddie ignored the taunt, his obsession a bulletproof mantle.

"You said, 'everybody else,'" he therefore commented, sliding forward slightly in his chair. "Who did you mean, exactly?"

"So," Willy asked Sam and Les as they entered the office and hung up their coats. "You two wrap this sucker up? Who dun it?"

It was dark by now, being winter in New England, but also late by normal working standards. No one here hardly noticed, however. One of the understandings of working for the VBI was that in exchange for attaining its lofty professional perch, any expectations of a nine-to-five schedule were hopeful at best.

Sam's only concession to that reality was to ask him instead, "Louise good with watching Emma?" referring to their long-standing babysitter, also an ex-cop.

"Happy as a clam," he answered. "I just called."

It was good to know, but did little to stem her regret at being unable to tuck her daughter into bed after hearing the day's adventures at school. Having a baby had been a big step for Sam, even with a partner like Willy, who—notwithstanding his reputation and occasional flights of misbehavior—was a devoted companion and father. But oddly, she knew only now, she hadn't factored in the longing that accompanied a child. She thought about Emma all the time, and still hadn't come to grips with the parental paradox of that feeling being both healthy and normal.

Lester addressed Willy's question. "It is looking like an old-fashioned mystery. If our dead guy had died of a blow to the head, I'd be looking for a candlestick in the library."

"Swell," Willy said dully, like Sam, sensing that Louise was going to be seeing a lot of their daughter for a while. As reckless as his early life had been, even by his own admission, the unexpected domesticity he enjoyed now was an awfully nice fit.

"Big house, I hear," Joe played along. "Probably *does* have a library."

"Or several," Les continued. "It's not a house. We didn't go through it—just to the top floor to meet the non-grieving widow and son—but I'd describe it more as a gated community under one roof, connected by hallways and staircases."

Sam agreed. "Yeah, that's good. Including three businesses, each belonging to a family member. Picture an old English movie where the whole village fits onto a gigantic soundstage."

"And only family lives there?" Joe asked.

Sam reached for her notepad. "Not entirely. One or two live off the premises, there are a couple of stay-over apartments where people can spend the night. A couple of employees also have one-room efficiencies, tucked into the far corners."

"We haven't gone door-to-door yet," Lester said. "but a rough estimate is maybe ten to fifteen full-time residents. The ones we met were Monica Tardy, the late Nathan's wife, and Rob Lyon, his son by another marriage."

"Another woman," Sam corrected. "We don't know yet who was married and who wasn't."

"What *do* we know?" Joe asked.

"Concerning Nathan's last day, not much," she admitted. "Husband and wife had separate bedrooms. Hospice nurse had clocked out for the day. Monica claims she last saw him watching TV one night, and found him cold and stiff the next morning. She called his doc, he told her he'd write the DC. End of story."

"So the doc killed him," Willy said, deadpan.

"Anyone could've," she countered. "According to Rob, who looks about Monica's age, people come and go throughout the building all the time. If anyone locks their doors, we didn't hear about it."

Joe indicated the whiteboard, speaking to Sam. "Take us through the cast of characters, if you got 'em."

Sam eyed her colleague. "Les took better notes than I did."

He'd risen from his desk and was already crossing the room. A caricature of a human being—too tall, too skinny, with far-too-flexible facial features—Lester had been made fun of since his police academy days and had a collection of stork-related cards, bobble heads, and figurines adorning his work area to prove it, including a gangly papier-mâché bird hanging above his desk.

He uncapped a marker and started at the top of the board. "Nathan Lyon," he told them. "Family patriarch, eighty-two, rich as Croesus, husband of Monica Tardy. Apparently made his pile in the food business many decades back, out of state, and retired to the soothing Green Mountains. Setting up first at a big spread out of town, he then bought and converted the mill building."

He drew a line connecting the couple and attached a dangling dropdown from it. There he wrote, *Mike*. "Michael Lyon," he intoned. "Bio-son of the happy twosome. Their only natural child, and co-owner with his wife of Food Flourish, one of the businesses."

Little by little, checking his notes as he went and taking the occasional cue from Sam, he laid out a crude family tree.

By the end, however, the board looked more like a Marx Brothers football play diagram from *Horse Feathers*.

Willy was rubbing his forehead. "Okay," he reviewed. "Tell me if I got anything wrong. Nathan had a kid, Rob, from before any of them moved here. He's the guy pretending to be the building manager. Mike, Nathan's son with Monica, is married to Michelle, and they have Debbie, a six-year-old, all of whom live in the mill. Monica also has an adult kid of *her* own, unrelated to Nathan, named Gene Russell, originally given up for adoption, but who now also lives in the mill, complete with a wife, Peggy, son, Mark, and a business named ER Ceramics. Plus, there's another relative named Penny Trick in there somehow." He gave Lester a hapless glance. "Am I getting this right? Who the hell's Penny Trick?"

Sam tried to help. "Gene's stepsister, the bio-daughter of the couple who adopted Gene."

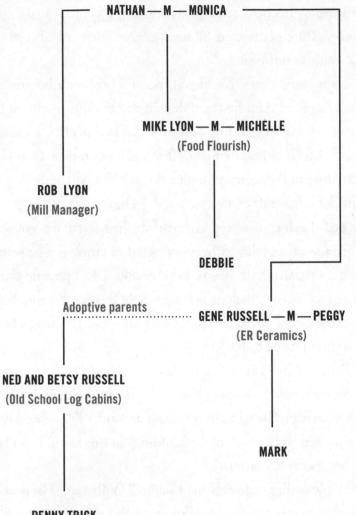

"Betsy and Ned Russell," Lester threw in helpfully.

"But the elder Russells do not live at the mill," Willy stated.

"Correct. They live in Brattleboro, nearby, and apparently almost caused World War III by resisting Nathan's invitation to co-locate. Their compromise was to move Ned's office and design studio into the mill. He owns Old School Log Cabins. You've probably seen his signs around the county. Nice-looking homes."

Willy shook his head silently, staring at the board.

"Penny Trick connected to anyone else?" Joe asked, reflecting some of Willy's confusion.

Sam answered that. "No, if you mean a husband, boyfriend, or kid. She's divorced. Has her own digs in the building—one of those apartments. According to Rob and Monica, Penny's thirty-nine. Les and I got the feeling that neither of them like her much. Don't know why yet. Also got the feeling Monica doesn't like Michelle."

Willy let out a puff of air and asked, "That it?"

"Nope," Lester answered cheerfully. "Just what we got so far. There're a few other folks, either contracted or employed full-time to handle the infrastructure needs. Rob mentioned in passing that the building's electricity bill alone averages eight thousand a month." He indicated the board covered in names. "This is like running a factory, which is what it used to be."

"What *did* it used to be?" Joe asked.

Lester gave Sam a delighted look. "I *told* you he'd ask." He faced his boss to answer, "Textiles. It was built around 1900, which is later than I expected, given most of the buildings in this town. I can't even guess what it cost to convert."

"Multiple millions, from what I heard," Willy said. His desk, unlike the others, was placed catty-corner to the room, facing out, his back almost wedged into the corner. The positioning spoke volumes about his comfort with, and attitude toward, the rest of the world. "And that was a long time ago."

"It is over-the-top fancy," Lester agreed. "We were told about an indoor pool, although we didn't get to see it."

"You will," Joe reassured him. "Sooner or later, we'll see every square inch of the place." He pointed at the confusion covering the whiteboard, adding, "And interview everyone having anything to do with it." He paused a moment, concluding, "How did you leave things vis-à-vis securing the scene and collecting items that were Nathan's?"

Sam answered, "We got the locals and the sheriff helping seal off what were strictly Nathan's private quarters. We bagged and tagged what made sense—computers, phones, et cetera—and we'll be applying for access to records, wills, trusts, and whatever. Be advised that the widow is not happy about a bunch of cops as twenty-four-hour roommates."

"She interest you in particular?" Joe asked.

"A woman in mourning, she is not," Lester told them. "We're gonna have our work cut out with her—that's my own two cents. And something tells me she won't be our only speed bump."

CHAPTER FOUR

"Sally Kravitz?"

Sally racked her mind, trying to pin down the woman's voice. The number on her cell's display hadn't meant anything, but few people beyond past clients and close friends knew this number.

"Yes," she answered cautiously.

"It's Annie Paget. You okay? You sound sort of . . . off."

The light came on in Sally's head. Paget was a CPA who'd hired her two years ago to dig into a possible embezzlement.

"I'm sorry, Annie. Just distracted. How've you been?"

"Boy-oh-boy, I'm not complaining. Busier than a one-armed paperhanger, if those people still exist."

Sally was now remembering Paget's fondness for hokey gollyisms. "I think they do," she replied. "What's up?"

"Well, there you go. Straight to business. Always liked that about you. Not a girl to let grass grow under her feet. Course, you're right. It is business, why I'm calling. You're still a private eye, aren't you? I get such a kick out of just saying that."

Sally resisted sighing. Although, in truth, if she were honest, she got a kick out of it, too. "Still employed, Annie. You have something for me?"

"Darned if I don't. A client who's worried one of her employees might have sticky fingers."

Sally frowned. "Shoplifting? Why doesn't she call the police? You told her my rates, didn't you? They've only gone up."

"Oh, oh," Paget reacted. "What a dummy. I should've set this up better. It's a wholesale business, so it's not just stealing toilet paper or something. My client doesn't want word getting out to her customers that she runs a sloppy shop. It's a food business, involving fancy condiments and ritzy appetizers like caviar, where people get paranoid about high standards being maintained."

"Your client changed pass codes, I hope, so whoever this is doesn't get at the books?"

"No, which really worries me. She doesn't want to spook whoever it is, and she doesn't want to fire the whole staff. You can see the fix she's in, and me, too, if she goes under. She's kind of desperate, and I don't want to lose a good client."

Aren't they always desperate, Sally mused. A woman still in her twenties, Sally didn't have decades of experience, but she'd seen her share of aberrant human behavior. In addition to her professional exposure, she'd spent her entire youth in the company of a deeply eccentric father who had chosen to live just shy of the street, moving them from place to place all over Brattleboro, in part to give his daughter a crash course in social inequality. This despite the fact that he could have simply moved them into a middle-class house like everyone else's.

"I can't make any promises," Sally told her caller. "But I'm happy to talk to her, if that would help you out."

Paget's relief almost poured out of the phone. "It's all I'm asking.

Her name's Michelle. Her business is called Food Flourish. Give me a second and I'll send you her contact info."

Sally waited until her screen lit up with an entry from Annie's virtual address book. "Michelle Lyon," she read aloud.

"You betcha. You'll like her. Good people. Can't thank you enough, Sally."

And can't get off the phone fast enough, Sally thought, her hot potato now squarely in someone else's lap.

"I call it an ant farm."

Reflective of his methodical style, Joe Gunther began his anthropological excavation of the House of Lyon from one of its outermost aspects, its so-called building superintendent. This was a woman somewhere between her thirties and forties, short-haired, trim and muscular, fingernails clipped close, dressed in practical wool, UMass ball cap, and fleece, wearing work boots, and equipped with a powerful handshake and good, penetrating eye contact.

Her name was Kimona Alin, and she'd worked for the Lyons for three years, assigned to monitor the heating, maintain the building transformer, attend to all repairs not demanding a major crew, paint, shovel snow, check the eight publicly available bathrooms, change the light bulbs, watch over contracted service providers, from rubbish haulers to internet providers, and otherwise patrol the building and respond to its residents' needs.

She'd introduced herself as the Jill-of-all-trades upon meeting Joe in her office, a corner of a room containing two industrially sized, oil-fired furnaces that stood roaring like chained dragons in the middle of a large concrete slab.

For all of that, it was warm, almost embracing, and had its own white noise cocoon for utter privacy. Alin had equipped her corner with a desk, two chairs, a small couch, and a dorm fridge. On the desk were three computer monitors, each split into four images connected to remote cameras placed around and inside the building.

It was his inquiry about that surveillance system that had prompted her comment about the ant farm.

"Are they hooked to a recorder?" he asked next, hoping for the best.

But of course, her answer was a shake of the head. "Not that I've been told." Reading his disappointment, she added, "I'm not saying they're not; that wouldn't make sense. I just can't say for sure."

He was intrigued by her precision and warmed to having chosen this woman as his first interview. "Please, go on."

She pursed her lips, thinking back. "The cameras are not hardwired to these," she pointed to the computers. "Meaning their signals can be captured by anyone with the proper access code."

"Who is . . . ," he asked.

She shrugged. "There you have it. Beats me. Why the interest? Something happen I should know about?"

Death certificates in Vermont are available to the public. Joe didn't think it would take long for Beverly's latest revelation to leak out. And he wanted Alin on his side.

But he was also in no rush. "Tell me first about Nathan Lyon."

"Creepy dude," she replied instantly. "I did everything I could to avoid being alone with him."

"He ever do anything to you?"

"Nope, which is why he died with his balls on. At least I guess he did."

Joe settled the issue for her. "He did, as far as I know. He misbehave with anyone you know of?"

"Never heard about it, but it wouldn't surprise me."

He studied her for a moment before asking, "You seem pretty confident. Based on what?"

She considered her answer carefully. "You get to know people." She shifted in her chair and asked him, "You live in this town long?"

"More years than I can remember."

"So you know all about how Brattleboro is the cradle of PC, hug the trees, love Bernie, all that?"

"I've heard the rumors."

"Well, I'm good with that, or most of it," she confessed. "But not when the true believers start ranting about pure evil, and how so-and-so or such-and-such is worse than Adolf Hitler or something. You know what I mean?"

"Okay," Joe said encouragingly.

She nodded. "Good. 'Cause where I'm going with that? Your man Nathan? He *was* evil, PC or no PC."

Interesting, Joe thought. "Tell me more."

"You know anything about this place?" she asked.

"I'm learning. Some kind of family compound under one roof?"

"That would be the polite description. I'm more inclined toward a one-man cult."

"And yet here you are, three years into it. Why stay, if this is the house of evil?"

She held up three fingers and folded each, one by one, as she answered, "One, he died just in time; two, the pay is unbeatable; and three, while these people may be off their rockers and mean to each other, they're good to me. I'm a college-educated, single woman who's handy and likes to work alone. They let me be that. Plus," she threw in, "they're wicked interesting, if you're into abnormal psychology."

She leaned forward and said, "So, spill. I know the VBI chases major crimes only. You're not here for a traffic ticket."

"Nathan's death has been recertified as a homicide," Joe told her.

She sat back. "Wow. Didn't see that coming. Maybe I shouldn't've been so blabby. I need a lawyer?"

Joe looked at her blandly. "You feel you need one?"

"No."

"Good. Were you here the day he was found dead?"

"Damn—this is like a TV show. Yeah, I was."

"Tell me about it."

Kimona Alin took her time, speaking slowly. "I arrived at six. Nathan always wanted me to live here, but I refused. I checked the usual meters, gauges, and readouts, including my roommates." She indicated the furnaces. "Then phone messages, emails, and any Post-it notes left on the door, which I keep locked, before you ask. Not that it matters, since in a top-down operation like this, anything I have—like access to camera footage—is probably available elsewhere, starting with Rob Lyon, but maybe the queen bee, too."

"Monica?"

"Right."

"And all appeared normal?"

"Yup. Not a hair out of place."

"Anything unusual on those?" Joe pointed to the monitors.

"Not when I looked at 'em, although I have to admit, I don't spend a ton of time channel surfing. I don't really want to know that much. I won't deny that late at night sometimes, if I've had to work overtime and I'm just chillin' before heading home, I'll put my feet up and watch for a while. But it's mostly with my brain turned off."

"You do that the night before Lyon died?"

"Nah. Sorry."

"Okay. Keep going."

"Not much to say. The work spaces and living quarters are out-side my orbit. The cameras don't cross those thresholds, nor do my duties, mostly. Sometimes a sink gets plugged or a toilet overflows, or whatever, and I fill in until outside help shows up, if needed, but that's about it. There are exceptions. The majority of the family is squirrely enough that they don't want me witnessing too much."

"We'll get back to that," Joe said. "Let's stick to the actual day for the moment."

"Right," Kimona replied. "Well, like I said, not much to tell. Monica called me on my cell, very businesslike, and said the funeral home would be showing up in fifteen minutes—this was about nine thirty or ten—and I was to escort them to the penthouse. She didn't tell me why till I asked. Even then, she just said, 'Nathan died in the night,' and hung up. That was it. They came, picked him up, and it was That's-All-Folks. I was out of the picture."

"No ceremony or family function or general announcement after-ward?"

"Just a short obit in the paper. The only shoe that dropped around here was Rob coming down a day later to tell me things would con-tinue as they had been, which I found hard to believe, given Nathan's personality."

Joe pursed his lips, thinking a moment. "Two things I'd like to hear more about: the comment you just made about life post-Nathan; and your description of the family being generally squirrely. You game?"

"Why quit now, right?"

"You're asking the wrong man. Start with how things changed—or didn't."

"That's a little hard to answer," she confessed. "It's been like liv-ing through the aftermath of Henry Ford's death, maybe, or some other bigger-than-life person who's suddenly, totally gone. It made me think of somebody turning off all the sound and lights at a concert, in the snap of a finger. Everything's still there, but you can't see anymore. The world didn't end, but there's that sense that life *is* different than it used to be."

"Good or bad?" Joe asked.

"I'm not talking about me," she stressed. "I'm the hired help. All the cannonballs go over my head. So when I say it was bad before, it wasn't for me. But I do think Nathan was a dark force of nature. That's why I feel in my bones that those cameras do run to a recorder someplace and that there're a bunch more of them. Nathan was a Big Brother type, as I saw it. Controlling, watchful, manipulative, cruel. In college, I took a course that talked about the difference between immorality and amorality. Nathan was the second. Human emotion didn't seem to be part of his DNA. And given his influence and the family he controlled, I can't believe his spirit isn't still alive in one or two of his descendants. But I can't really answer your question."

"Nobody pulled up stakes? Some of them must've gotten sick of it."

"You'd think that, wouldn't you?" she pondered as if equally mystified. "The conversations I overheard always centered on the money— how he'd made them so reliant on him financially. But that wasn't true for when Ned Russell moved his log cabin business in here. He seemed to be doing okay on his own. That would be a good question for you to ask: What did Nathan have on Ned? It had to've been a doozy, 'cause anytime I ever mentioned Nathan to him in passing, he'd growl like a pissed-off pit bull."

"You ever witness any of this?" Joe asked. "Nathan pressuring anyone?"

"Just the fallout. People crying or swearing. Furious body language. Cars squealing out of the parking lot. Amazing how people, especially rich ones, don't care when you're standing on a ladder nearby. Made me think sometimes I was trying out for *Downton Abbey*—the invisible servant."

"Anyone come under fire more than others?"

"I guess Monica was spared. She probably knew where the bodies were buried. Not," she quickly added, "that I know anything about bodies. I just always figured a character like Nathan must've had blood on his hands, regardless of any cover story about how he made his millions."

"Which was what?"

She made a face. "Pretty vague. Something about specialty food products. I figure that's where his kid Michael got the idea for Food Flourish. You know about that, don't you?"

Joe nodded. "Yeah. Okay, second question, which now probably ties into the first about life after Nathan. You said the family was squirrely. The implication being that it's gotten worse in the vacuum he left behind."

Not for the first time, Kimona looked philosophical—his local observer of human nature.

"Well, that's sort of what I meant by this being the death of Henry Ford. A mean-spirited super-controller all of a sudden leaving a bunch of gelded lieutenants in charge. What do they do now? Who's the new alpha dog—or bitch?"

"Is Monica pretty dominant?"

"Yes and no. She's got company. The other women in the building seem to be angling for advantage. Mike's wife, Michelle. Gene's better half, Peggy. And of course Penny Trick, who ain't fueled by the milk of human kindness."

"How 'bout Rob Lyon? Is he a comanaging partner, so to speak? That's how he appeared to my colleagues."

"He's my direct boss, and he spends a lot of time with Monica these days. You may be right. He shares some sort of history with her that came before all this." She raised her eyes to the rough wooden ceiling high above, crisscrossed with pipes and conduits. "I always got the feeling that Nathan, Rob, and she had an advantage over the others, because they'd been schooled in the old ways by elders only they got to meet."

"You make it sound like *Lord of the Rings*," Joe said.

She made that face again as she countered, "Yeah, meets *Lord of the Flies*."

"Was there any scuttlebutt about how he might've died? Other than natural causes?"

"Not that I heard. What you just told me doesn't come as a huge shock, now that I think about it, but that's not based on anything."

"Were you aware of his doctor coming by to check him out, or his going to the hospital for any complaints? In the last week, let's say?"

"I'm not sure. It was almost a year ago. I remember the big details, but that? Nothing comes to mind. Why?"

"I'm just thinking about the hospice angle. What they did, how often they visited. All that. The patient has to be pretty far gone for them to be called in. We'll be talking to them, but I was curious about your take on it."

But she was shaking her head. "He may've seen his doc. I don't know about that, and I know nothing about hospice's involvement. You'll have to go straight to the source. Sorry."

Joe nodded in response before asking, "You still okay for time? I don't want to get you in trouble. You've been a huge help."

She checked her watch. "I'm good for a bit more."

"I just have one last favor, at least for now. I'd like you to take me through all the residents, one by one, top to bottom, including any employees you've gotten to know." He quickly interpreted how she took that and added, "Just thumbnail sketches. You described this place as an ant farm. They're still looking a bit like ants to me now. I only want enough to tell one from the other. Can you do that?"

She could. "Sure. I'll give it a shot, but it's all gonna be too short to do any of them justice, and it's all from my perspective."

"Fair enough."

Half an hour later, Joe and Kimona parted ways, leaving him at the end of the first floor's almost three-hundred-foot-long, twenty-foot-high hallway. His head full of verbal portraits of the residents of this eccentric building, he paused to take in his surroundings, looking and listening as if willing himself to absorb what it had to impart.

In his decades as an investigator, he'd become intimate with people exhibiting a propensity for camouflage—often reflected in their chosen environs. Similar to a countercultural tattoo glimpsed beneath an establishment, button-down business shirt, contrasting personality traits dart and hide like furtive animals behind what people show in public. Tales of unhappiness, abuse, or even contentment may go unnoticed, masked by blandness or longing, lust or rage. Social posturings are too often substitutes for lives fenced off.

That left explorers like Joe to decipher which conjurings might be real, while ignoring the disguises.

And so he absorbed the setting around him, as sensitive to what it told him as to what it hid.

It did carry some information, elliptical in nature, just in the way it was presented. As a lifelong New Englander, Joe had been inside any number of old factories—abandoned, resurrected as affordable housing, turned into shopping malls or office buildings. But never as a private home, or whatever this was.

He walked ahead slowly, taking it in. As Sam and Lester had reported, it maintained its prior identity clearly, with the exposed utilities overhead, the tall windows, the broad-planked floor of massive hardwood boards, kept in place with square nails and exposed bolt heads the size of his palm. But it had all been coated over, visibly and not, by the application of uncountable wads of money.

The windowpanes had been swapped for thermal replacements, the surrounding beams and floor carefully restored to something grander, smoother, and more soothing to the eye than the rough, timeworn lumber originally encasing machinery and exhausted workers. The very air, now lavishly filtered through a topflight circulatory system, had been purged of its reek of oil, sweat, and a fog of cast-off lint from spinning miles of thread revolving at high speed.

And it was quiet, reminiscent of museums, churches, or funeral parlors.

How much of this was telling, and how much simply subterfuge, remained to be seen.

Given the sensitive nature of their proposed meeting, Michelle Lyon hadn't wanted to meet Sally at her place of business, suggesting instead the café section of the famed Brattleboro Food Co-Op, one of the largest in the state and a deserving crown jewel of the town's self-consciously progressive image. This was even truer now that it had torn down its shabby previous quarters—an old, adapted cookie-cutter grocery—and replaced it with a much larger, ballyhooed, environmentally friendly marketplace, complete with affordable housing apartments overhead. Some old die-hard hippies hadn't loved the transformation, calling the new digs a rip-off and a sellout to corporate America, but that was partly what gave the whole town its vibrancy—what many termed its crankiness.

Whatever its reputation, the co-op's food was good, the location convenient, and the atmosphere convivial. One almost forgot that years ago, in a seeming paradox, one inter-employee dispute had ended in gunfire, with one dead and the shooter in prison.

Michelle Lyon had described herself as a chunky redhead with glasses, which had struck Sally as an unusually frank self-portrait. It also wasn't wrong, as she discovered upon entering the store's deli section and scanning the seated customers. Michelle's chosen venue perhaps helped to explain her present appearance; she was sitting by the window, both hands wrapped around a remarkably large sandwich. It was nowhere near lunchtime.

Sally wove a path between the mostly empty tables until she stood before her potential employer. "Michelle Lyon?"

Lyon took her eyes off the snow-clad scenery of one of the town's malfunctioning traffic intersections, glanced up at her inquirer, put the sandwich down, and licked her fingers clean before wiping them on her napkin.

"Yes. Sorry. You're a little early."

Sally sat down without offering to shake hands. "Sally Kravitz," she introduced herself. "Annie Paget recommended me?"

Michelle was correct. Sally was early by five minutes, not that it seemed to matter. "Right. Thanks for coming. You want something to eat? My treat."

"No, thank you. I'm fine. Annie said you might be having problems with one of your employees."

Michelle took a sip of her soda and pushed her plate half an inch away, clearing her throat and seemingly gathering her thoughts. "I think so."

"Why not call the police?" Sally asked. "They're pretty good at things like this. They'd also be free."

Michelle was already frowning. "No. I want this done quietly. It's worth it to me to pay. What do you charge?"

Normally, Sally asked to know more about a case before reaching this point, but here she didn't hesitate. "A hundred and twenty-five an hour. One thousand in advance as a retainer."

Michelle gave a half smile, her eyes hard. "My credit no good?"

"I don't know you."

That wasn't entirely true. In fact, Sally had used the databases available to her to check this woman out, including several reserved by subscription to those of her profession. She knew Michelle Lyon to be twenty-nine years old, the mother of a girl, aged six, owner of a two-year-old Prius, married for seven years, co-owner of Food Flourish with her husband, Michael, and—yes—with good credit.

"I don't know you, either," Michelle replied.

"You like the UPS driver who delivers your packages?"

"What? I guess."

"You know his name?"

Michelle smirked. "Okay, fine. I get it. You'll deliver, too, even if we're strangers."

"But only if you hire me."

In response, Michelle dipped into her nearby purse and extracted a checkbook. "This okay?"

"Yup. Make it out to Sally Kravitz LLC."

As part of the same process, Sally slid across the table her standard employment contract, which Michelle also signed, virtually unread.

"Cool," Sally said, folding both check and contract and placing them in her pocket. "What would you like done?"

"Well, that's it, isn't it? I'm not sure. I run a food product business, mostly high-end packaged sauces, flavorings, and spices supplied to restaurants, along with specialty items like caviar, red snapper, olive oil, fancy parmesan cheese and paprika. Almost anything I can sell for wholesale that has a good shelf life and can be used to enhance a restaurant's choice of tasty accessories. Not the fancy chef trade—they charge a fortune and shop for source products directly—but the eateries regular folks splurge on for special occasions. Some of this we even make ourselves; the rest we import and relabel for domestic distribution."

"Sounds very involved."

"I know. It's not, which is how we can do it. We're not Beatrice Foods. We've got a pretty stable, greater Northeast customer base. We're not greedy or trying to take over the world. We've built a niche, almost by word of mouth, and we try to be fast, available, and reliable, versus some faceless, huge outfit where nobody's accountable."

"Okay," Sally said patiently. Now that she was on the clock, she was content with Lyon wasting paid time.

"All that means there's a fair amount of autonomy among the staff. We know how to do everyone else's jobs, more or less, barring bookkeeping and other specialty things, but we're not pigeonholed generally. The phone rings or an email comes through, it's whoever's closest who grabs it and puts it into play."

"Meaning your supervision can get a little murky?" Sally suggested.

Michelle's response was wry. "You could say that. Inventory and income expectations have taken a dip for no definable reason, and I can't pin the tail on any donkey because of the way we operate."

Sally pulled out a notepad and flipped it open to a blank page. "Okay. You better lay it out—who're your employees, their backgrounds, how do you manage your money, what comes in and what goes out."

Presumably to brace herself, Michelle took another bite before beginning.

CHAPTER FIVE

Joe Gunther wasn't the only one to occasionally avoid a direct approach. One of the hallmarks of the VBI was that their investigators were culled from Vermont's law enforcement community precisely because of their ingenuity. Acceptance to the agency was less a reward for ambition and a high solve rate, and more a reflection of consistent thoughtfulness being put to original use. By and large, VBI special agents were independent, not given to comfort in numbers, and prone to following good hunches.

As Willy Kunkle was doing now.

Unknowingly duplicating his boss's reaction, Willy's instinct following the Lyon clan squad briefing was to ponder how best to approach what was looking like a quagmire. Sam, Lester, and—he presumed—Joe, would all be wading in and conducting a near-endless number of primary interviews.

Willy would join them in that soon enough—they did have to be done—but he chose to begin with a more global approach, and for that, he had the perfect man in mind.

Dan Kravitz had been an informant of Willy's for years—a CI, in police jargon. At one time the ubiquitous employee no one ever noticed working in the backs of garages or truck terminals, shoveling, sweeping, or repairing machinery, Dan had moved from job to job all over Brattleboro. So quiet he was sometimes mistaken for a mute, he remained unnervingly clean, despite the filthiness of his surroundings, forever watching, listening, and remembering. These last traits had initially brought him to Willy's attention, coupled with Dan's readiness to help the cop in righting the wrongs around them.

There evolved an irony to this, however, which Willy had only started suspecting before his CI changed careers and largely vanished from sight. Dan, at first unknown to everyone except his young and observant daughter, Sally, had throughout been living a second life as a skilled and specialized burglar, entering high-end homes not for material goods, but for the data stored on people's electronic platforms—data he was now exploiting far from the public eye. He remained an invaluable source to Willy, who now simply made a point of never questioning the source of Dan's information.

Adding to this need for diplomacy, that daughter, of course, had later become a private investigator.

Willy and Dan met, as was their habit, in some out-of-the-way corner of town, deserving of a scene from *All the President's Men*. It wasn't in a public garage, but, because of the weather, it did occur inside Willy's heated car. Climate change notwithstanding, Vermont's next-door neighbor remained Canada, so while the temperatures had been flukily warm this year, they still hadn't forestalled icicles hanging from the eaves.

"Hello," Dan said after sliding into the passenger seat, seemingly addressing the front window. They didn't shake hands—neither liked the habit—and Willy had grown used to the other's refusal to meet his eyes, along with his propensity for having a vocabulary like

Mr. Chips's, if and when he spoke at all. Willy often wondered how Sally had turned out as genial as she appeared.

"Hello, yourself," he couldn't resist replying.

Dan left it there, not moving or speaking more, waiting for Willy to explain his summons.

"You know about the Lyon family?" Willy therefore started off.

"Nathan Lyon?"

"Yes."

"I do."

"Tell me about them. I've got the family tree, the rats-in-a-can setup, and the fact that the old man died a year ago, but I want to know what makes 'em tick before I start with the interviews."

"Why would you be interviewing them?" Dan asked reasonably.

But Willy had his doubts about the legitimacy of the question. He knew this man well enough to imagine that Dan was asking something for which he already knew the answer.

That was Dan's ace in the hole, of course, which again he'd only fully shared with Sally. Dan hadn't simply collected people's information during his break-ins. He'd implanted viruses in their electronics. After his purported retirement, he'd sat back in a sealed-off location full of his own computers, and eavesdropped on the exponentially expanding traffic between those tapped machines and their brethren, since each of his viruses had been designed to go forth and multiply with any other device it contacted. Dan's database had thus supplied him in short order a view of the surrounding world that the NSA would have envied.

Only vaguely suspecting the truth of all this, however, Willy was reduced to playing the straight man. "That death is looking like a homicide."

That drew a slight turn of Dan's head toward him, along with a surprised, "Really?"

"You never caught a whiff of that?" Willy asked doubtfully.

Dan's answer was a cautious, "I was aware that his passing shook the family tree."

"Ah," Willy said. "What about that?"

"Nathan was an egomaniacal autocrat," Dan began, "which wore on some, less so on others."

Willy consulted his notepad. "Start with Rob, the eldest."

"He's one of the less-so's," Dan told him. "Unmarried, no children, I think Rob enjoyed the limitations, especially now that he and Monica are comanagers of the tribe."

"That was another thing I wanted confirmed," Willy said. "So the two of them are Nathan reborn?"

Dan was back to speaking directly to the windshield, his hands motionless in his lap. "Hardly. It's more like they're sharing the street sweeping after Nathan's parade. There's quite a bit of unhappiness under that big roof and a considerable amount of conspiring. The money was the fire keeping everyone warm, and Nathan the iron lid on top of the pot. Now only the money's left, and from what you're telling me about a murder—or the acknowledgment of it—I imagine things will start boiling over soon enough."

Willy wanted confirmation. "But Rob and Monica do control the cash."

"For the time being," Dan confirmed, "through a trust. But to switch metaphors, if Nathan, as the leader of the pack, finally earned being killed, what does that say about the rest of the pack's restlessness?"

"Why stop with Nathan?" Willy asked rhetorically.

"Precisely."

"Is there any particular member who's hungrier than the others?" Willy asked.

Dan hesitated, belying the notion that police informants couldn't be as careful and calculating as their handlers. Dan, after all, was engaged in a highly illegal—and very lucrative—activity. Given that he was ignorant about who had killed Nathan Lyon, being overly generous with his opinions could only further expose him to Willy's professional curiosity.

"That would be guesswork," he therefore replied.

"It's okay," Willy reassured him. "Give me some probabilities. I won't come back to haunt you."

That, Dan could live with. "Well, from what I've learned over time, Monica is one to watch. She goes back a long way and has expensive tastes. Keeping with the women for a moment, Michelle, Mike's wife, might be a bit of an operator, although perhaps just more obvious than Mike himself. Gene's wife, Peggy, is restless and un-happy, I know. And I like Penny Trick for her natural complexity, if not for being subtle or devious. More a tortured soul, that one. She's the daughter of a hardworking, middle-class couple, and stepsister to Monica's now hyper-wealthy son—Gene. She fits neither camp, is torn between cultures, has no husband or child to distract her from a mixed bag of self-destructive desires." He paused before adding, "As I said, tortured. Crooked? Perhaps. Confused? Definitely. I person-ally hope she's only an innocent if damaged bystander. She's suffered enough."

Dan lapsed into silence, which was Willy's cue to move on. "The guys," he said. "What about them?"

After a thoughtful pause, Dan recited from memory, "Rob is the most buttoned-down. Wary, watchful, probably clinically repressed. I would say his contents are under extreme pressure, but what they are and how they'll find expression—if ever—I have no idea."

"Okay," Willy said half to himself.

"Gene," Dan continued, "is a dreamer. A sweet soul surrounded by prickly, needy malcontents. He's most like his adoptive mother,

Betsy. He's a good businessman, mostly because it's easy for him, but he doesn't care about ambition or money. He's the proverbial square peg, his art being his only perfect fit."

He continued without prompting. "That puts him at odds with the youngest of Nathan's three boys, Michael, who is as crude, careless, and unoriginal as a frat party drunkard. He is not blessed with Nathan's or even his wife's, Michelle's, brains, but is greedy and angry nevertheless. I would fully expect him to misbehave at some point. In what manner remains to be seen."

"There are three businesses run out of the mill," Willy said, impressed by the depth of Dan's insight, while respectful of his not revealing too much. "The food supplies operation, Gene's pottery studio, and old man Russell's log cabin outfit. Any of those got meat on 'em?"

Dan reflected for a moment. His answer, when it came, was elusive enough that Willy knew especially not to press him. "I wouldn't ignore Food Flourish."

Fredo eyed his cousin angrily staring from a park bench at the murky water drifting by, his collar turned up and his hands jammed into his coat pockets.

"God, that man's an asshole," Eddie said.

"He gave you something, didn't he?"

Eddie nodded once. "Yeah. Thanks for that."

Fredo had driven them to behind a warehouse overlooking the Providence River, hoping the long, open view of distant cranes and storage tanks of the Exxon terminal in East Providence would help calm Eddie down. Unpredictably, it seemed to be working, if slowly— along with the cold breeze pushing the odd sailboat along.

"We're family, Eddie," Fredo said. "You'd help me in a jam. Hell, your going inside was only to be useful to your daughter."

Eddie's response was bitter. "Yeah. That turned out real good.

Now she's got me around her neck with all her other problems. Just what I didn't want."

Fredo thought of Marie's own daughter, developmentally delayed and in a special school whose costs had forced Marie to take a second job working nights. He was about to ask about her, but changed his mind, not wanting to drive home Eddie's very point of having become an additional burden.

"What d'ya wanna do now?" he asked instead.

Eddie was still distracted by self-pity. "What d'ya mean?"

"Well, hell. Neri said it was Zucco who put out the hit on Vito for screwin' up his arrangement with Bianchi. And it was Zucco who sent a go-between to you to take the fall, wasn't it? That's where I'd start."

"Assuming Neri wasn't full of it, Fredo. Plus, Zucco's dead. You know that."

"Some of his people aren't. You told me you wanted to get who killed Vito. I'll guarantee you it wasn't Zucco. It was one of his boys. You wanna learn how this went down—who did what to who—you need to find some lieutenant of Zucco's who's still breathing. What was the name Neri gave us at the end, after you pushed him for more?"

Eddie's voice was flat, but Fredo could recognize a flicker of interest. "Moretti."

"Right. Phil Moretti. We just need to find somebody who knows where he's at."

For the first time, Eddie took his eyes off the river and looked at him. "I suppose."

That was good enough for Fredo. He rose from the bench and returned to the car.

"I love that smell."

Lester ushered Sam through the door labeled ER CERAMICS, into a slightly damp fug that to him had the odor of wet dirt, tinged by a faint tang of hot electrical wiring. "You a potter?" he asked in surprise.

"In my dreams," she replied, twisting her neck to take in a room of over two thousand square feet. It was on the first floor of the Lyon mill, as the team was calling it, and thus equipped with a two-story-high ceiling. Its train station dimensions had been cut up and channeled by rows of shelving, long tables, and islands clustered around key pieces of equipment. A couple of people in clay- and color-stained clothing were working or moving about, but no one paid the newcomers any attention as they stood in the doorway and took in their surroundings.

"It's laid out well," Sam commented. "I'll give them that."

Lester wasn't convinced. He just saw dust covering most surfaces, a stained floor, and what appeared to be a confusion of arcane tools, either lying around or hanging from pegboards. Not to mention row upon row of shelves packed with thousands of unglazed pots, mugs, plates, bowls, and those cute sayings people buy to hang on the wall.

"Could fool me," he said under his breath.

Sam pointed to one corner and swung her arm slowly as she spoke. "Start with wet clay storage, then to wedging tables, throwing and/or rolling, sculpting, drying, glazing, firing. It's a progression. It changes depending on what you're making, but it goes from wet to dry to packing and shipping. This is a big operation, and well equipped. Multiples of everything, including kilns."

By now, they'd taken advantage of being ignored to advance into the room, seeing more of it revealed. It was, in fact, a small factory, making Lester think of pictures he'd seen of big European studios in history or art books.

"Sorry," said a man from behind them. "This is actually not a retail space. My insurance company would have a fit if they caught you in here."

They turned to see a wiry man of medium height in his forties, with a retreating hairline and a ponytail, dressed in clothes so covered with clay byproducts that he seemed qualified for one of the drying racks.

"You Gene Russell?" Lester asked.

"I am, but I'm afraid I still have to ask you to leave."

By instinct, both cops opened their coats to reveal their badges.

"Police, Mr. Russell," Sam told him. "I'm Special Agent Martens. This is Special Agent Spinney. We're from the VBI."

"Ah," the man replied, caught off guard. He wiped a hand ineffectually on his jeans and offered to shake. "I heard you were around. Something about Nathan's death."

They each greeted him formally, Sam still talking. "That's correct. You were Mr. Lyon's stepson. Isn't that right?"

Russell looked from one of them to the other. "Technically. None of this makes sense, though. Are you positive somebody killed him?"

"Yeah," Lester dragged out the word slightly, for emphasis.

The potter rubbed both hands against his pants this time, a gesture Sam sometimes associated with sweaty palms. "What do you want to know?"

She took the long way around to answering that, indicating the room surrounding them. "This is a big setup. You must be doing well."

He frowned slightly. "I'm not complaining."

"Still," she persisted. "Two of everything, top of the line, if I'm any judge."

He nodded. "We split the business between the champagne trade and the tourists." He took a few steps to his right to remove an item from the nearest rack and held it up. "Vermont-y log cabin, complete with removable roof." He demonstrated before replacing it, adding, "We glaze it cheaply and colorfully. It sells like crazy, even though only millionaires can afford real log cabins in this state."

"Like what your adoptive dad builds," Lester said.

"Oh," Gene reacted. "I guess you're right. He builds affordable ones, too. Small ones." He opened his mouth to add something, but then reconsidered.

"What?" Lester prompted him. "What were you going to say?"

"Nothing, really. I consider Ned my dad, period, and Betsy, my mom. Nathan was just my bio-mom's donor, and as for her, Monica . . ." He hesitated. "Well, we've figured out a relationship."

"That's got to be tough," Sam commented. They all three stepped aside as a worker walked by carrying a large tray of mugs.

"I know this is inconvenient," she continued, "and we promise to get out of your hair soon, but do you have a corner where we can talk some more?"

"Sure," Gene said, turning on his heel and leading them to a small, open-ceiling office in a far corner, complete with a view of the snow-clotted parking lot. It was far from pristine, and jammed with a hodgepodge of filing cabinets, catalogs, pottery odds and ends, along with a desk, a computer, and three chairs.

"Excuse the mess," he requested, removing a few items from one of the seats.

"Not a problem," Sam assured him as they settled down. She immediately followed up on what had just piqued her interest. "You mentioned how you were balancing two sets of parents under one roof. On top of so many other family members in this building, that must get tricky."

His kind and friendly face looked mildly pained. "Ah. *The Waltons* on mood stabilizers," he said, referring to the old sentimental TV show. "Yeah. Well, it's never been like that. Not even close. I should make it clear, though, Dad—Ned to you—only has his office here. He and Mom live off campus, in the real world."

"Tell us about your dad," Lester requested, enjoying his easy manner. "Having him in the mill, even if it's only during working hours, is pretty unusual, isn't it? Did he even know Nathan Lyon when you were growing up with him and Betsy and your sister, Penny?"

"For that matter," Sam threw in, "did any of you know Monica? Or did she give you up without strings?"

Gene was already shaking his head. "No, no. I was clueless about all of it. Mom and Dad told me I'd been adopted. They thought that was only fair, that I should know. It didn't come as a total shock, since Penny and I are almost the same age and in no way alike. We always figured something was off. But I doubt our parents ever knew Monica's identity. That's usually a rule in adoptions, isn't it?"

"Who found who?" Lester asked. "Did you dig up Monica, or did she come hunting for you?"

"Neither," was the response. "It was Nathan. He probably hired someone, or more likely bribed them, to find out. I figured that's why Monica's always been pretty cool around me. She wasn't interested in the first place."

"How's she as a mom to Mike?" Lester asked, who had two kids of his own, one an adult, the other an older teen.

Gene saw some humor in that. "Good point. I shouldn't complain she's playing favorites." He reflected a moment before admitting, "I have no idea why she had any kids. Now, technically, she's stuck with three sons and two grandkids. Might as well saddle a cat with a litter of puppies."

"Can I go back to why Ned's got his office here?" Sam asked.

"It's your party," Gene replied. "The answer is, you'll have to ask him. It'll either be money or blackmail. Or both. That's why most of us're here."

Lester asked the obvious question. "Including you?"

Gene looked rueful. "Better add spinelessness."

Ooh, that hurts, Sam thought, who was coming to enjoy this man's apparent honesty, even if she didn't like his ponytail.

Gene sighed. "You know, it's funny. When Nathan died, I thought a mantle would fall, that the world would change and we'd all wake up, like in some fairy tale. But now I know better. Nathan was a manipulative, vainglorious man. But none of us called him out on it; we ignored it in exchange for money and all this." He spread his arms wide. "Or because of the threat of having him take it away."

He looked at them with pent-up passion. "But the power he had was the power we gave him. He may've been a jerk, but we fed that in him, to a point where his being alive didn't matter anymore."

"The jail survived the jailer," Lester suggested.

Gene nodded. "I know it's ridiculous to complain. All this excess and the money it represents. Everyone should be so lucky. But all of us except the two little kids have surrendered, first to Nathan and now to the trust he left behind."

He paused before adding, "Monica's a different story, since she's pre-Brattleboro—she and Rob. I never figured her out, even though she's the only hundred percent relative I have here. And Rob's a total mystery. As for Dad, to finally answer your question, I did ask him once, since I'd always thought he was made of stronger stuff. He told me it was bigger than he could fight and to let it go."

"What did that mean?" Sam asked.

"Like I said, ask him. It sure implied Nathan had gotten to him somehow, and I doubt it was through flattery."

"He threatened him?"

"Good luck finding out. Dad's an old-fashioned New Englander. But look at the business he's in, building specialty houses for upscale people. That's a natural marketplace for Nathan."

"How did Nathan make his money?" Lester asked, seemingly out of the blue.

"Go to Mike and Michelle for that one," Gene said. "Nathan weighed in heavily when they set up their food business ten years ago. I'm guessing he was into something similar back in the day, on a much bigger level."

"Around here?"

"Nope. Someplace south. That was one of the forbidden subjects." Gene drew his finger across his lips.

"Did he lean on you, too, when you were setting up this business?" Sam asked.

"You have to understand," he answered, "I already admitted to the weakness of our natures. The flip side is who's feeding that, even bankrolling it. And who better than a sociopath? That was Nathan, through and through. He could be as seductive as he was ruthless and groom the most stubborn man in any room. Or cripple him if he didn't yield."

He shifted in his seat. "I love Dad. He's a man's man, self-taught, tough as nails, proud, and responsible. He puts value on honor and the flag and family, and bringing yourself up by your own bootstraps, to quote him. But when the time came, and Nathan showed up with his money and his wily ways, Dad's influence on me didn't stand a chance. I sold out like that." He snapped his fingers.

"Before you ask," he added. "Penny did the same thing, but then she and Dad were always oil and water. She hates him to this day. Me? I wish I could turn the clock back, to be honest. I love what I do, when I'm talking about working a lump of clay with my hands, all alone. But to make a living doing something as uncommercial as that? Good luck unless you have somebody like Nathan greasing the skids. I kidded myself that my son, Mark, and wife, Peggy, would be the beneficiaries. That's certainly how Nathan pitched it to me early on. Before I knew it, I'd isolated myself from Dad, sold my soul to Nathan, and ended up with no father at all, with only myself to blame."

He gazed at the floor meditatively. "After that, it just became a habit, I think for all of us. In the end, Nathan's dying barely caused a ripple. We'd already been bought and paid for."

There was a knock on the door, and one of Gene's employees stuck his head in. "Paul's got a question about the Williston order. There's something screwy with the paperwork."

Gene half rose and glanced questioningly at his guests, both of whom were already getting up.

"Go," Sam told him. "And thanks. We'll probably be back, if that's okay."

"Anytime," he said from the doorway. "It's never gonna be pretty, but I'll tell you what I know."

The two cops were left standing in the empty office.

"What do you think?" Sam asked.

"We didn't ask him what he was doing on the night Nathan died."

"We will," she said. "Not that I see him as the doer. He talks too much for that."

Lester looked up to take in the building overhead. "The house of evil," he said half to himself.

Sam seconded him. "Certainly the house that Nathan built."

CHAPTER SIX

Gene Russell was taking his own advice, sitting in the darkened studio, a single lamp on above the kick wheel. The dark room was so vast and tall that no light reflected back, although he could make out the barest image of himself in one of the distant windowpanes, looking like a sole voyager hunkered over a late-night campfire, far off in the distance.

It felt a little like floating in space, alone with his memories, his hands wet and slimy against the spinning clay, his foot rhythmically and unconsciously keeping the wheel going. Stimulated by what he'd been telling the police officers earlier, he'd begun yearning for at least the barest touch of his origins, when there'd been no business, deadlines, or payroll to worry about.

And no haunting sense of self-betrayal.

He wasn't truly making anything. The kilns were off, the place silent apart from the sounds of his own labor. He kept this one wheel off in a corner, under a tarp, ignored except by him. Indeed, he was among only a few of them who even knew how to operate it, the rest having yielded to the convenience of electric motors.

But this was Gene's preference. In his imagination, he could transport this simple machine, despite its modern ball bearings and steel sleeving, all the way back to prehistory. And even earlier, to cavemen placing their hands against rock walls and daubing them with paint to leave an outline. Humans had always valued the mold-able qualities of river mud and clay, and applying them to create the likes of bowls, dishes, and mugs. What, after all, ranked among the oldest of archeological finds, along with flints and bones and circled stones stained with soot? Pottery shards.

What he was doing now, this moment, took him away from kitschy log cabin boxes, putting him back in touch with the fundamentals that had first drawn him to this art form—its earthiness, usefulness, and primordial history. This was the best of all therapies for him, far from the pressures of modernity and the weight of compromise.

It put him in such a place of calm that all he could experience was the slippery substance between his fingers and the hum of the wheel.

He felt nothing of the blow that killed him aside from a painless explosion of light. He was dead before toppling from his seat.

The Vermont State Police Crime Scene Search Team, shortened, thankfully, to CSST, consists of plainclothes detectives and field force troopers who, when needed, respond as a unit from their other assigned duties to process crime scenes throughout Vermont, regard-less of whether those scenes "belong" to the VSP or not. It was a good way to maximize resources, be supportive of other agencies, and give a telling counter-push to the notion that the state police didn't play well with others.

Vermont's total complement of full-time officers, border to bor-der, across all agencies, was about a thousand, or one-fortieth of the NYPD's. The state's population was also admittedly tiny, meaning that not only did a pragmatic attitude generally prevail, but that someone of Joe's extraordinarily long tenure, coupled with the VBI's ubiquity, had probably met or worked with 60 percent of Vermont's law enforcement community.

Including Sergeant Jim Collins, who was one of only two troopers permanently assigned to the CSST, and thus responsible for responding with his team, as well as keeping it up, running, certified, and trained. He and Joe had worked together, off and on, for almost fifteen years.

As they were now, side by side, dressed in white Tyvek suits, booties, and nitrile gloves, looking down at the supine body of the late Eugene "Gene" Russell.

They had been here for a couple of hours already, dividing the jobs of interviewing, photographing, collecting, measuring, documenting, and checking for any and all video footage, electronic texts, emails, usage logs, and eyewitnesses. They were barely warming up to these tasks when they found themselves by coincidence gazing down at the body slowly stiffening in their midst.

"First impressions?" Joe asked, fresh from having read Lester and Sam's report on their interview of this man the day before.

Collins pushed his lower lip out thoughtfully. "First? Slip and fall." He began pointing things out as he spoke. "The floor's wet because of the clay-and-water mix by the wheel. His sneakers are smooth-soled and worn, essentially making them skates. You can see the furrows on the floor leading to the feet, and how their directionality supports his heels having gone out from under him."

He shifted position slightly before continuing. "At the head, there's not just one but several of these pastry roller thingies that seem to have come off the pegboard over there and landed on the floor, including the one he hit with the nape of his neck when he landed on his back. The windows were all closed, the one door locked, and there are no other footprints in this puddle of slime. Plus, I gather this fella had a habit of burning the midnight oil all by himself, just like it seems he was doing last night."

Joe was nodding throughout this recitation, acknowledging its apparent accuracy. Now he peered at his colleague to suggest with a touch of humor, "But . . ."

Collins acknowledged the implication. "Well, like you said, those're first impressions, maybe carefully arranged for our benefit. Didn't you say you were already crawling around this building, checking out another homicide?"

"You think this is a new one?" Joe asked.

"I'm not saying a word," Collins replied. "You know me better than that. It's too early to say."

"What's bugging you about it?" Joe asked.

"Those." Collins pointed at the rolling pins, of which there were three, all made of gray granite, including the one dramatically lodged under Russell's neck. "We're being asked to believe," he explained, "that in this otherwise undisturbed section, they fell off the wall just as Mr. Russell was returning to his pottery wheel, startling him, and causing him to fall, whereupon he struck one of them just right and broke his neck."

Joe played along. "And your problem with that?"

"Big picture? Not much. Little details? A lot. Start with the pins. If that's what happened, they came off the pegboard, bounced off the worktable below, rolled or bounced again onto the floor, and then rolled out to here. Or at least one of them did. In the world of action and reaction, that's a really long sequence—a lot longer than the startle reflex that causes a man to twist in surprise at the noise, and then slip and fall."

"In other words, Gene would've been on the floor before the first pin reached where he could've caught it with the back of his head."

"Exactamundo. And look at the skid marks. They look familiar?"

Joe was unsure what he was being asked. "They don't look unusual."

Collins was pleased. "*Bingo.* Just like they look when your feet go out from under you as you're walking downhill and you hit an icy patch."

"Except there's no hill here," Joe suggested.

Collins squatted down to get nearer. "Look at them," he urged. "Parallel. Same starting point, like when you suddenly stop after a running start. Not after you've been slowly walking through the dark. In that scenario, one foot starts first, and the other follows, usually going out at an angle as you twist in surprise."

"Was he walking through the dark?" Joe asked.

Collins pointed out the lamp hanging over the wheel. "That was the only light on when we got here."

He rose and approached the wheel. "Which brings up what he was doing walking around in the first place. Look at his hands," he ordered Joe.

"Dirty."

"As if he stopped working the clay in mid-project," Collins confirmed. "If he'd wanted to go pee, he'd have headed in the other direction; if he'd just gone and was coming back, his hands would be clean. Maybe you don't wash after taking a leak. But I'll almost guarantee you that if your hands were that sloppy, you'd at least rinse 'em before grabbing your pecker to do your business. Human nature."

"What else?"

Collins was staring at the evidence before him, gently shaking his head. "I know throwing clay is messy, and you gotta keep it wet as you go. I saw that movie with Swayze and Demi Moore. But look at how the water's distributed on the floor. It goes out like a smoke plume, toward where the body's lying. Shouldn't there be less of it? And shouldn't it be splashed around where he was sitting, in a circle? This is a total mess."

Finally, he stooped over the actual wheel, studying the lump of air-dried clay in its middle. "And last but not least, you got this. No potter I know half makes a mug, or whatever this was, and walks away. Not unless somebody yells, 'Fire!' from down the hall, which we know didn't happen. So, what's the story here?"

Joe's reservations echoed Collins's. "I don't disagree. Problem is, it's all interpretive," he said. "Someone else could say he just slipped and fell."

Collins sighed. "Yep." He then straightened and took in the rest of the room—a general appraising the field of battle. "But," he emphasized, "we've barely scratched the surface. Talk to me later. We haven't even rolled him over yet. Might be he has a knife in his back, complete with fingerprints."

Joe patted his Tyvek-clad back. "We can only hope."

Sally sat in her car, as ensconced and comfortable as a bookkeeper before a computer screen. Her view was of the passing world, however, and of fellow human beings. Also, unlike in an office, she had a choice of creature comforts and professional aids within easy reach to lighten her tedium and ease any discomfort. Water bottles, snacks, a urinal, binoculars, camera, various hats, scarves, and coats to change her appearance. Essentially, her purposefully nondescript car was like a miniature camper—cramped, perhaps, but with all the necessities for a snug sleepover.

She didn't need most of it today. She was parked for a short time only on a low hill overlooking the distant Lyon family mill, watching the Food Flourish entrance.

Michelle Lyon had supplied a list of nine people who worked

various shifts at the business. Sally had run all their names—not using her father's alluring resources, which she rarely tapped into for legal and ethical reasons—and she'd driven by their various homes and apartments, learning about them anecdotally. Did they drive? Did they have kids or spouses or intimate others? Did they own or rent where they lived? Were they semiretired or just starting out? What were their politics? Did they have a checkered financial or criminal past? The list of options available to her were many, and her expertise at ferreting out such details considerable. The data didn't include everything available to law enforcement—or to Dan—but it was enough to give her the insights she sought, at least early on.

Now came the more tedious phase of putting faces to names. This didn't mean merely taking pictures of them as they came and went from Food Flourish; it involved tailing the most interesting selections to better learn of their habits, friends, and possibly unsavory enthusiasms.

This initial list numbered five of the nine. She'd scratched off one woman she actually knew and another who was near her dotage and working to pay her husband's medical bills. And there were a couple of others whose profiles simply didn't trigger her alarms.

Of the remainder, as far as she could tell so far, it was a crapshoot. They were the usual assortment of men and women who lived more or less messy lives and were capable, if not culpable, of yielding to temptation and crossing that thin line into committing a criminal act.

The questions were, who among them was the one she was after? What exactly were they up to? And how was she going to close her case rapidly and affordably?

And now, of course, there was an extra wrinkle, evidenced by the messy cluster of official vehicles jamming up the parking lot below. As Sally had determined by monitoring local electronic smartphone traffic—a sea of text-happy busybodies that seemed to cover the earth nowadays, watching, recording, and broadcasting over chat rooms— there'd been a death at the mill, in a business down the way from Food Flourish, belonging to one of Michelle's relatives.

Since there wasn't anything she could do to ease this complication, and an extra pair of eyes might be handy because of it, and—finally—because it would benefit the best friend she had, Sally reached for her phone and speed-dialed it.

"*Brattleboro Reformer.* Rachel Reiling speaking. How may I help you?"

"Hey there," Sally said. "You dying for a hot tip?"

"Ooh," the reporter replied, her pleasure obvious at hearing Sally's voice. "What've you got?"

"You been eavesdropping on scannerland?" Sally asked, referring in older terms to the newfangled news feed she'd been monitoring.

"No," Rachel said. "I was just wrapping up a piece. What's going on?"

"A death at ER Ceramics, at the Lyon mill. Cops and crime lab people are crawling all over it."

"Who is it?"

"Dunno yet."

"A homicide?"

"Dunno that, either. I'm working something else in the neighborhood. But I know how you love your bodies."

Rachel read between the lines, and asked, "Is Joe Gunther there? Or any of his team?"

It was a telling two-pronged question. Joe was virtually Rachel's stepfather, being her mother's romantic partner, and the VBI was only called upon for major cases.

Sally's pleasure at being the messenger grew. "Yep," she said.

"I'm on my way."

"You got it. Don't look for me. I'm playing invisible."

"Roger that."

Rhode Islanders, who are more prone than other lowlander New Englanders to call themselves Swamp Yankees, resent the hell out of the Mafia, in the same vein as New Jerseyites. In Rhode Island's case, however, the reputation that the Mob stamped on the state and obsessive media attention to its hoodlums, kept it from being heralded for its more laudatory attributes. Faded America's Cup glory notwithstanding, or the paler ghosts inhabiting Newport's echoing mansions, Little Rhody, in the regional vernacular, is a justly proud repository of history, culture, cuisine, commerce, and multiracial commingling that makes Vermont look like a child's start-up kit.

The fact that the Mob chose this diminutive collection of islands to set down roots right in time for the Roaring Twenties and Prohibition largely just pisses locals off.

Fredo and Eddie were driving in Johnston, west of Providence and the Woonasquatucket River, distinctive for having eighteen dams along its fifteen-mile length, all of which used to supply hydropower to the plants and mills lining its shores.

As suggestive as that was of nineteenth-century sweatshop factories, spewing pollution and working women and children to death, the reality today was mostly modern American Bland—shopping malls, commercial strips, auto graveyards, and converted factories, closing around pockets of sedate, middle-class neighborhoods that stuck like barnacles to the river's banks.

These suburban enclaves were fenced in between two major, parallel "miracle miles," Woonasquatucket Avenue in West Providence, and George Waterman Road in Johnston, creating a swath of homes for that economic stratum between those who own everything and those barely making ends meet.

From what the two cousins had learned, this was where old wise-guy Phil Moretti had chosen to live out his days.

There was a sour irony for Eddie, being here, surrounded by shade trees and residential split-levels, lining quiet, almost suburban streets. This was what he'd aspired to in his grand scheme, instead of living off Marie. By the same token, that a drone like Moretti had ended up here drove home what Neri had thrown in Eddie's face: Eddie was a have-not—not a made man, not connected, and with a piss-poor sense of timing. Just a wannabe who'd gambled and lost.

"You ready?" Fredo asked him, eyeing the modest, tidy home they'd parked opposite.

"You sure he lives here?"

Fredo masked his irritation. "That's what we were told, Eddie. You were there. Did you believe what you heard or not?"

He was referring to the classic guy-who-knows-a-guy—a minor-league gangster with whom they'd had a cup of coffee hours earlier, and who'd claimed to know where Moretti lived.

"What's the worst that can happen?" Fredo asked.

"He could shoot us through the door," Eddie answered.

That, Fredo hadn't been expecting. He punched his cousin lightly in the shoulder. "There you go—a hero's send-off. Christ Almighty. Why do I spend time with you?"

For once, Eddie showed a glimmer of humor, patting the back of the other man's hand. "Must be my love of life."

Fredo snorted. "Get your ass outta the car. Let's do this."

They navigated the small barrier of soiled, icy snow by the curb and reached the sidewalk, Eddie in fact wondering, if briefly, why indeed Fredo was keeping him company—not that he wasn't grateful. Fredo's attention was in many ways the first true show of friendship he'd received in decades, his long-suffering daughter's tolerance of him notwithstanding.

In fact, he'd never been visited by Fredo while in prison, not that he blamed him. It would have only been awkward anyhow. They were like old VFW buddies in that way—linked by kinship, nostalgia, and, now especially, maybe a pinch of realization that their own mortality was looming nigh.

But neither one of them went in for much sentimentality.

"Here goes nuthin'," Fredo said quietly, heading toward the building's front walk.

Eddie pressed the doorbell, hearing its chime from within. He was about to repeat the gesture a full minute later when a muffled male voice demanded, "Who're you?"

"Eddie Moscone and Fredo Sindaco," he answered.

There was a long pause, followed by, "Eddie 'the Mouse'?"

"Ignore it," Fredo urged in a whisper.

Eddie's response was flat, almost bored. "Yeah."

The door opened a crack. "The fuck do you want?" Neither of them could see the speaker.

Fredo spoke up, not trusting Eddie's choice of comebacks. "Hey, Mr. Moretti. Sorry to bother. We're just trying to piece together some ancient history. From the old days—Al Zucco, Knuckles Alfano. Stuff like that."

"They're dead."

"Which is why we're here."

"This my reward for livin' long?"

Filling in Eddie's stony silence, Fredo maintained his patter. "C'mon, Mr. Moretti. Give us a break. It would mean a lot."

Another silence before their possible host said, "One at a time. Mouse first. You know the drill. Come in with your coats open."

Fredo gave his cousin an encouraging look and a small tap on the back. "Go for it."

Eddie followed instructions, pushing the door open with his toe, stepping inside and standing still, the edges of his coat held wide. He was alone in a vestibule with a side table, a mirror, and a couple of closets, facing the doorway to a hall beyond. Unlike the building's exterior, the décor had conspicuously cost a bundle—beveled edges to the mirror, the table Queen Anne, adorned with two vases. The ceiling molding was hand carved and ornate.

The voice came from around the edge of the distant doorframe, its harsh tone scratching against such surroundings. "Drop the coat on the ground, lift up your shirt, turn around easy."

Silently, now working on a slow burn, Eddie did as he'd been told, thinking back to uncounted hundreds of times he'd undergone searches in prison.

"Lift up your pant legs."

He did that, too, displaying socks and no ankle holsters. "Want me to take the whole shirt off?" he asked, still without inflection.

"I want you to give me shit, I'll tell you. Unbutton it, so I can see if you're wired."

Without a change of expression, Eddie did remove the shirt, his undershirt, and finally dropped his pants.

"Okay, okay," Moretti conceded. "I get it. Stayin' alive takes practice, you know?"

Silently, Eddie put his clothes back on.

Moretti showed himself, at least halfway, a gun hanging loose by his side. He was short, powerfully built, and with a thick tuft of hair protruding above his partially unbuttoned, custom-made shirt. "Have a seat over there." He nodded to the most distant chair from the door.

After Eddie had done so, Moretti yelled to Fredo and had him repeat the same ritual.

Moretti waited until both men were ready before gesturing to them. "Follow me," he said, and preceded them down the hall.

He brought them to an expensively furnished living room, whose windows overlooked an in-ground, tarp-covered swimming pool, weighted down by remnants of old snow, and accessorized by a cluster of nearby all-weather chairs and tables.

"Sit," he ordered, gesturing to a couple of easy chairs. After they'd complied, he chose the sofa opposite them for himself. Eddie recognized that he and Fredo had been directed toward constraining seating, leaving their host the ability to rise fast and cut in either direction, if need be. There was also a low coffee table between them, and, as if more emphasis were needed, Moretti nonchalantly laid his pistol on the pillow beside him.

"What about Zucco and Knuckles?" he asked. "Haven't heard those names in a while."

Eddie finally spoke. "I did time for Vito Alfano's murder. I didn't do it, but I paid the ticket. I want to know the details."

Moretti looked confused. "*You* wanna know? I'm supposed to care?"

"It was a contract," Fredo explained politely. "Eddie did his end; he was told he'd be taken care of after."

"Who by?"

"Zucco's boy. De Luca."

"Manny?" Moretti repeated. "Damn. You two're like a walking obit. Another dead man."

"But he worked for Zucco," Fredo said.

"So? I did, too—over Manny." Moretti made himself more comfortable, crossing his legs and stretching his arms out to either side, along the top of the sofa. It was the kind of gesture Eddie had been hoping for.

"Was he told to talk to me or not?" he asked, trying to sound conversational.

Moretti lifted his chin a fraction of an inch—a man in control.

"Course. That's why you're here, right? You know a guy like De Luca wouldn't twitch unless I knew about it. Chain of command, boys."

"Which means you know who *did* whack Vito."

Moretti didn't immediately answer, looking from one of them to the other, assessing where this was going. His answer was cautious, as it might have been if a tape recorder were running. "I heard a lot of things back then. Doesn't *mean* anything."

Eddie waited for Moretti to shift his gaze to Fredo before he gripped the arms of his chair, launched himself forward, swept his hands before him like a diver headed into a pool, and grabbed the edge of the coffee table. Flipping the table up, he followed it across the space separating him from Moretti. The upside-down table hit the other man first, covering his lap, hiding the gun, and cutting into his waist, while Eddie landed on top of it, his hands around Moretti's throat. Bracing his foot for leverage, Eddie twisted Moretti like a rag doll, away from the gun's location, off the sofa entirely, and onto the floor.

Fredo, at first stunned by the maneuver, knew better than to hesitate. He, too, leaped from his chair, tossed the table off the couch, grabbed the gun, and fell to the floor beside the other two, pressing its barrel against Moretti's cheek.

"Pretty quick for an old man," Fredo complimented Eddie.

"The fuck're you doin'?" Moretti managed to get out. "You'll die for this."

Eddie got close to him. "You'll never know, fatso. Let's do this again. Who ordered the hit on Vito?"

Moretti seemed genuinely confused. "Why do you care? It's done. You followed old rules in a new game. You got screwed."

Eddie slapped him. "*Damn*, I'm getting sick of hearing that. Answer the fuckin' question or die right here. I don't care anymore."

Fredo cut him a fast look, thinking he didn't share the same opinion. But he kept his mouth shut. He had the gun, after all.

Moretti got him off the hook. "Zucco did. You *know* that, fer Chrissake."

"Why?"

Despite his poor bargaining position, Moretti grew impatient. "Why? Why? Why the fuck d'ya think, asshole? Vito crossed the wrong people. Same ol' story. He got greedy and stupid, both, and he pissed off the bosses."

Eddie had by then repositioned himself, placing one knee in the middle of Moretti's chest. He took advantage of that now by applying his weight, making the other man wince.

"Details, Phil," he ordered.

The answer came following a gasp for air after Eddie let up. "It ain't rocket surgery. Zucco was pissed off. The original deal was, Knuckles had asked him to do something for his kid, Vito, even though Vito was a waste of time and everybody knew it. But Knuckles and Zucco were old pals, so what the hell? That's how the little bastard ended up working for Bianchi. For a long time, that was it. Everything was good. Vito felt important, Knuckles felt like he'd done a fatherly thing, and Zucco didn't care 'cause what Bianchi was doin' wasn't technically Family business."

Eddie scowled. "Nick Bianchi wasn't Family?"

"Nah. His dad ran a popular restaurant. Patriarcha and the rest of 'em loved the place, the food, and the old man. And they loved little Nicky after he was part of the picture. The father finally retired, Nicky grew up and got ambitious, and the next thing you know, he's got all the old guys backing him in some restaurant supplies business or something. Point is, it filled a gap the Family needed filled."

"Even though Bianchi wasn't connected," Fredo said.

"It happens," Moretti replied. "There were others like that. As long as you kept your nose clean, showed respect, paid your dues, and didn't get too cocky, you could be good to go. And Nicky was smart. He knew how to play the game."

"Till Vito showed up," Eddie suggested, barely leaning on Moretti by this point. Overlooking the gun, the trashed furniture, and the body language, this almost could have been a simple conversation.

"Right," Moretti agreed. "Vito was as stupid as Nicky wasn't, and he finally pulled some shit nobody could overlook, including Knuckles, his own old man."

"What was that?"

"Dunno. Don't care. What mattered was Zucco got a snoot full and ordered him gone."

Eddie's interest piqued. He removed his knee and leaned in closer. "Who got that order?"

Moretti again showed his impatience. "C'mon. I told you already. De Luca. But he didn't assign the contract. Somebody beat 'em all to it. That's what got you messed up."

Eddie straightened. "What? What're you talkin' about? You don't know?"

"Nobody does. That's why they needed you."

"De Luca told me I was covering for somebody high up. That's why I'd be taken care of."

Moretti looked at him pityingly. "You poor slob. It was a deal— with the brass, the cops, the DA, the politicians. They needed somebody they didn't give a shit about. You got the Kewpie doll. De Luca even got a bump for making you plan B. You were a gift from God."

"I didn't even know him," Eddie said, rocking back on his heels. "Not till he came to me with the deal."

Sensing the shift in mood, Moretti gently brushed aside Fredo's gun with the back of his hand and struggled to sit up, rubbing his neck.

"That was the idea," he said. "You weren't supposed to know anybody."

He then eyed Fredo more thoughtfully. "You say your name was Sindaco?"

"Yeah."

"You worked for Bianchi, didn't you? It's an unusual name."

"Not directly," Fredo explained. "I did some grunt work for him a couple of times, early on. We all got shuffled around." He pointed to Eddie, adding, "Him, too."

In confirmation, Eddie said tonelessly, "I saw Vito once. Treated everybody like dirt."

"That's the boy," Moretti, said, slowly rising to his feet and smoothing his shirt. He looked around, assessing the damage. "Moscone," he addressed Eddie.

The other two had also stood up.

"Yeah."

Moretti was restoring his self-respect. He indicated the scene in general. "I'll give you a pass on this. One time only. You remember that like I'll remember your names. Get the fuck outta my house and don't never come back."

Fredo tossed the gun onto a chair as they headed out.

CHAPTER SEVEN

"*Gilbert*," Beverly murmured, crouching down and gathering up Joe's cat.

"You came," Joe said, greeting her with a kiss that Gilbert tried to break up with a paw.

"Hey, you," Beverly addressed Gilbert, dropping him on the nearby couch to wrap her arms around Joe.

They'd been hoping to meet at Beverly's Windsor house, an hour north and much closer to her part-time teaching job at Dartmouth, but as usual, something had cropped up with one or the other of them, in this case the late lamented Gene Russell. Normally, that would've meant a rain check, but yielding to impulse, Beverly had kept driving when she'd reached Windsor, calling Joe from the road.

It was a rare treat for him to host her at his small Green Street carriage house in Brattleboro. Windsor aside, when his job called him to Vermont's largest city, he stayed with her near Burlington, where she had a home on the lake. But having her here had become almost a thing of the past—and thus a show of true devotion now.

Stepping away from him to remove her coat, she therefore took in her surroundings, as if visiting a sentimental haunt. "I always think of you here," she said fondly. "When we're on the phone, even when I know you're someplace else, I see you here, surrounded by your things."

She returned to his embrace. "I am so happy we ended up together."

"I am, too, sweetheart," he replied, understanding what she meant. They were a couple of life's veterans, survivors of loss and sorrow, exposed through their jobs to more than an average portion of trauma and viciousness. They'd also known and trusted each other for decades. Their love was a settled, solid thing, as reliable as the cast-iron woodworking tools he had in his next-door shop, responsible for many of the objects she so dearly associated with him.

He kissed her again and asked, "Is that why you made the extra trip?"

She gazed at him before answering, "Yes, as un–New England as that sounds. I came prepared to tell you what I found with Gene Russell at autopsy, but that's pure pretense."

He put his hands on her waist. "Then let's address first things first. You can tell me about Gene over ice cream."

Smiling, she responded, "Take me to bed."

An hour later, dressed in robes and thick socks, the woodstove stoked, they sat on the couch, one pint of Cherry Garcia and two spoons between them.

"So," he began, licking the last dollop off his spoon, "now that we've addressed our priorities, speak to me about our friend Mr. Russell."

"You first," she said, rooting around toward the bottom of the pint. "I take it you're harboring suspicions."

"God, I love it when you talk fancy," he said with genuine pleasure. "I'm harboring just that. We think he might've been whacked. But why, we have no clue, and we also have no proof that we're right."

"Proof, I can't give you," she told him unsurprisingly. "But I can tell you that based on my experience with these types of injuries, it's quite possible Mr. Russell's were not sustained by falling on the floor, even onto a rolling pin. The subdermal hemorrhaging and type of bony fracture better indicate the energy from a swinging baseball bat, say, delivered with considerable force. But if I were asked to testify to that in court, I'd have to say that I couldn't tell one way or the other. We both know how hard you can land when your feet suddenly go out from under you. The misfortune of having a rolling pin on the floor at the right time in the right place is improbable, but possible."

Gilbert hopped up from under the coffee table and offered himself up for a stomach rub, which Beverly happily supplied after handing the pint to Joe.

"I take it," she said, pursing her lips at the purring cat, "that you think the deaths of Messieurs Lyon and Russell are in some way connected."

"I do, but there again, I'm damned if I know how or why."

"Would it help to talk it through?" she asked.

He nodded. "They were related, kind of. Gene was Monica Tardy's son. She's Nathan's widow, and they were living under the same roof."

"I heard tell that's some fancy roof."

His eyebrows shot up. "You should see the place. Outside, it's pure New England Rust Belt history, but inside, 'fancy' doesn't touch it. It's been totally redone. Marble, granite, slate, hardwood trim up the wazoo, stainless steel and iron fixtures tastefully accenting everything. Indirect lighting like at an art museum. Quiet, efficient, temperature-controlled, cutting-edge noise suppression. On and on. Millions went into it. And all conceived and paid for by what's beginning to sound like one of the world's great fascist bastards."

"Mr. Lyon."

"The one and only. We're only at the start of interviewing everybody. That's why I couldn't get up to Windsor this weekend. There's a cast of dozens to talk to, especially now that we're suddenly no longer talking about a one-year-old suspected homicide. And it's looking like there might be a power vacuum we'll need to sort out, too. That could help us figure out why the bodies are beginning to drop."

Beverly looked up from her cat massage. "Good Lord. You think there'll be more?"

"Too early to tell. The widow and Nathan's son Rob appear to be running the roost. That's the impression they gave Lester and Sam when we broke the news about Nathan's COD. News they took remarkably well, I might add. But when I spoke with the building manager, an impressively observant young woman named Kimona Alin, I picked up on a calming official line hiding some potentially lethal turmoil, as perhaps evidenced by Gene's death."

"Who benefits from that?"

Joe gently pulled on Gilbert's tail a few times, which only added to his hedonistic near delirium. "Hard to tell this early. We're getting hold of any and all wills, trusts, et cetera, to help us with that, at least from the financial side. The pottery business Gene ran looks profitable. Does that make it a motive? Kimona hinted at some possible hanky-panky among and between the various entities in the building. Was Gene fooling around with someone he shouldn't have been? He has a wife and a kid. Maybe *she's* got an ax to grind. Too many choices for the moment."

"Does that mean you're just going to do a massive sweep of all occupants and compare notes?" she asked. "See where the discrepancies are and have them explained?"

"That and conduct some serious background checks," Joe agreed. "You know how it goes: money, lust, or loathing. One or all of them are usually in play somewhere. We just need to find out who best fits that frame."

"If it's only one person."

He could tell, as was often the case, that she was fascinated with his procedural process. She'd even told him once that the similarities between her methodology, inspecting what the body has to tell, and his with the living counterparts, were surprisingly similar.

"Correct," he agreed.

"Who are you going to start with?" she asked, her keenness disturbing Gilbert, who reminded her of his need for her complete concentration with a head bump.

In medical school, her inclination had been toward psychiatry. Forensic pathology had only later ignited the same passion and beyond, due to its additional hands-on nature. And so she'd switched, discovering afterward that the same evolution was common to many pathologists. She'd mused this was perhaps due to both disciplines being heavily dependent on investigative problem-solving. But that still didn't account for the pure joy she still felt—even so many years later—when confronted by a body in the morgue, poised to reveal the secrets of its demise.

"I should probably go after Monica and Rob," Joe was saying, "since they're the supposed top dogs, but I'm more interested in Gene's adoptive father, Ned Russell."

"Adoptive? I thought Gene lived in the same building as his mom."

Joe nodded. "I warned you. Complicated. Monica gave him up as a baby. The Russells adopted him. Nathan then scooped everybody up as part of his all-in-one-tent campaign."

Her incredulity was plain. "And the Russells went along with this?"

He was pleased. "Exactly why I want to start there. Ned Russell and his wife don't physically live at the mill, but he did move his office there, I guess as a compromise. And their natural daughter, Penny Trick, moved into one of the apartments Nathan offered."

"Penny Trick? What a wonderful name. Sounds like a girl from a children's book."

Gilbert had tired of the lack of attention and wandered off.

"Maybe she is," Joe replied. "And maybe she ain't."

Joe had always liked log cabins. It might have been the woodworker in him, or the fancier of history books detailing the origins of the United States, but their solidity combined with their clear connection to the surrounding woods had always made of the style a visceral touchstone to Joe's romantic side.

And of course, there was that smell. After Joe carefully picked his way across the slippery, snowy path from the packed-earth parking lot and entered a large, two-story, two-chimney, balcony-and-porch-equipped wooden monster of a new home overlooking Spofford Lake in Chesterfield, New Hampshire—just across the river from Brattle-boro—he was immersed in the intoxicating sweet and pungent aroma of freshly worked softwood.

He paused a moment to breathe it in and get his bearings. He'd phoned Ned Russell earlier for an appointment and been told to come here, where Russell was doing what most well-organized regional contractors did during winter: working on the heated insides of projects they'd enclosed during the warmer months.

And this house was toasty. As Joe opened his coat and stamped his boots free of the snow stuck to their treads, he appreciated how the builder had made a point of installing the customer-ordered pellet stoves first, even before attacking major projects like interior walls and the main staircase, which at the moment was a ladder.

The building, cathedral-ceilinged, French-windowed, accented with emphatic if unnecessary brick chimneys, was full of the sound of hammers, saws, routers, and the obligatory radio blasting rock and roll.

"*You Gunther?*" he heard a shout from overhead.

Joe looked up to see a burly, gray-bearded man wearing a worn tool belt attached to red suspenders staring down at him from an overhang with no railings.

"Ned Russell?" he replied.

The other man opened his mouth to respond, but was drowned out by the howl of a nearby circular saw. He held up his palm as if to stop traffic and began making his way toward the ladder down to the main floor.

Upon arriving, he beckoned to Joe to follow him into the depths of the building, among a cross-cutting of blond studs, lintels, and support beams—a forest of machined trees—until they reached the intended kitchen. Here, the walls had been closed in, a door installed, and while there was much work to be done, at least it was quiet. Joe noticed a scattering of plans and work orders covering the room's island, flanked by a few stools.

"Take a pew," Russell recommended, following his own advice.

Joe removed his coat and draped it carefully across the back of the stool. "Thanks for meeting with me," he began, sitting down.

Russell had taken a box cutter from his belt and was scraping the remnants of some dried foam insulation from the back of one of his thumbs. He was a square-built man with ruddy cheekbones above the beard, his glasses plastic-rimmed throwbacks, and flecked with speckles of dried paint.

"No problem," he replied, not looking up. "What's on your mind?"

"I wanted to first offer my condolences over your son's death."

Russell kept at his handiwork. "Thanks."

"How's your wife taking it?" Joe asked.

"Like you'd expect."

"And Penny?"

That brought his eyes up. They were also gray, very steady, and gave nothing away. "Wouldn't know."

"You haven't seen her?"

"Nope."

Joe was reminded of his own late father, an up-country farmer who made this man look chatty. "I'm going to take a flyer here and guess you two don't talk much at the best of times."

"You'd be right."

There was a loud crash from above, most likely from a dropped two-by-four. Russell didn't even blink.

"What do you think happened to Gene?" Joe asked.

Russell returned to his gentle carving. "Isn't that your department?"

"Did he tend to be a night owl, working on his own projects after hours?"

"Probably got that from me."

"It was a well-known habit?"

Again, the gray eyes rose to meet Joe's. "His wife knew it."

"Peggy," Joe confirmed. "How did they get along?"

"Wouldn't know."

"How did you get along?"

The eyes widened a fraction. "With Peggy?" He paused to consider his answer, which Joe appreciated. Even over so brief an acquaintance, he suspected that whatever this man told him would be the truth as best he knew it.

"We give each other room," Russell finally offered.

"How's her character differ from Gene's?"

The man lifted his chin slightly, clearly caught by surprise. "Restless," he said.

"Gene was more settled?"

"Maybe. Maybe resigned."

Joe moved on. "Unusual setup you all have at the mill."

The thumb drew Ned's attention once more, although its problem appeared to have been addressed. "You say so."

"Well, we're starting to connect a few of the dots there. Dominant, filthy-rich father figure. Possible tyrant, possibly not shy about getting what he wants, regardless of the method. Tell me when I step off the path."

"You're okay."

"That style works on people either dependent or vulnerable. Strikes me you fit neither category, and you used to have your office elsewhere. What happened?"

Russell retracted the cutter's blade, put it back into his tool belt, and straightened his back. Joe feared he was about to stand and leave the room.

Instead, he answered, "I'm a businessman. It was a good offer. Rent-free."

This time, it was Joe's turn to watch silently, his face still.

In response, the other man removed his glasses and rubbed his eyes, admitting, "There might've been more."

Joe was happy to have trusted Russell's fundamental integrity. "He had something on you," he suggested.

"*Over* me," was the response.

Joe concentrated on what he knew, what he had, and what he could possibly decipher from it. He sensed he had one shot before this man either walked or opened up. He pursued the one detail he'd learned the least about so far. "Penny?"

Russell slumped, his hands for once completely still. "She's had some troubles."

Joe softened his voice. "Ned, I'm sorry to be making you do this, and it might not sound relevant to you, but things look to be going a little haywire at the mill. I need to sort through what I can before figuring out what matters and what doesn't."

Ned sounded defeated, as if the loss of his son had finally settled on him. "I know."

"Tell me what Nathan did."

"Penny got into a fix. He got her out. The price was me. I had to move into the mill. First, he wanted me to live there, but we compromised on the business only."

Joe's next question almost asked itself. "What kind of fix?"

"She killed somebody."

Joe waited, his silence once more working for him.

Ned explained. "She was driving under the influence, forced a bicyclist off the road. For some reason, she called Lyon, and he fixed it."

"How?"

"Made it look like the guy lost control and went over a guardrail into the river."

"Hard to fake," Joe suggested doubtfully.

"Whatever. She claims she didn't actually hit him, so in a way, that's what really happened. It just went beyond a simple accident with no complications. You can look up the story. It was in the paper, or at least their cooked-up version was."

"Did she help the guy?"

He shook his head. "She didn't even stop. She barely knows anything about it. She called from down the road, Nathan asked where she was, told her to wait for him at some distance away and stop driving. The next thing you know, it was in the paper as a solo accident.

Then Nathan got her and me in a room together and laid out his price tag."

Joe imagined the complications of reconstructing the scene credibly, and had a hard time fitting the aging Nathan Lyon to the tasks required.

"What else did it cost you?" he asked.

Ned looked befuddled, even given the passage of years. "That was it. I moved the business. It's all he wanted."

And to blackmail you with your own silence, Joe thought. For a puppet master like Nathan, control over a strong, proud, righteous man like Ned Russell must have felt like a worthy conquest—up there with owning a prized and rare possession that is never publicly displayed. But there had to be more.

"You must've wondered," he asked, "why Penny called him that night. Why not you, or 911?"

"She hates me and the cops about the same. Plus, she was drunk."

"There's got to be more to it. Why Nathan, specifically?"

"She was already living at the mill, like Gene was."

"That only makes her his tenant, Ned."

Russell scowled briefly. "Fine. I get it. I think maybe they were seeing each other."

"Sexually," Joe filled in.

He could barely hear the response. "Yeah."

"You ever talk to her about that?"

"No."

"Was it still going on when he died?"

"Doubt it. Lyon wasn't seeing anybody at the end."

Joe's mind was filled with possibilities. "Did Gene know about any of this?"

"I never told him."

"Your wife, Betsy?"

"Nobody."

"Might Penny have told her?"

"Ask one of them."

"And in the years since it happened, it's never come up?"

"It wasn't something to talk about."

That comment was revealing of Ned's character, Joe thought. Here was a man used to tools, wood, load-bearing structures with capacities and limitations, who, upon hearing of his son's death, had gone straight back to work. So-called old New England stock.

"How did Penny and Gene get along?" Joe wanted to know.

Ned thought before answering. "They were okay when they were little. He was a bit older. We had Penny after we adopted him. Betsy had complications getting pregnant, and then it happened. We decided not to have any more."

He paused, as if exhausted by having said so much. "You hear sometimes," he unexpectedly resumed, "about how an adopted child turns out wrong. They talk about genetics and stuff. But for us, that was Penny. Gene was always solid. A bit of a dreamer, but a hard worker, and never difficult. Penny," he sighed, "was a handful. No boundary she wouldn't push, no self-control. If she wanted something, she went for it. At first, it was okay. She raced bikes, got into sports like rugby, even boxed some. It seemed physical. But in her teens . . ." His voice dropped off.

Joe stayed quiet, letting him pull more from his trunk of memories if he chose.

"She married as soon as she could. Some loser named Matty Trick. He died of an OD a year later. I think maybe they were together at the time. I always wondered if she played a role in that, bad as it sounds to say. Afterward, it was like watching a slow-motion car crash, like they do in the movies. Parts flying off, spinning through the air. That little girl just crumpled into something else."

"But you loved her enough to agree to Nathan's terms."

Ned had been staring into some middle distance and returned to Joe's face. "They're your children," he answered simply.

Joe wanted to end it there, at least for the moment. He felt sorry for Ned Russell and wanted to grant him a little peace in which to mourn.

But that wasn't his job.

"How did Nathan find you in the first place?"

Ned looked up quickly at the ceiling. "Oh, you know. He pretty much got anything he wanted. Monica had given Gene up at birth—I'm not sure why—and Nathan wanted to close that circle. I doubt Monica gave a damn either way, but to Nathan, Gene was family, and family had to be kept close."

"Whether they liked it or not," Joe filled in, breaking a cardinal rule of such interviews not to supply your own answers. But this didn't seem like much of a breach.

"Yeah," Ned agreed.

Joe stood up and removed his coat from the stool's back. "I'll leave you be, Ned. Again, I'm sorry about Gene."

Ned didn't say anything. Joe moved toward the door but stopped shy of it to ask, "Why do you stay there? At the mill? Nathan's been dead almost a year."

"I told you. Good business deal. The terms haven't changed. It's still rent-free."

"That's Penny's kind of thinking," Joe suggested.

Ned turned in his seat and allowed for the hint of a smile. "Yeah," he agreed. "Suppose it is."

"So?"

The big man sighed for a second time. "I guess it was Gene. I didn't want to leave him alone, even with his own little family. It was too strange a place."

Neither one of them referenced how well that had turned out.

Joe continued to the door. "Thanks for your time."

"Hey," Ned said quietly.

Joe dropped his hand from the doorknob. "What's up?"

"They told me it was an accident, that he slipped and fell. Was it?"

Now it was Joe's turn to ponder telling what he suspected to a grieving father.

Suspicions however, wouldn't be of much comfort. "I can't answer that right now. But I won't quit digging till I can."

Russell nodded without further comment.

There are friendships—a few—vaunted in literature, noted in history, and envied in everyday life, that transcend what most people get to enjoy. They are founded on a harmony beyond kinship or marriage and are perhaps better explained as a spiritual melding. The beneficiaries of such linkages don't usually question their provenance, or fine-tune what makes them work. They do, however, respect what they've received and nurture its upkeep with as much distance as proximity. People with a connection like this frequently live apart, pursue separate interests, but are forever cannily aware of the strength and comfort that each supplies the other, even in absentia.

Sally Kravitz and Rachel Reiling had such a bond.

They were dissimilar young women by upbringing and experience. In contrast to Sally's peripatetic wanderings around Brattleboro in her eccentric father's wake, Rachel had basked in upper-class privilege in one of Burlington's comfier suburbs, the child of a now-divorced doctor and a lawyer. That mother, however, being Beverly Hillstrom, trucked no favors with entitlement and had made it a point to influence her daughter accordingly. Furthermore, tagging along with Joe Gunther on a couple of cases as a teenage photographer and videographer, Rachel had already witnessed beyond an average helping of mayhem, murder, and heartbreak.

It had, in large part, influenced her later to sign up with the *Brattleboro Reformer*, where the editor had quickly put her photographic talents to use, and paid her semiofficially to practice some investigative journalism, even though the paper had no budget for such extravagance.

This job perk was in part why Sally had called her upon discovering the emergency vehicles outside the Lyon mill, just as their mutual attraction for unconventional food now lured them to the warmth of Sally's car on the same day Joe met with Ned Russell.

The venue for lunch was a favorite: Fast Eddie's on the Putney Road, progressive Brattleboro's much-debated miracle mile, which many loved to disparage and everyone frequented.

Fast Eddie's suited them because, especially in winter, they could skip the sparse seating and repair to one of their vehicles to watch the snow falling in privacy, as it was doing now. Also, a little sentimentally, it re-created the memory of their first encounter, when a few years ago, Sally had picked up Rachel on that same editor's recommendation, to see if they might occasionally collaborate on stories— one as a source, the other as the writer.

That had been an awkward meeting. Sally, the veteran, Rachel, the newcomer; one sworn to confidentiality and bound by laws and rules, the other hired to expose all she could to public scrutiny. And yet their friendship had begun then and there, to be strengthened upon every subsequent encounter.

"You get anything out of that death at the mill?" Sally asked, working on a double dog, multiple napkins spread across her lap.

Rachel had opted for a hot pretzel and a frappe, the former layered with mustard. Sally's father, Dan, had once commented that they had the foraging instincts of a pair of goats.

She licked a finger before answering, "Gene Russell, son of the late owner's widow, owner of ER Ceramics. From what I could get, it looks like he was working late at his potter's wheel, slipped as he crossed the wet floor, and cracked his head, never to throw a pot again."

"An accident, then?"

"They're doing an autopsy, but that's what they're saying. Why were you there?"

That, of course, defined the fine line between them, free to be inquired about, not always to be crossed. Rachel therefore had no expectation that her question would snare an answer.

"Something cooking at the mill," Sally said vaguely. She added, "Doing an old client a favor, more than anything. You gonna write a piece about the slip and fall, or let it drop?"

Rachel had her mouth open to receive a bite, and extracted the dripping pretzel quickly enough to say, "You know me. I'll poke at it a bit more, then give it a few column inches. He was part of the business community, after all."

Sally eyed the passing traffic for a moment, through the delicate dusting of fresh snowflakes, not the only one wondering if there might be a connection between this and other activities at the mill.

She seized on that notion to give her friend something she thought would do no harm and might also benefit the world by appearing in print. Sally was not too fond of organizations like the police holding cards exclusively to their chest. Despite her respect for individual officers, including most of Gunther's unit, she tended to believe that privately held knowledge often led to corruption and/or injustice. She'd seen that borne out too often in the past.

"One small extra detail," she therefore volunteered.

"Yeah? You been holding out on me?"

"No, but while I've been looking into the goings-on at the mill, I tripped over the fact that the VBI is very discreetly investigating the death of the paterfamilias, Nathan Lyon. He died almost a year ago of supposedly natural causes. I looked up his death certificate, which is likely being amended as we speak. The building's certainly full of rumors it might've been something else. If that whets your appetite any," she added with a raised eyebrow.

Rachel responded in kind. "That it does, Ms. Kravitz. Thank you very much."

"I hate to say this," Willy announced, transparently unrepentant, "but it's not clear to me that we have any homicides here at all, either fresh or growing weeds."

"You know the mantra," Lester replied.

"Yeah, yeah, yeah—'They're all homicides till they're not.' Blah, blah. I get it. But two in a row with no smoking gun? It's not like we don't have a caseload, guys. We're not starving for work."

"Two in a row at the same address?" Sam rephrased without looking up from her computer screen. "And since when did you not want to chase a homicide?"

Willy laughed. "Okay, call me devil's advocate. What d'we really have?"

"Fair enough," Joe said from his desk. "We've been running interviews and background checks. What've we found so far?"

Lester began, since he'd been updating the computerized case file, including background results from the state fusion center outside Burlington. "No smoking guns yet, and I'll grant you Gene Russell's death is the least suspicious of the two, but there's gotta be fire under all this smoke. If nothing else, we have to explain how Nathan Lyon got his hyoid snapped and those bruises over his carotids."

"Not to mention the Benadryl cocktail," Sammie contributed.

"From what I'm hearing," Joe said, "Nathan was not a popular man. Les, what did the fusion center have to say about him?"

"Basically that he was a miracle baby, born in his late forties."

"You're kidding," Willy reacted. "Lyon's not his real name?"

"Apparently not," Lester confirmed. "I sent his prints to the FBI and put out what we got on him, but so far, nuthin'."

"Guess I'm about to get better acquainted with Monica Tardy," Joe said, half to himself.

"What about his eldest?" Willy asked. "Rob. His age puts him back before then."

"You take him," Joe said. "We can compare notes afterward."

"I'll make sure you both get background on Nathan's will and trust paperwork," Lester told them. "I asked Tausha Greenblott at the AG's office to assign one of her experts to that. Nothing too surprising, though, minus a couple of interesting details."

Greenblott was their permanently assigned prosecutor, VBI being a statewide unit unassociated with any county.

"Like what?" Joe asked.

Lester explained. "Rob and Monica end up in the driver's seat, as co-trustees, as expected, and the others get proportional sums based on who knows what—favoritism or past squabbles. It's not like most documents of the type, where everybody gets an equal slice. Also, there's a proviso across the board that to get the cash, each recipient has to stay living in the mill, for a long stretch. And the money," he continued, "doesn't come in a bag. Rob and Monica are ordered to disburse it on a timetable."

"A dead man's provision," Willy suggested. "Legally keeping his hand on the controls."

"Right," Les agreed. "The biggest anomaly to my eye—which should be of special interest, given the two deaths—is that Gene got special treatment."

"Are his widow and kid next in line?" Joe asked. "Or did the old man see that coming and screw them over?"

"No, no. They get his piece." Lester paused before adding, "It's almost corporate in structure. All of them, whether it's for a lot or a lot less, get regular deposits in their accounts, like they were being paid an allowance. I'll print out a cheat sheet with the important stats."

"Must be nice," Willy said, almost inaudibly.

"What did you get out of Ned Russell?" Sam asked her boss, changing the subject based on Lester's lapsing into silence.

"Good man coerced by a manipulative narcissist, from what I can tell. We'll have to vet his story, but he told me his drunk daughter killed a bicyclist with her car some years ago and Nathan covered it up, making it look like a solo accident. His price tag was that Ned had to move his business into the mill."

Willy wasn't buying it. "That was the total price tag?"

"No argument from me," Joe reassured him. "That's just what he owned up to. The deal's rent-free. My suspicion is that there might've been more to come, except that Nathan died."

"That puts Ned in a good place to have hurried things up," Willy suggested.

"It's also convoluted by Penny Trick having been Nathan's lover for a while."

"Jesus," Willy let out. "Now we're cooking. No way we shouldn't go back to the car-versus-bicyclist face-off and give it extra scrutiny. Sounds like Nathan made out just by moving a body around a little."

Lester tapped his monitor screen. "She has been a bad girl," he emphasized. "All the way back to her sealed juvie records. She may've done worse than what her father told Joe."

"Does that make her someone who also might've wanted Nathan gone?" Sam asked.

"Or how 'bout Monica and/or Rob, in order to take over the reins?" Joe added. "The list goes on. Look, it's no good playing twenty questions here. It seems fair to say that just meeting Nathan Lyon was enough to make people want to kill him. We actually have to pin this on someone."

"What *is* it with everybody having to live under one roof?" Sam asked almost at random. "It's so screwy."

"To answer that," Joe responded, "I think we need to find out who he was and where he came from. As we were just saying, it looks like Rob and Monica are the only ones who might know about that. Everyone else is too young."

Lester returned them to square one. "So what about Gene Russell?"

"Did we finish interviewing the pottery shop's neighbors?" Joe asked.

"Yes," Sam answered him. "And met with Gene's wife, Peggy, checked out their apartment—within limits, since she and the son're living there—and knocked on doors of anybody who might've seen any comings or goings from the parking lot that late. Nothing. We also collected a portable computer from Gene's office. I think it's for personal use, since he already had a desktop unit. The laptop was password protected, so Jim Collins is having one of his techies break it open for us. Might be interesting in light of what Les said about the cash disbursements."

"What was the new widow like?" Willy asked. "Peggy?"

"Stunned, tearful, seemed to be legitimately torn up." Sam paused before tacking on, "I'd like another crack at her, though. She fell apart enough to be incoherent, so I finally let her be."

"Too much snot?" Willy said.

Sam couldn't argue his point, even if his imagery was typically raw. Everyone there had experienced moments where their diet of violence made empathy feel awkward. Cops are not universally hard;

they can in fact be quite sentimental. But their professions do numb them protectively.

"You should talk with her again," Joe recommended. "It may be that the year-old homicide of Nathan Lyon is our stronger case right now, but we should neither ignore Gene Russell, nor overlook that both deaths are likely connected. There's a lot on our plates, folks."

CHAPTER EIGHT

There are many little known crannies in Brattleboro, even to the locals, that constitute neighborhoods almost literally cut off from the rest of town. Geography, topography, and old-fashioned urban planning—or the lack of it—have allowed enclaves of from one to three streets to develop virtually on their own, slowly establishing socioeconomic or architectural identities that a tried-and-true neighborhood crawler like a cop, or Sally Kravitz, instantly recognized simply by glancing around. What appeared as a string of bland houses to an outsider struck these connoisseurs with the familiarity of a well-known face.

The confluence in east Brattleboro of the West and Connecticut Rivers had formed two such pockets, each clinging to opposite flanks of the Putney Road, which charged up the middle of a peninsula to leap across the water and join with the town's primary commercial strip. There is a blur of houses lining this heavily traveled stretch, and tucked behind each row are the two pockets in question—the west-facing one overlooking a vast, shallow, popular fishing backwater called the Retreat Meadows, and the eastern one, set lower down, paralleling the railroad and the broad Connecticut River just beyond it.

This latter forgotten corner is called Wantastiquet Drive, after the massive, ancient mountain that looms above it from the New Hampshire side of the river.

To Sally's eye, it fit her father's fond memories of a TV show she'd never seen, called *Leave It to Beaver*, which apparently represented a suburban America Sally knew only from history books.

Despite her personal ignorance, however, she saw the appeal. Even sandwiched between the tracks and the busy road, although well situated above one and below the other, the noise and bustle of both went largely unnoticed. And the mostly 1950s houses, each fronting a string of tidy front lawns, spoke of contentedness and peace, regardless of any contrasting larger world.

She was following Alexandra Lloyd, who had become her favorite suspect as Michelle Lyon's nemesis. Since winnowing her list down to five, the number of likely parties had melted further, allowing Sally to more surgically use Michelle's employee files to dig deeper and in more detail.

Lloyd, predictably called Alex, had only surprised her in one regard, which was that she lived on reliably middle-class Wantastiquet Drive—an oddity set right when it turned out she in fact rented a small garage apartment belonging to an older couple named Cullins, who probably would have been horrified by their tenant's past criminal history of drugs, burglary, DUIs, vagrancy, and assault.

Given her own exposure to society's darker corners, Sally was more understanding than most of such backgrounds. By the same token, she was no Pollyanna about people changing merely because they landed a good job. Somehow, she suspected, either Alex had felt herself under pressure and fallen back onto old habits, or simply yielded to temptation.

The house was on the east side of the street, with the garage farther back on the lot, meaning that while it perched above the embankment overlooking the tracks, it also had the property's best view of the ice-choked river. A decent trade-off for putting up with the clatter of two or three trains per day—assuming you were there to even hear them.

Sally had seen Lloyd pull up and park, and witnessed her climbing the exterior staircase to get home. The stairs were not covered, and perhaps unsurprisingly, Lloyd had made no effort to shovel them off, opting instead to kick the snow out of the way, or simply squash it underfoot, creating a series of small, icy moguls. As a result, Sally hung on to both railings and stepped carefully as she ascended to the tiny deck fronting the apartment's entrance.

There, she knocked without force, hoping to be confused with one of the elderly landlords. Whether she was or not, the door quickly swung back to reveal a young woman with cigarette smoke on her breath—a presumed violation given her guilty expression—and a compromise Goth haircut above conventional jeans and a Henley shirt. Sally had already witnessed Alex in her nonwork clothes—a far cry from this tame outfit.

Lloyd looked startled. "Oh," she said. "I didn't . . . Who're you?"

Sally gave her an unblinking stare. "Not someone you ever wanted to meet, but too late for that now. Let me in, unless the Cullinses pay for the heat."

"What? The Cullinses? Did they send you?"

"Worse." Sally brushed by her nonplussed hostess and entered the one-room apartment, looking around. There were more belongings scattered across the floor and unmade bed than she imagined could fill any drawer or closet.

"*Hey,*" Lloyd protested. "What the fuck? Who *are* you?"

Sally crossed to the bathroom and glanced in. Satisfied they were alone, she answered, "I represent the business you've been ripping off." She crossed the room, retrieved a tin from the windowsill, and held it up, continuing, "Of items like this, among other things, unless caviar is something you eat regularly on a Ritz."

Lloyd protested, "That's mine," but her voice lacked conviction.

Sally put the tin back down. "The complaint isn't that it's not yours now. The complaint is that you stole it. That can is only available from one place around here, and you sure didn't buy it."

Sally made a panoramic sweep of all the flat surfaces she could see and added, "Same is true for the fancy tea I see over there, the bag of saffron in your kitchenette, the several cases of primo olive oil, and whatever else you got stashed or have already sold. Jesus, girl, you could've made this a little harder, you know?"

Her approach was working. Lloyd was beginning to melt before her. "We get an employee discount."

"Please. Don't think I didn't check that out. The only thing you ever bought from Food Flourish was a T-shirt, when you were hired eighteen months ago—bright pink, size small. You really want to challenge me here?"

"Are you the police?" Alex asked in a monotone, her shoulders slumped in resignation.

Sally pointed to the bed. "Sit."

The girl did as she was told, her knees angled in like a child's.

"That," Sally told her, "is the only good news you're looking at. No, I'm private. But if after our conversation, I get the feeling you're jerking me around, the cops'll be my next phone call."

Alex cupped her face in her hands. "This is so not fair. Those people make more money than they know what to do with. It's all dirty and it's all going to hell anyhow, especially since the big man died. I just wanted to protect myself. It's not like they'll miss it."

Sally was incredulous. "Why do you think I'm here? They knew what you were doing. They just didn't know who you were."

"I'm a nobody," Alex complained. "Why do I always get shit on?"

This was a familiar refrain, but Sally was curious about something else, especially given what had been going on at the mill. "Explain how they're all going to hell anyhow."

Alex stared at her in astonishment. "They're *killing* each other. That place is a snake pit, dude. It's like . . . the whatchamacallits. That feuding family."

"Hatfields and McCoys? Montagues and Capulets?"

The latter certainly drew a blank. "Okay, well, whatever. They fight all the time, and the old guy's death really did it. They murdered him, you know? The cops're all over it."

"Who murdered him?"

"One of them. That crazy family. *That's* why I stole stuff. I mean, look at Gene Russell. He's dead. How d'you think that happened? Old age? I don't *think* so."

"The funny thing is, Alex," Sally told her, "none of that changes what you did, unless you know something more than what you just told me."

That perked her up. "I *do*. I swear to God." She jumped to her feet and grabbed up the tin of caviar Sally had replaced on the windowsill. "What do you think this is? Caviar? Not hardly. It's eggs from some Mississippi shit fish. I heard 'em talking about it."

She moved quickly over to her corner kitchenette and snatched up a jar of paprika Sally hadn't even noticed. "And this? It's got brick dust in it, to make it red. We do some of this in the shop, when we're packaging. They fake everything at that place. The canned fish isn't what they say it is, the spices are all messed up, the olive oil and honey are fake. Nobody knows the difference."

Sally wasn't stunned to hear this. It was common knowledge that in some areas of the country, red snapper was almost exclusively counterfeited. Salmon, tuna, and hundreds of other foods were routinely mislabeled, and sometimes contained toxins and heavy metals as well. What caught her attention was the depth of Alex's purported knowledge.

"And they do all this in the open, where you and the other employees can see it and potentially blackmail them?"

Alex looked at her pityingly. "Look, whoever you are, I know you think I'm just a trailer trash dumbass. I can hear it in your voice. But I know what I know, and I seen what I saw. You can take any of this garbage and have it tested. You'll see I'm right. Maybe I did steal it, but those assholes are poisoning people. You check if I'm not right."

She sat back down, this time in a ratty armchair covered with dirty laundry, her self-confidence recovered, despite the defeat of her surroundings. "No, they don't do it in the open. They're like you. They think we're all stupid woodchucks who don't know what we're doing. But I notice stuff. Always have." She touched her forehead. "That's how I've kept alive all this time."

Sally resisted pointing out how Alex hadn't reached thirty yet, knowing that in some quarters, that milestone was considered late middle age.

But this conversation had created a well-worn dilemma between the duty Sally owed her client and her obligation to obey the law. Morally and ethically, it wasn't a choice, nor was this the first time she'd been so confronted. The trick was in landing a solution that at once righted a wrong, while keeping her—and her reputation—untarnished. She didn't want to become known either as the PI who squealed to the cops, or the one who winked at proof of a crime.

Thus, she steered for a middle course. "Tell you what. We both know what's going on here, so let's show each other a little respect. I'll keep you in the clear if you hand over what you've still got on hand *and* tell a cop friend of mine what you just told me. No muss, no fuss. You get to keep whatever money you made on the side, and I'll do my best to make sure you don't get charged. Of course, you will lose your job, which doesn't sound like it'll be a big deal anyhow."

"A cop?" Alex demanded. "How the hell's that gonna work? Of *course* he'll lock me up. That's what they do."

"He's not the kind who'll be interested in what you've done," she answered.

"Fuck that," Alex said. "No cops."

Sally played her trump card, pulling out a pair of handcuffs from her rear pocket. "Fine. Then we'll go traditional. I'll throw you to the local PD and the two of you can dance the dance. The Cullinses'll throw you out, you'll go to jail, and nobody'll give a damn about what you know, 'cause they'll say you're lying to get off. Not only that, but it'll give Food Flourish time to clean up their act and make everything look squeaky clean.

"Let me put it in simple terms: My way, you're off the hook and pick up brownie points talking to a grateful major crime unit. Your way, you get to play tag with a bunch of horny people behind bars. Me? I don't care either way."

As hoped, Alex didn't think to challenge the fine points of Sally's proposal. Instead, fatalistic by virtue of past experience, yet canny enough to recognize a lifeline when she saw it, she reluctantly conceded. "Fine," she said dully. "Whatever."

"That's what you're eating? Johnnycakes and a cabinet? You got a death wish, Eddie. You'll never live to put things right."

Eddie wasn't amused. "Says you with a hot wiener and a Gansett. I'll dance on your grave."

They were back in Cranston, on Broad Street, not far from Roger Williams Park Zoo, at a restaurant Fredo had recommended because of its peculiar lineup of Rhode Island foods. He'd done this largely for his cousin, who he knew loved the stuff, proven by what was now before him. Fredo was perfectly happy with gussied-up hot dogs and a local beer for lunch. That seemed normal to him. But this local version of Eddie's pancakes, plus a milkshake—the former supposedly a holdover from pioneer times and made with cornmeal gruel—was something he could live without.

He waited until their waitress had walked away before saying, "Speaking of that, assuming Phil Moretti doesn't change his mind and have you knocked off for old times' sake, what d'you wanna do next? Like he said, everybody's dead. You found out what happened. Feels like we're kinda done, don't it?"

Eddie silently poured syrup over his cakes. He'd been very quiet since their encounter with Moretti, visibly steeped in thought. But the results of that effort had been lost on Fredo, who was privately hoping his involvement in this nostalgic quest might be nearing an end.

He loved his cousin, falsely played by a system he'd supported all his life, and was committed to supporting him to the end. But none of that meant Fredo didn't also hope the whole problem wouldn't run out of gas.

Clearly, however, Eddie had other ideas. "I wanna know who killed Vito."

Fredo considered protesting, quoting Moretti's opinion on the subject, but he knew better. He was also enjoying how Eddie had tucked into his meal, as disgusting as he found it personally, and didn't want to put him off.

"You mean actually pulled the trigger?" he asked. "Probably some mope who's long dead, too. One of De Luca's crew. I bet we could still find out, like we did from Moretti."

Eddie surprised him then by sounding almost philosophical. "That would be good, 'cause I got it in my guts we're not being told somethin'. What we heard wasn't the straight dope. I can feel it."

Fredo sat back from his meal. "What?"

Eddie explained, "What Moretti said Vito did wasn't a killing offense. And you're telling me Vito's own father just took it on the chin, without saying a word? His own kid? It had to've been more than skimming the business—like spitting on the flag, or cursing God. You know what I'm sayin'? What do you remember hearing from Knuckles back then, when Vito was found dead? Nuthin'. Am I right or what?"

Fredo couldn't argue the point. He also remembered a distinct lack of histrionics from any of the mobsters at the time.

"And another thing," Eddie went on. "De Luca got the call, like Moretti says, and got somebody to do the job. Then why come to me to pay the bill? I got nuthin' to do with any of it. That's unusual, isn't it? I mean, I heard of a cold gun being dropped at the scene—no prints, no history, no serial number. But a cold guy? A guy who knows less than zip about anything? That smacks of everybody except him knowing way more than they're letting on."

"What're you saying, Eddie?"

"I'm sayin' the guy who goes under the bus on a deal like this is usually a volunteer. But De Luca came to me. Made me a deal I thought was like money in the bank. Why not whoever really pulled the trigger?"

The whole notion had put him off his johnnycakes, if not the coffee cabinet, of which he now took a long pull through his straw.

Fredo couldn't see much daylight through the tangle. "Guess we keep on diggin', then," he conceded unhappily, all interest in his own meal suddenly evaporated.

Lester Spinney looked up at the knock on the office door. A young trooper, still awkward in his new uniform, was standing on the threshold holding a package.

"Hi," Lester greeted him. "I help you?"

"My sergeant told me to drop this off?" his visitor said hesitantly.

"Sure. What is it?" Lester asked, rising.

The trooper glanced at the unmarked package as if it were a cue card with instructions. "A laptop connected to your homicide, I think?"

Lester reached out and took it from him. "Right. Gene Russell. We'd asked to have the password cracked. Cool. I am curious about this little item. You got the chain of custody form?"

He did. They conducted the transfer, and as the young man faded away, Lester tore into the package, extracted the computer, opened it up, plugged it in, turned it on, and immediately copied its contents onto a backup disk, leaving the original as pristine as when they'd seized it.

Satisfied, he locked the laptop in his desk and turned his attention to Gene's duplicated desktop screen, which featured a photograph of his wife, Peggy, and their child, Mark.

"Okay, Mr. Russell," he addressed the image. "Let's get better acquainted."

Befitting a fledgling reporter of ambition and curiosity, Rachel Reiling had not needed further prompting to dig deeper into the activities at the Lyons' mill. But she knew that her approach would have to be subtle and carefully considered. Three separate drive-by visits to the mill had revealed unmarked police vehicles in the parking lot, indicating not only that something was indeed underway, as Sally had suggested, but that the place itself was nowhere a reporter would be welcomed.

Rachel needed to find an alternate key to opening her investigation, and, as she emerged from her car and took in the small, tidy, snowcapped house before her, perched on an immaculate white lawn, she was hoping she'd found it. The modest home was set back from

Upper Dummerston Road, north of Brattleboro's downtown, and be-
longed to Betsy and Ned Russell, the late Gene Russell's parents.

It was reasonable she should be here. Gene had been a wealthy
and successful local businessman, abruptly taken in the highly touted
prime of life. Rachel could have knocked on the Russells' door in a
journalistic cold call, hoping to get lucky. However, a little digging
had revealed that none other than her boss, *Reformer* editor Stan
Katz, was an old and close friend of the Russells, dating back to when
Ned had been a freelance carpenter, eking out a living at work sites
across Windham County.

Rachel had asked Katz to phone Betsy Russell and give her a
heads-up about Rachel's desire for an interview. There may be limitations for an aggressive journalist whose beat is small, mostly rural,
and thinly populated. But lack of people knowing one another is
not one.

The woman who opened the door therefore smiled wanly upon
seeing her. She was small, sparely built, haggard in appearance, and
her eyes were red-rimmed and looked exhausted. "Rachel Reiling?"
she asked.

"Yes, ma'am," Rachel answered, shaking a damp, almost lifeless
hand. "I'm so sorry to be invading your privacy at a time like this."

Russell stared at her silently for a moment, as if separating reality
from a vision. "Call me Betsy," she said, but then threw Rachel's best-
laid plans awry by stating, "I can't do this."

Psychologically poised to be invited in, Rachel was momentarily
stumped. "What?"

"Do this. Be interviewed. I know I said I would, as a favor to Stan.
But no good can come from it. Gene will still be dead."

"I'm just here to write a memorial, Mrs. Russell," Rachel countered. "I've heard he was a wonderful man—kind and generous and
talented. I was hoping you could draw me a fuller portrait."

She in fact knew none of those things with any certitude. But they fit what most parents think of their children, she thought, and didn't run afoul of the little she had heard.

Betsy, however, was clearly on a tangent at odds with traditional grieving. "You're not supposed to play favorites with your children," Betsy continued, unknowingly echoing what her husband had told Joe, "but Gene was a perfect son, right up to the end, while Penny . . ." Her voice trailed off.

"Yes?"

She finished the sentence. "Was the child from hell."

Rachel's surprise helped her ignore the awkwardness of still standing in the open doorway, fully dressed for the cold, while Betsy Russell—seemingly impervious—was wearing only a light cardigan.

"That must make losing Gene even harder," Rachel prompted her.

"Yes and no," Betsy admitted candidly. "Ever since Nathan Lyon appeared in our lives, I've become numb to loss."

Rachel had not seen that coming. Her knowledge of Lyon was scant at best. "What do you mean?"

Betsy had been staring into the lawn beyond her and now fixed the young reporter with a hard eye. "Did you ever meet him?"

"Lyon? No. He was before my time."

"He was a monster," she said simply. "And he destroyed my family. My son, my daughter, my husband. All of them."

Rachel abandoned her previous plan of attack, which had only really been an excuse to expand on the suspicions she'd learned from Sally. "Can you explain that?" she asked.

Betsy gave her a wan smile. "Gene had a good mind and a generous heart. But . . . I wish a lot of his success hadn't happened. Most of it wasn't really his doing."

"Oh?"

Betsy sighed. "Yes. Nathan again. At first, it was very attractive, his taking Gene so much to heart, unlike Monica—there's a cold fish. But Nathan was charming and supportive, very encouraging of Gene's potential. Later on, too late, he made me think of a spider, spinning his web. And Gene . . . Well, he just went along. That was his nature, too, I think—he accepted Ned and his bad moods, he went along with what Nathan told him to do, he married a woman, Peggy, who seemed more interested in what he could give her than in who he was. He was too trusting for his own good."

She added, as if startled, "I took advantage of that, too, relying on him for the love I couldn't get from Ned or Penny."

Rachel tried building on a confessional mood. "Did he ever grow resentful of Lyon?"

Betsy didn't answer at first, seemingly searching for the right answer. "I'd say resigned," she finally said.

Rachel decided to swing for the bleachers. "The reason I ask is that there's a rumor Nathan was murdered. That he didn't die of natural causes, like they said."

Once more, the other woman surprised her. "Yes, well, that's God taking care of one thing well, I guess." Her expression hardened. "I can tell you without a doubt, though: It wasn't Gene."

"How long have you known about it?" Rachel asked.

Betsy's answer was dismissive. "Not long, ever since the police started asking questions. I was happy to hear it. I didn't like the idea of that man simply dying in his sleep."

"What did Gene say about it? You must have discussed it."

"He was very conflicted."

"Because Nathan was so unpleasant, despite his generosity?"

Betsy let out a short laugh. "No. Because Nathan's death made him even richer through no effort of his own." She placed her hand on her forehead, as if steadying herself. "Gene told me he wished he could give it all away and start over."

Unfortunately for Rachel, that touched some additional emotion in Betsy, for she abruptly straightened, shivered once, and said, "I'm sorry. I have to stop. Please thank Stanley for wanting to print something nice, but I don't want to go on. I need this to end, and for you to go. It's too much. It was hard to live through, for years without end. But it's over, and I'm done."

Rachel opened her mouth to divert her, but was cut off.

"Goodbye," Betsy said, and closed the door.

Rachel retreated from the front step and began heading back to her car. Not to worry, she thought. It hadn't gone as she'd expected, but she now had something to work with, and knew what to do with it.

CHAPTER NINE

Joe had been told what to expect upon visiting the mill's penthouse, and—for that matter—its sole occupant, but as he stepped free of the elevator, he was struck by how the place triggered memories of photographs of Hearst's San Simeon palace in California or, better still, its parody as featured in *Citizen Kane*. It was all lofty airspace, extended flooring, sweeping windows, and what Joe could only silently term "antique bling."

He counted his hostess among the latter, posed as she was in a chaise longue, an ornate wooden box of tissues near her manicured hand. She was dressed in something long, ornate, and not too revealing, a gown of sorts, designed to make her look slinky while hiding most imperfections. Her face, lacking such easy cover, had been attended to by a plastic surgeon and the best of cosmetics.

Joe did hand it to her: Monica Tardy—as living sculptural art, if nothing else—was a masterpiece. Dolly Parton she was not. She lacked that icon's honesty and humor. But what Joe could see of her was immaculate, even while he wondered what damage a sudden sneeze might cause.

"Mr. Gunther?" she inquired as he crossed what felt like a carpeted tennis court to reach her.

He didn't extend a hand in greeting, knowing it would only throw her. "Ms. Tardy," he responded. "Thanks for agreeing to see me. I am very sorry about the circumstances."

She waved vaguely. "You're very kind. Please, have a seat. Would you like something to eat or drink?"

The hand hovered over an electric button placed beside the box of tissues.

He sat. "No, thank you very much."

He did admire her spunk. Given, per his research, that she'd been born over six decades earlier in Rhode Island as Mona Gomes, a Portuguese long-haul trucker's daughter, Monica Tardy was comporting herself like the movie star she'd apparently modeled herself on.

"I'm assuming you're here about poor Gene," she began, following with, "I hope you're not thinking his death was anything other than an accident."

"We haven't reached a conclusion, one way or the other," Joe said. "Regardless, it is routine to ask some basic questions about an unexpected death."

"Of course," she said. "And please thank whoever it was who broke the news to me earlier. They were very kind and tactful."

That ruled out Willy, Joe thought, saying, "Of course. If I may start, then, Gene was your son by a relationship prior to your meeting Nathan Lyon, is that right?"

He'd opted for a blunt opener on purpose, to gauge her reaction as much as to get an answer. He was looking to improve on her bland interview with Lester and Sam, days ago. Since then, the squad had gathered a stockpile of information, including an FBI report stimulated by Nathan Lyon's fingerprints, establishing his true identity.

She gave him the satisfaction of a telling pause before responding, "Close enough."

"And Gene was born in Rhode Island?"

Her eyes narrowed less than a fraction, nevertheless revealing that he'd hit a nerve.

Her answer was studiously careless. "Providence, that's right. Forty-two years ago."

Almost upon reflection, she extracted a tissue and gestured with it under her eye, although Joe noticed it didn't make actual contact, sparing her makeup.

"Did he know his biological father?"

"No."

He crossed his legs, noting her lack of expansion. He decided to stick to that course of inquiry. "Is Rhode Island where you met Nathan?"

"Yes."

"Under what circumstances?"

A growing tension was beginning to tell in her restrained gestures. "Oh, you know," she said airily, attempting to override her body language. "One thing leads to another."

"He already had Rob from a previous relationship? You and Rob are about the same age, no?"

That stung. She shifted, straightening somewhat from her languid pose, and avoided answering altogether. "Nathan and I were introduced by a mutual friend."

"What was he doing in those days?"

"He was in the food business." She risked having a small scowl crease her alabaster forehead. "What does any of this have to do with Gene's dying?"

Joe played that down. "Maybe nothing, Ms. Tardy."

"Then why are you going on about it?"

"Why are you objecting?"

She pressed her mouth tight before countering, "I'm not. I just don't see the point."

"The point is that your son and husband have both recently died under less than crystal-clear circumstances. Had you already given birth to Gene when you met Nathan?"

The response was a sullen, "Yes."

"Who was his father?"

"Nobody. A fling. He's dead."

Joe was silent, watching her.

She looked away, glanced out the window, studied her nails for a split moment.

"Nathan was Gene's father," she finally corrected herself, barely audibly.

"What happened there?" Joe pressed her.

She took a deep breath, put an end to the remains of her pose, and sat up all the way, her voice clearer. "I was a teenager, married, and Nathan was running a business, trying to get ahead. Having Gene would just complicate everything. I loved my husband, but we were barely starting out, and things were already shaky. It was just one of those choices."

"Plus," Joe said, "Nathan already had Rob."

Her face flushed. "Of course."

"And a wife?"

"No. That *was* a fling. And she died of an overdose soon afterward. That's how Nathan ended up with Rob."

"Nathan Lyon wasn't his name in those days."

It was said as a statement, not a question.

Another hesitation. "No," she finally said.

"What was it?"

She flashed anger for a split second. "You already know, don't you? Why the games?"

Joe waited her out again, silent until she conceded, "Nick Bianchi."

"Thank you. Why the change?"

"He wanted to reinvent himself. He'd made his money. He wanted to see how it felt to start fresh."

"Tough time coming up through the ranks?" Joe suggested. "Complete with skeletons in the closet?"

She looked away. "I wouldn't know."

Joe returned to his previous line of questioning. "So, instead of telling anyone about the pregnancy, you disappeared, had the baby, and put Gene up for adoption. Nathan never knew he was the father?"

"He had no idea. I told everyone, including my husband, that I'd left town for a few months to take a job. The marriage was pretty much over anyhow."

The flaw in that story almost announced itself. "Ms. Tardy," he began. "I don't want to pick a fight here, but you're not being very forthcoming. Not a smart move in a murder investigation."

"What do you mean?"

"You give up Gene, and he just happens to end up with an adoptive Brattleboro family, living under your roof some forty years later?"

Again, he let silence work for him.

"Nathan made that happen," she conceded after a pause. "For my sake, after he retired, he made sure we moved to wherever Gene was living. We didn't choose Brattleboro. It could've been Seattle for all we cared."

"What happened to Nathan not knowing about Gene?"

"I told him later. He found out about the pregnancy by accident. I don't know how, but I admitted everything."

"And Gene meant that much to him, even as an unknown ab-straction, years later?"

"*Family* meant that much," she emphasized. "That's why this place was created." She expanded her arms to include the walls around them. "Maybe because of something in his childhood, maybe because I gave up Gene for his sake . . . I'm not sure. But Nathan was a maniac on the subject."

"What about his childhood?"

"I was using a turn of phrase," she said. "He never talked about it, and I never asked."

"So Nathan pulls up stakes and moves everybody here just to create a relationship with Gene? You have to admit, that's hard to swallow."

"Still."

"Where was Mike born?"

"Here, right after we moved."

"Was Nathan tough to get along with? I heard he could be de-manding."

She wasn't coy, to Joe's surprise. "No marriage is a cakewalk."

He contemplated a young woman falling for an older man, domineering by nature and short on patience, whose personality was enough to have made her act as she had. Assuming what she'd said was true.

What did that reveal about each of them, then and now? The thought brought him back to how people layer and disguise who and what they are.

What wasn't being addressed here, he wondered, and how might it link the two deaths facing him? He began considering examining Nathan's Rhode Island roots in detail.

"Tell me how he was to live with," he pressed her.

"The hardest thing about Nathan for most people," she explained, "was that he was usually right, and he knew it. My husband didn't suffer fools, and he was used to getting what he wanted. To me, he was kind, thoughtful, and generous. And look what he did for Gene. Who else would've done that?"

Joe instead thought of what Lyon had done "for" Penny Trick. However, he seized on her comment to pursue a different angle, asking innocently, "He seems to have set all of you up well. What was that? A trust? A will? I mean, this place alone has to cost a fortune to keep running."

A hint of wariness crossed her features, as if she could sense his duplicity. "It's a trust," she answered shortly.

"Smart," he complimented her. "Was Gene mentioned in it?"

"Of course. We all are."

Joe pushed slightly harder. "As you're aware, your son's death is being treated as a homicide. Subpoenas and warrants will give us access to what may help solve it. So this is your opportunity to be open and honest with me, which I think you know will look best in the long run."

Despite their having just touched on her tolerating her late husband's bullying, she was clearly put out by Joe's mild suggestion.

"Everyone is taken care of," she said testily. "Some more than others. I'm to live here for as long as I choose, as is everyone else. Rob and I share managing partner status, and are compensated accordingly. I really don't know what to tell you. It's like running a business and managing a portfolio, which is Rob's primary role. Nothing's too complex or confusing, but there is a lot of it, which is why we employ accountants and bookkeepers and the rest."

"You said some of you are better taken care of than others," Joe pointed out. "How did the apportionment of funds differ among the kids—Gene, Michael, their wives and children? I realize that Rob, while also an offspring, fits a different category."

She spoke tersely. "Gene did slightly better, and he was named a successor trustee."

"How much did he get?"

"Enough to never have to worry."

Joe took a wild guess. "In excess of several million dollars."

A flash of impatience made her eyes sharpen again. "There's a lot to go around, as you'll find out soon enough."

"Not to mention a successor," Joe commented. "That put Gene in management. Was that over Mike?"

"I suppose so."

"With his death, do all the same benefits transfer to Peggy?"

"I don't recall," she said stubbornly.

"Who knows the contents of the trust?"

"Just Rob and me." She hesitated before throwing in, "And the others I mentioned, of course—lawyers, accountants, et cetera."

"Does Mike know? Peggy's not even a blood relation."

Her jaw muscles tightened. "Not that I'm aware."

"How will he take it? Did he and Gene get along?"

"You'll have to ask Michael."

Joe smiled at her tone. "Okaaay. Since Gene got special treatment, what happens when one of the others dies, spouses and grandchildren?"

"The money's redistributed."

"That'll make for interesting reading," he commented, eyeing her closely.

But she'd been well trained. "I hope you enjoy yourself."

"Along the same lines," he said, "how did things change otherwise with Nathan's death?"

"Otherwise?"

"Not to sound like a broken record, but the consensus is that

Nathan was a tyrant and a control freak, Ms. Tardy. You and he may have come to an accommodation, but clearly few others did."

She finally angrily broke role and stood up, marching to a nearby table rivaling an aircraft carrier and snatching up another wooden box that turned out to contain cigarettes and a lighter.

"You're not going to get me to trash my husband," she said grimly, igniting the end of a cigarette and drawing on it deeply. Joe hadn't smelled any lingering smoke upon entering, and so figured this was a habit she largely kept to herself—an artifact, perhaps, of the younger Mona Gomes.

"You sit on top of this oversized nest," he said, "complete with closed-circuit cameras, financial control, and whatever arrangements you or Nathan put together to keep everyone in line. I'm less interested in trashing his memory than in finding out who killed him, which is a goal you don't seem to share."

"I want this conversation to end," she stated, blowing out smoke.

He remained seated. "I'm sure you do. You should know before it does, though, that until we're convinced otherwise, that presumption of homicide in Gene's case isn't academic. We have good reasons encouraging us."

"You're full of crap. You're using a tragic, heartbreaking accident so you can get me to say things that aren't true."

Her previous mask transformed by fury, she stabbed the cigarette at him, adding, "If you think poking and prodding is going to somehow knock me over, you've got another thing coming. I've been pushed around by experts, and you don't even come close."

Joe slowly got up and draped his coat over his arm. "I'm going to take an educated guess. I think you've been less pushed around by me than educated. Someone is killing your family, Ms. Tardy. One by one. Possibly you, but I'm betting not. Which means you've got at least one long, sleepless night ahead of you, trying to figure out what's happening and how to control it."

He moved toward the elevator, pausing midway. "Imagining for a moment, unlike for Nathan, that there's more in your heart than maintaining control and using money as a hammer, remember this: What you come up with after all that head-scratching might save lives. But only if you tell me about it."

He reached into his pocket and extracted a business card. "Nathan had an old bullet wound in him, going back years. We'll find the source of that, along with a lot more you'd prefer we didn't. I've been at this long enough to sense where things are headed, and they aren't looking good for you and yours. Storm clouds are gathering, from us and whoever's targeted you. That makes the math pretty simple: You work with us, and we defeat them together. You go solo . . ." He paused to let her imagination fill in the blank, before adding, "Well, I think you know better than I about what comes next."

He placed the card on the far end of the long table's flight deck.

"Call me. Anytime."

"Rob Lyon?"

"Yes."

"This is Bart Nelson, at the King's Keg."

"Okay."

"I'm the bartender here. I was told to call you if there was a problem."

Rob rubbed his forehead. "Okay."

The man on the phone was hesitant. "Look, if this doesn't mean anything, I'll just call the cops, okay? It's what I'm supposed to do anyhow. But your dad told me a few years ago—paid me a retainer—to phone this number at the mill if I ever had something I couldn't handle."

"Okay. What's it about?"

"Penny Trick. That ring a bell? She needs to go."

"Ah," Rob said.

"You gonna come over? I'll give you fifteen minutes, 'cause it's snowin' again, but after that, it's 911. I don't need to get fired over shit like this."

"I'll be there, Mr. Nelson. Thank you for calling."

"Whatever." The line went dead.

Rob sighed as he hung up. Trust Nathan to have set up a safety net. He wondered how many other bars across the county had the same arrangement, and for how long into the future it was supposed to extend.

He'd been swimming, as he tried to do every day, and so finished dressing before stepping out of the locker room into the subterranean space that housed the ghostly, blue-lit pool, which extended into the gloomy distance like an azure, alien swamp of clear liquid. He'd come here from outdoors and so had his winter coat available. He therefore accessed the parking lot without detouring to his apartment down the hall from Monica's penthouse.

Although it occupied the same floor as hers, his bachelor lair was smaller, darker, wood-lined, bookish, Turkish-carpeted, and lacking the monumental, garish bric-a-brac she favored. In the midst of a Pentagon-sized structure inhabited by people he sometimes considered mad, Rob saw his apartment as a refuge akin to a space capsule.

Which brought him back to his current mission. Penny, to his organized, orderly, fastidious mind, had long since ceased teetering on the edge. She'd toppled over years earlier, perhaps genetically encouraged, perhaps pushed by Nathan's nonstop, compulsive intrusiveness.

The fact that his father had playfully arranged to have people call Rob whenever she crashed and burned was another example of the old man's capriciousness.

Turning up his collar, he stepped out into the parking lot and into one of those beautiful, silent, windless New England snowfalls of Bing Crosby fame, where the fat white flakes, flashing by the nearby streetlamps, seemed poured from an enormous box of old-fashioned laundry soap, high above. Rob pulled out his keys, hit the fob that unlocked his Audi, and headed downtown to retrieve Penny from her latest meltdown, accompanied by the soothing strains of stereophonic Mozart.

In its boisterous 1970s heyday, Brattleboro had contained more bars than most could count, making of Friday and Saturday nights regular brawls between police and hard-core drinkers who'd been turned into the streets by closing hours. That was an embarrassing memory to the more genteel, progressively minded population claiming the town now. But claiming did not mean full possession, and Brattleboro still had a complement of citizens whose ideas of progressivism extended only to how many drinks they could consume before passing out.

That's who the King's Keg catered to, along with Penny Trick.

It was located on Flat Street, not far from the brook that fed the Connecticut River a few hundred yards downstream. Years before, the whole area had been flooded in a storm, and the Keg submerged in mud. Many wished it had stayed there; many more believed it had never resurfaced.

Rob parked by the curb, negotiated the icy snow in the gutter, and regained his footing in front of an entrance scarred with dents, stains, gouges, and plastered with ads and job offerings for temporary work. The dull music from within thudded through the walls like the heartbeat of a gasping dinosaur. Rob pushed open the door and entered a dark den of hot, stinking, pulsing air.

He heard Penny before seeing her, her shouting arcing over the top of a huddle of drunken men in a geyser of abuse. The bartender, standing behind his beer- and booze-slick barricade, eyed Rob warily as he walked in, instantly seeing by his dress and demeanor that his purpose here transcended the norm.

Not challenging the fog of noise, Rob merely gestured questioningly toward the cluster and received a nodded and relieved acknowledgment from the barkeep.

Little did either of them realize how little relief was coming.

Rob unhappily approached the group and began easing his way through the jostling, malodorous bodies, catching sight of the main attraction. Penny, clad only in a low-cut halter top and tight jeans, was competing with a young man remarkable for his array of facial tattoos and piercings. Both were working their way along a line of shot glasses and beer mugs, in some sort of game Rob wanted to know nothing about, pausing only to scream at each other or the world in general, accompanying each outburst with a bang of glass on bar top.

Rob's intention had been to suggest a ride home to Penny—a notion, he now realized, he'd clearly have to reconsider.

Fortunately or not, she removed all such conjuring. Once her crazed, bloodshot eyes landed on him, she shoved her drinking buddy off his stool with one hand and threw a shot glass at Rob's head with the other, hitting him over his right eye.

"*You piece of shit!*" she screamed, and came out of her seat swinging.

CHAPTER TEN

Sam and Willy chose to divide and conquer, or at least divide and interview, while still at the hospital ER. Willy steered Rob into the tastefully lighted room the hospital used for fretful relatives, with comfortable chairs and Kleenex; Sam drew the short straw of the treatment room and a stool on wheels, given that Penny's injuries, from the bar fight she'd instigated, were more numerous, though superficial, and her state of inebriation deserving of an IV. Fortunately for Sam, enough time had passed by for her subject's last blood tests to proclaim her adequately sober for a legally sanctioned conversation. It was past dawn.

That was not the only official consideration, of course. The fallout from Penny's explosion at the bar had involved two ambulances and the local police, the second of which had not bothered laying blame for who'd thrown the first punch. Virtually everyone there had been more than delighted to join in once the fight started, and nobody was pointing fingers, including the barkeep, who didn't want to lose that many patrons. The state's attorney, rousted from bed for a consultation, had recommended issuing disturbing-the-peace citations across the board.

Not that Sam was going to bring Penny up to date. She was happy to let the younger woman think she might be facing assault charges.

She sat beside the gurney, using a nearby cabinet as a backrest. "Hey," she said by way of introduction. "I'm a cop. You feeling better than you look?"

Penny smiled despite a swollen upper lip. "How *do* I look?"

"Like you been in a bar fight."

"Well, if that's the baseline, I've felt worse."

"Do this often?"

"Now and then. It beats exercising."

"They have a decent exercise yard at the jail. And you could learn to snowshoe around the baseball field. It's become very trendy."

"Fuck that. You here to arrest me?"

"I'm way worse than that," Sam told her. "I only chase A-level felonies, like murder."

Penny eyed her silently for a moment. "Who did you say you were?" she then asked.

"You want a lawyer?"

"No."

Sam pulled out her credentials. "Samantha Martens. Vermont Bureau of Investigation."

Penny's expression cleared. "Oh yeah. I heard you people were around. Checking out who killed Nathan."

"We're also looking into Gene's death."

"He was *murdered*?"

"The way we look at these things," Sam explained, "they're all murders until we prove they're not. Gene hasn't reached that yet."

"Wow," Penny said. "Cool job."

"It has its moments."

"You ever been shot at?"

Sam wondered if she were speaking to a thirteen-year-old.

"Worse," she answered. "Everybody lies to my face and thinks they're being clever."

Penny had nothing to say.

"That's a clue, in case you missed it," Sam added. "Tonight? Here and now? Don't lie. It'll only piss me off and put you in even deeper shit."

Up the hallway, Willy and Rob Lyon settled into the next-of-kin waiting room, which had always struck Willy with a funeral home's aura of grim finality, at odds with a hospital's mission.

Rob was showing minimal effects from the evening's spontaneous brawl, shy of a few stains on his expensive clothing and a welt over his eye. From what he'd told Willy during introductions, he'd ended up on the bottom of the pile almost immediately and suffered less abuse than the carpeting underfoot. Still, his clothes were not looking cleanable to Willy, who shared Rob's attraction to quality and cleanliness. Willy, for all his more controversial characteristics, bordered on being a neat freak by preference, not that he ever held that over Sam and Emma at home.

It did cause him to consider the purported second-in-command of the Lyon dynasty in a new light, however. As extravagant and theatrical as was Monica Tardy, Rob Lyon presented more as either a Mormon lookalike or a retired, if successful, accountant. Tall, blond, clean-cut, with a tamped-down personality to match, he struck Willy as the aging Ken doll to Monica's Zsa Zsa Gabor.

The question was, did a lack of theatricality imply any less of an inclination to hide the truth?

"You sure you're feeling all right?" he now asked, settling into an armchair opposite Rob's couch. "Things can start hurting after the adrenaline wears off."

"No, I'm fine," Rob reassured him. "More embarrassed than

injured. I should have known better than to go there alone. I'm more distracted than usual, I suppose."

"Gene's death on top of our looking into Nathan?"

Rob gave him a wry expression. "I'm used to family squabbles more aspiring to murder than committing it."

"Looks like you were almost the victim tonight," Willy said. "What was that all about? I heard from the locals that Penny lit up as soon as she saw you." He pointed at Rob's injury. "And beaned you with a glass. Sounds like more than a squabble."

"We're a complicated family."

Willy bit back a laugh. "The Corleones were a complicated family, Mr. Lyon. What the hell's going on?"

The seriousness of his question made its impact. Rob paused to think carefully before responding. "May I ask you a question first?"

"You can ask."

"Are you treating Gene's death like Nathan's?"

"Right now? Yes."

He didn't look surprised. "I was afraid of that. Who do you suspect?"

"That, Rob," Willy said, "is what I'd like to talk about."

"So what've you got against Rob Lyon that you tried taking his head off?" Sam asked.

Penny scowled. "He's an asshole—Nathan's Mini-Me."

"Really? I heard Nathan was pretty bad. And full disclosure? Your dad told us about what he did to you guys, back when—why Ned was forced to move his business into the mill."

Penny was silent, more thoughtful than surprised. "Poor Dad," she said mournfully.

"What?" Sam asked.

"He told you about the bicyclist?"

"Yeah."

"That's only part of it."

"What's the rest?"

"I had to fuck Nathan so he wouldn't tell you guys. Putting Dad into the mill was a way to make him look like an accomplice if I didn't play along. Double blackmail. Nathan, through and through. Also, when Dad was having problems, early on, Nathan lined up jobs for him, did him favors, stuff like that—things he wouldn't let Dad forget after. You wanna find out who killed him, though, look at Monica, for justifiable homicide, except she's such a bitch herself. She probably even knew about Nathan and me."

"Sounds like we could look at you, too," Sam said.

Penny's eyes blazed. "*Fine.* Knock yourself out. You think I give a rat's ass? I'm already in prison. A change of scenery's not gonna make any difference."

"Why do you still live there? Nathan's been dead almost a year."

Penny's look of self-loathing was telling. "That's on me. Call it an extension of the same barrel Nathan had me over."

"Explain."

Her face flushed with anger. "The money, duh. That's the deal. I leave, they cut me off. It's the same with all of us."

Sam pretended she'd been caught off guard. "And Rob keeps that going?"

"It's not up to him, limp dick that he is. There's a trust or something. Some deal Nathan set up before he died that lasts forever and nobody can change."

"What were you doing on the night Nathan died?" Sam asked.

"Like I can remember."

Sam believed her, seeing how she was acting right now. Penny Trick seemed to be living from one bender to the next—probably not a journey where keeping track was a priority.

"Try," Sam urged nevertheless. "Where were you when you heard he was dead?"

"In bed," she responded without hesitation. "Mom came to my apartment and told me."

"Your mother? She and Ned don't even live at the mill."

"Credit my dad for that. He was at the office when they found Nathan. I guess Monica told him. Anyhow, Dad phoned Mom, who came over to tell me."

"Your dad didn't just climb the stairs to do it himself?"

For once, Penny looked empathetic. "That kind of thing's hard for him. You shouldn't blame him. He does the best he can."

"All right. Now that we've established the morning after, what were you doing the night before?"

But Penny shook her head. "Probably getting blasted somewhere. I sure as hell wasn't near him. Nobody was, toward the end, 'cept maybe Rob and Monica. He'd been going downhill. That's why this whole murder thing is so crazy. We all *knew* he was dying."

Sam realized she wasn't going to be able to jog Penny's recall about a night so long ago, and her instincts were telling her that Penny—guilty as she might have been for so much chaos and clamor—was probably innocent of strangling someone, including the man who'd exploited her the most.

Which, in part, brought her back to her opening question. "If you think Rob is such a nebbish, why did you lash out at him at the bar? Why bother?"

Penny stared at her pityingly. "Jesus, you just don't get it, do you? Rob's a nobody. A nothing. He's a suit who wears shoes and a hat."

"Okay . . ."

"Well, that's it, right? It makes him the perfect yes-man for an evil corpse. Nathan's frigging gofer, even now. You take the nastiest piece of crap in the world and you make Rob his representative. Of all people."

She pounded the gurney with her fist. "Damn straight, I tried to knock his block off."

"Let me turn the tables on you, Rob," Willy said. "Who do you suspect killed Nathan?"

Rob looked nonplussed. "Where to start?" he asked rhetorically. "And who knows how much another person will take?"

"Like you?"

That startled him. "Me? Why would I do that? How would it benefit me?"

Surprisingly logical answer, Willy thought, and reasonable. Nevertheless, he took a stab at suggesting, "He humiliated you?"

Rob made a face. "He did that to stray animals. He did it to everyone. It finally became irrelevant. Besides, the worst was over before he died."

"What's that mean?"

"He had Alzheimer's. For the last year of his life, he had no meaningful interactions with anyone."

"That didn't appear on his death certificate," Willy said.

Rob was sympathetic. "Ah yes. Official documents. They do so often stand in for the truth."

Willy frowned. "We talked to his physician. Looked at his records."

Rob rubbed his thumb and index together, back and forth. "Money, Detective. It's a powerful lubricant. Nathan made sure what appeared on paper was only what he wanted. His doctor was no different than anyone else whose wallets were fattened to help Nathan create the life he chose." He shifted in his seat to emphasize, "Including me."

Willy laughed and waved his one hand dismissively, while tuck-ing away the reference to a fabricated life for later on. "Okay, okay. I get it. The great Svengali. The Wizard of Oz. Whatever. Answer the question: Who do you think had it in for him?"

Rob answered indirectly. "I think the solution there is in the here and now. Your question should be: Who's come out ahead because he died a year ahead of schedule?"

"And?" Willy prompted him, impressed by the comeback. It was becoming clear why Rob had the responsibilities he did.

"We were all living rich before he died, and still are. None of us benefits from having a murder charge hanging overhead."

Willy conceded the point. "All right. So who's come out ahead emotionally?" He jerked his thumb at the door. "How 'bout Penny?"

"Her life may not be pretty, but it's unchanged from a year ago, when Nathan was still breathing. His torturing of her had already stopped."

"You knew about that?"

Rob was patience personified. "You need to understand that real-world experiences didn't apply to life in the mill. Nathan Lyon had the money, the ruthlessness, and the force of character to do as he wished. Call him a cult leader, if that helps, although it's not accu-rate. He was a psychopath, with the charm and intelligence ramped up. Add a vast amount of cash, and you have a magic formula for complete control, along with a corresponding lack of guile. Nathan Lyon didn't care who knew about his activities, especially ones like that."

"But the son of a bitch is dead," Willy protested. "Isn't it time people snapped out of it?"

Rob's voice was almost soothing. "His legacy lives on. It won't last forever. Clearly, with Gene's death, it's already showing cracks.

But Nathan's legacy is a little like one of those supertankers, the size of a floating skyscraper. It just keeps steaming ahead, long after the engines have been cut."

"You're saying your entire family is a bunch of zombies."

"Rich, privileged, insulated zombies, with no immediate incentive to change."

"Holy cow," Willy muttered.

"We will change," Rob went on, "and some of it won't be pretty. Penny's a good example. Gene was a holdout. He kept his soul intact, even while he sold out for the sake of his wife and child. But that's because he was a Russell at heart, if not by blood, and the Russells did well by him, even if they lost their daughter to Nathan."

A horrifying thought occurred to Willy, who spoke against better instinct. "You think Nathan could've had Gene killed after his own death, as revenge against Ned Russell's influence?"

Rob looked dubious. "The man was evil, Detective. Not the devil. But I'm glad you said that; it reveals Nathan's secret weapon. He allowed the paranoia of others to act on his behalf."

Willy was embarrassed. "You're coming out smiling."

"I would have in any case. But you are right. I'm happier now that he's dead. Monica's no bowl of cherries, but she's predictably unimaginative, which in this case is a good thing."

"And she wouldn't have gained anything by killing him, for what he did to Penny, for example?"

Rob's short answer was paradoxically eloquent. "No."

"Okay, okay," Willy reflected. "Let's go back in time, speaking of you, Monica, and Nathan. Or should I say, Nick?"

Rob was still for a half beat. "Ah. Didn't know that cat had gotten out."

"Tell me about Rhode Island and the story of Nick Bianchi—our Nathan Lyon."

"What would you like to know?"

"Very clever. Instead of my asking twenty questions, why don't you just give me a history lesson?"

"He was the son of a restaurant owner who ran a popular place outside downtown Providence, and when it came time to take it over, he opted for something else. Related, but not the restaurant."

"We heard a food business."

"Correct. A much larger version of what Mike and Michelle operate at the mill. That's where the idea of Food Flourish came from. He did keep the restaurant running for a few years with hired help, as a form of brand identity, like a monstrously twisted and ironic Newman's Own."

"And he made that much money?" Willy asked him.

"Those were the old days."

Willy wasn't about to leave it at that. "Explain. What's that mean?"

"I didn't tell you my grandfather's restaurant was a gathering place for the Mob, back when it ruled the roost. Little Nick Bianchi—Nathan—was like a miniature padrone, zipping from table to table, talking up old, sentimental crooks like a pro. They loved him, slipped him money, talked him up to his dad. That's why it was assumed he'd take over the restaurant. But he came up with this supply-side model instead, where he could stand between the producers like fishermen, lobstermen, spice and exotic condiment sellers, and the rest, and sell to Mob-vetted outlets like the restaurant he'd been brought up in, all across the northeast and beyond. It was a way to expand exponentially without having to cook and wait tables. All he needed was to reach out to the same people he used to suck up to as a kid. They couldn't give him enough money, contracts, and protection." Rob spread his hands, concluding, "Perfect match."

"But it had to be more than that," Willy pushed him. "You're making it sound legitimate."

"You mean adulterating the product?" Rob asked, although Willy had said no such thing. "You bet. Nathan took the notion of adding a little water to the wine to extremes. Everything he sold he fiddled with to fatten profits. Nobody cared as long as it didn't cause problems, and who was going to complain, even if a customer did get sick?"

"So he was a mobster," Willy stated.

Rob laughed outright. "Nick? Not even close. A fellow traveler. There was a lot of that back then, especially in Little Rhody. He gave them a piece of the business; they gave him access to outlets under their control. It was simple and worked for everyone. The whole idea that the Mob ran everything outright is nonsense. They made accommodations all the time. Self-serving ones, but still . . . He was a pilot fish."

Knowing this could be checked later, Willy was content to largely sit and listen—a patient man when he needed to be, willing to wait out his target's small meanderings.

"All right," he therefore said, "so now we've got Nick up and running in business. Where, how, and when do you and Monica come in?"

"I was born in Providence," Rob answered easily. "Never knew my mother. I was told she died shortly after my birth. Monica appeared on the scene when she and I were both in our teens. Nathan took a liking to her."

"And made her pregnant with Gene?"

"That's what I heard."

Willy had been briefed on what Monica had told Joe, and found Rob's terse response interesting—his easy portrayal of openness notwithstanding.

"Go on," he prompted him.

"Monica was married at the time. I think they cooked up a story to keep things vague. Monica went away to give birth and gave up the baby. I don't know if her husband was in on it or not. I don't even know his name. They didn't last, surprise, surprise."

"You say 'they,' but Nathan was kept in the dark, too, wasn't he?"

For the first time, Rob caught a glance of Willy's insight.

"You've done your homework."

"We're doing a lot of interviews," Willy countered. "Plus, you learn when to take a lucky guess, now and then."

"Right," Rob said slowly. "Okay, you're right. Only Monica knew about Gene."

"Must've been interesting when she finally fessed up. Who tracked him to Vermont and the Russells? I'm guessing Nathan."

"Correct."

Willy was silent, letting that drift between them briefly. "And finally, there were three bouncing boys," he said. "You, Gene, and, after you'd all reached Vermont, Mike."

Rob waited in turn.

"Here's a question, then," Willy proposed. "Who else do you think might've traveled north? To kill Nathan, for instance?"

Rob seemed genuinely startled. "From Rhode Island? Decades later? Why would anyone do that?"

"Why indeed?" Willy agreed. "A manipulative, nasty con man who works with the Mafia and makes a pile of dough illegally, changes his name, runs from the scene of the crime, and ends up murdered. It does seem like a stretch that he pissed off somebody who never forgot."

He paused before adding, "Or maybe it doesn't. What d'you think, Rob?"

"You're making more of this than it deserves, Detective."

Willy once more took in the smoothness of Rob's face, as untouched as a mannequin's by creases, wrinkles, or any landmarks of concern.

"Let me ask you," he said. "Given Monica's presence in Nick's life, before and after his rebirth as Nathan, and just humoring me that there might be bodies buried in his past, could Monica be the keeper of such secrets?"

Willy expected him to say, "Ask her," so his answer surprised him. "She'll know more than I do," Rob responded. "That's part of her power in the hierarchy. But Nathan never considered her an equal, and he felt free to betray her as much as he did the rest of us. He made her *feel* special. That always seemed to be enough."

Willy scratched his head and decided to move on. "Let's talk about Gene some more."

"You've already implied you think he was murdered."

"Let's say he was," Willy suggested.

"Why?"

"I'm asking you."

Rob was agreeable. "Fair enough. My answer would be money, which is another reason why I don't think Nathan reached out of his grave to kill him."

Willy was incredulous. "Money? You've all *got* money."

"Gene had more of it than most, myself and Monica aside. I take it you haven't had enough time to disassemble the Lyon finances. I'm not surprised."

Willy wouldn't concede anything, not wanting to show what in fact he did know. "We're working on it."

"I'm saying the trust explicitly states that once Nathan dies, Gene becomes a successor trustee, which he did—probably at Monica's insistence. Anyhow, millions of dollars became his as a result. A variation on inheriting a dead man's shoes, even though Gene didn't care."

"What do you mean?"

"You know the expression," Rob explained. "It's no longer common, but back in time, you couldn't improve your station in life until the man above you died."

"Except you're saying it was lost on Gene," Willy interpreted. "The prospect of upward mobility was Nathan's, not Gene's."

"Precisely." Rob lifted his chin like a lecturing professor. "There was other shifting around at the same time, by the way. Monica lost her power of attorney status, certain provisions kicked in, like Ned having his rent permanently made free and his debts wiped out, Michelle and Mike's business underwent a fundamental financial change. And so on down the line."

"Who gains by Gene's death, then? More dead man's shoes?"

"No. Only his family. Nothing nefarious there, I don't think. I said money earlier because things are in flux and there's no telling what a hermetically sealed-off group of spoiled, suspicious, jealous people might do. At our financial level, Detective, it's less the amount of money that matters, and more where in the pecking order it puts you. That's why Donald Trump always lied about his worth."

Willy was nearing the end of his tolerance for this. But as with the fascination one has for things repellent, he couldn't quite walk away. Not yet.

"What you said about Ned Russell's debts being forgiven. What was that about?"

Rob was amused as he said, "Ah yes. He told you of the leverage Nathan used to get him into the mill? The unfortunate episode of young Penny with her car?"

"Yeah."

"That's the face-saving story—the noble father stepping up to protect the wastrel child, even though she doesn't deserve it. True as far as it goes, and very Ned Russell, our own living John Wayne."

"But . . . ," Willy suggested.

"Indeed. 'But.' It turns out that Ned is a better builder than a businessman. Years ago, he was far from the square-jawed model of resolve and integrity we see today. That may partly explain Penny's obvious daddy issues. He was a failure and a drunk, and he owes his rebirth to none other than his nemesis, Nathan Lyon, who appeared from nowhere to bail him out, steady him on his course, supply him with some starter projects, and even make sure he stuck with AA."

"Why?" Willy asked, feeling himself increasingly in the presence of an unattractive alien life-form—programmed to reflect human emotions with almost robotic affect.

"Gene, of course. It was Nathan's gesture to his own ego. When he discovered that Monica had given up a child for adoption, it was incumbent upon him to locate it and own it. It and its family, lock, stock, and stalwart father, as it turned out."

"It," Willy echoed.

"Revealing pronoun, no? Factually reflective, however. To fully grasp that is to better understand Nathan. And Monica, when you come down to it."

As if such a thing were possible or desirable, Willy thought. Harking back to Joe's notes about his interview with Monica and her initial equivocations about Gene's parentage, he asked, "When in all this did Monica tell Nathan he was Gene's father? Before or after the move to Vermont?"

Heightening Willy's dislike of the man, Rob smiled wordlessly and shrugged.

"And Penny's relationship with Nathan?"

Rob was more rueful there. "Ah. That was a little more sordid. If it's any comfort, Nathan didn't play favorites. He saw all women pretty much the same, barring Monica, who didn't care about his dalliances."

"How old was Penny when they started?"

"Thirteen or fourteen," Rob answered carelessly. "Nothing defensible about it, of course. Utterly revolting. But she was a precocious girl. I will give her that."

Willy briefly considered punching him in the face. For all his own inner conflicts and emotional turmoil, some of which had cost him dearly, Willy had always managed to keep hold of certain key principles, mostly involving integrity and loyalty. In this instance, what floated in his brain was an image of his own Emma, whose welfare and happiness were, in his eyes, worth his life. To hear of another daughter so casually dismissed brought him to the edge of violence.

He rose stiffly to his feet. "We'll leave it there, Mr. Lyon. I'll be in touch."

Leaving Rob with his mouth half-open, Willy stepped into the hallway and closed the door behind him.

Fifteen minutes later, with Sam driving, she turned to him and asked, "You want to tell me what happened, or should we just drop by a pet store and drown a few puppies?"

Usually quick with a comeback, Willy remained silent at first, before quietly replying, "We see a lot of bad things in this job, don't we?"

Intrigued, she glanced at his profile to find him gazing ahead almost peacefully. "True."

"And more times than not, we write them off to bad parenting, poverty, drugs and alcohol, social disadvantages. Things like that."

"Yes," she answered neutrally, wondering where he was headed.

"So what happens when none of that's there? Where do you go when the person in front of you is just bad, like other people are naturally kind or generous or thoughtful?"

The latter image made her think of Joe, who'd always exhibited such traits, even when things were going poorly for him. "You talking about Rob?"

"Nah," he said, before correcting himself. "Well, yeah, in a way. I meant Nathan, but Rob made me think of it. The guy's like a loan officer, you know? As bland as a cucumber, all neat and squared away. Sleek and without feeling. But dependable. His dad? Holy Christ, what a unit he must've been. And it doesn't sound like changing his name from Nick to Nathan did anyone much good."

Willy twisted in his seat to look at her fully. She'd never seen him so philosophically wound up; he was such a poster boy for the dispassionate sniper he'd once been—a calculating assessor of human targets. To hear him now, she half expected him to quote scripture.

He spared her that, returning to his analytical norm. "And Rob's got the same DNA. Talking to him, I suddenly felt like you do when a cabin door flies open in the face of a blizzard. That blast of coldness . . ."

"You think he's dirty?"

Again, he hesitated. "He could be. Hard to tell. It's like all these people we been talking to, every one of them seems to be living in a tar pit, built for them by Nathan Lyon. I just can't separate the ones he pushed, versus the ones who jumped in with both feet."

CHAPTER ELEVEN

"He had dementia?" Joe asked.

"According to what Rob told Willy," Sam said.

Lester was studying the case notes. "It fits," he weighed in. "All the interviews I been indexing, nobody except Nathan's doc, Rob, and Monica claim they saw him within months of his death. He could've been a vegetable for a year or more, with no one the wiser."

"He did a Woodrow Wilson," Willy said, flipping through a gun magazine at his desk.

Everyone stared at him for the pure randomness of such a reference, even for him, before Joe spoke again. "Correct. Which—as with Wilson—brings up the doctor. Can't you disbar a doc for pulling a stunt like that? Or whatever they call it. Cooking up a phony death certificate?"

Lester had already looked into that. "He didn't," he reported. "There was no autopsy. He lists general decompensation as a secondary cause. Dementia qualifies. We have no idea how many times a death certificate has nothing to do with what killed a patient—just so long as the wording passes muster."

"Ask your girlfriend," Willy said without looking up. "She'll tell you. I bet we bury a lot of homicides."

"We almost did this time," Joe conceded, adding in a more upbeat tone, "but we didn't, so here we are, and from what I'm hearing, instead of missing a murder, we now have a building full of suspects. Correct me if I'm wrong, but the plant manager, Kimona Alin, may be the only one who didn't have an ax to grind against the dearly departed."

"That we know of," Willy threw in.

"Something else has popped up that might have a bearing," Joe told them. "A young woman named Alex Lloyd has come forward via the good graces of our friend Sally Kravitz, with information about Food Flourish and how they may be up to no good."

"Dan Kravitz's baby girl," Willy said, at last taking them in. "What the hell's *that* about?"

"Call it a coerced good citizen complaint. Under contract to Michelle, Sally caught Lloyd pilfering, but then through Lloyd, she discovered Mike and Michelle Lyon are cranking out counterfeit food products. Sally's hoping we'll give Lloyd a pass in exchange for the intel, which I'm inclined to do."

Lester greeted the news with typical enthusiasm. "I've heard about this scam. It's wild. Mississippi fish eggs sold as Russian caviar, sea bass that's not."

"Good news if you're a sea bass," Willy said, recalling Rob detailing how his father pulled the same lucrative scam decades earlier.

Sam broke in with, "Why do we care, other than making a phone call to the health department and the secretary of state's office?"

"We care," Joe explained, "because of two things. Number one is the potential leverage this gives us with Mike or Michelle, which is what Sally was thinking might be more valuable than a larceny charge. Number two is a small piece of evidence I got from the lab twenty minutes ago." He held up a photograph of the granite rolling pin found under Gene Russell's head. "They put this into their fuming chamber to see what fingerprints they could raise, and got a nice match to Michelle Lyon."

"Her shop's just down the hall from Gene's," Willy countered. "I bet you'll find some of his prints at her place, too."

"Maybe," Joe partially agreed. "But they collected prints from all over ER Ceramics. Hers only surfaced here." He waved the picture in the air for emphasis.

"I did hear there wasn't much love lost between family members," Lester said.

"Without Nathan, his moolah, and the trust tying them together like rats on a raft," Willy commented, "I bet none of them would be caught dead within spitting distance of one another."

"Maybe," Joe repeated. "Maybe not. A few of them are rats. I'll give you that. But if that place is a raft, after a while, even rats get lonely."

"Or hungry," Willy suggested.

The implication made them all think of Nathan's relationship with Penny and the pressures used to bring Ned Russell into the familial tent.

"This is like doing an autopsy on an evil cult," Sam said distastefully.

"Perhaps," Joe agreed. "But it also suggests that Michelle or Mike should be on top of our interview list."

"It's becoming less of a stretch why Michelle hired a PI instead of calling the cops," Lester said.

"Good for us her integrity wasn't for sale, too," Joe commented.

"This remind you of somethin'?"

Fredo snorted gently, his eyes fixed on the sprawling, six-story, low-rent apartment complex across the street. "What? Spending another all-nighter with you, waiting for some poor bastard to step into the open to get whacked?"

Eddie chuckled and patted the dashboard. "Hey. The heater's workin'. That wasn't always true back when. What're you complainin' about?"

"My butt's not as forgiving as it used to be," Fredo replied.

Eddie checked his watch, having killed the van's dash lights to eliminate any possible interior glow. Can't have the lookers being looked at.

"You sure your information's good?"

Fredo's voice was flat. "Sure as last time you asked."

"It's just the name that gets to me. Dan Silver. What kind of Italian is that?"

"Told you. I heard he changed it."

"Why would you do that?" Eddie complained. "Like he lives in a WASPy neighborhood and wants to join the country club? Spare me."

Fredo saw his point. They were in Central Falls, north of Providence, one of the most densely populated, least advantaged communities in Rhode Island, which was saying something. Fredo had heard once that a long time ago, Central Falls's population numbers had rivaled parts of urban India, where people were as crowded into houses as parakeets in cages. Probably bullshit, of course. But it had stuck in his mind forever.

That being said, God only knew how many people were crammed into the building facing them. The complex was enormous, clad in boring beige brick, dotted with hundreds of tiny windows. There was a massive jail facility up the street that made him wonder how many people had spent their lives migrating between both structures. One with windows, one without.

Central Falls had attracted all the wrong attention over time, from leadership corruption scandals to the entire staff of one of its schools being fired during a contract negotiation. Not long ago, the whole city had declared bankruptcy.

Calling the town home was usually not reflective of your rolling in riches.

"Maybe he wanted to lay low," Fredo suggested.

"That him?" Eddie suddenly asked, checking his watch again. "It's eleven on the dot. Just as advertised. And this one's wearing a black fedora. Old-style."

"That's what I was told," Fredo confirmed. "Every Wednesday, same time. You'd think he'd know better. It's dumb not to mix up a routine."

Eddie put the van into gear but left his headlights off. "Maybe he thought changing his name was enough."

Silver was on foot, as Fredo had been told he would be. Wearing a long dark coat and boots, he looked like a black polar bear, shuffling through the unshoveled snow on the sidewalk, courtesy of a flailing municipal service.

The panel van had been chosen for its rough and forgettable appearance, and earned its expectations as the cousins crept along the near empty street unnoticed, tailing their quarry in the middle of the night.

Fredo didn't fault Silver for making his foray this late at night, and in midweek. Fredo's source had told him the old hit man collected a check once a week, and journeyed out only now to tender it at a check-cashing kiosk, when chances of being robbed were lower.

"There he goes," Eddie confirmed, as Silver left the sidewalk to enter Broad Street, heading toward Clay and the kiosk, which sat in the center of a parking lot, glowing like a discarded, garish Christmas ornament.

Slowly, the tiny parade crawled alongside a large pharmacy, its windows long ago blocked up with solid panels to ward off vandalism, reflecting the area's architectural theme of blank, almost featureless walls. The cousins watched as Silver entered the glittering, shedlike building, covered with advertisements touting an ATM, food and drink, money orders, and including an eyebrow-threading service.

"The fuck is that?" Eddie wanted to know, steering around a dumped and mangled grocery cart in the middle of the street, and rolling to a gentle stop.

"Eyebrow threading?" Fredo asked, amused. "It's how women pluck their eyebrows using twisted thread. They sort of lasso the hairs and yank."

Eddie shifted violently in his seat to stare at him. "The hell you talkin' about?"

"It's like using tweezers or hot wax, but supposedly quicker and less painful. It's a Middle Eastern thing or something. Maybe Asian."

Eddie scowled. "You gotten weird on me?"

"I had a girlfriend who did it. It's crazy to watch."

Eddie regained his composure. "I don't wanna hear about it."

"Showtime," Fredo said instead, still watching the entrance.

Dan Silver appeared there, an envelope in his hand, which he buried in his pocket, and began walking in the same direction he'd taken earlier.

"Where's he going?" Eddie asked, beginning to inch forward.

"I told you. He likes to go in a circle. He comes up Broad, does his business, and goes back home using Railroad Street. Man of habit."

"I see 'man like a trained dog.'"

They escorted him to the back side of the pharmacy, where, indeed, he cut down a wide, dimly lit, empty street paralleling the abandoned Pawtucket / Central Falls railroad station, which sat astride the tracks below like a fallen tree trunk left to rot.

Eddie looked around uncomfortably. "Startin' to see why you thought of grabbin' him here. Creepy."

Fredo didn't argue. "Yeah. Who know why he does it, 'specially in this neighborhood."

"Well," Eddie said philosophically, "guess it's up to us to educate him, right? Ready?"

Fredo smoothly slipped a balaclava over his head and moved between the two seats, into the back. "Go."

Eddie finally sped up alongside their shambling target, coming to a halt as Fredo slid open the side door, reached out, and grabbed Silver by the collar. He hauled him into the van like a piece of luggage and whipped the door shut again.

Silver made no sound, but his right hand flew out of his coat pocket bearing a small automatic pistol.

Fredo was expecting it. He grabbed the man's wrist, smashed it against a part of the van's frame, and ripped the gun free as Silver shouted in pain.

By this time, Eddie had also donned a mask and joined them. He shoved his own gun into Silver's face. "Move and die, Danny Boy. It's real simple."

"And so you know," Fredo added. "We don't want your money."

"You cocksuckers know who you're dealing with?" Silver demanded, his outrage replacing any residual surprise.

"Birds of a feather, asshole. You're just another old, fat, Italian deadbeat to us. So don't cop a 'tude."

Despite the circumstances, Eddie's response seemed to settle Silver down a notch. "You're shittin' me," he said, struggling to get more comfortable. "This is like memory row."

Fredo helped him wedge his back against the van's wall. "Don't get all weepy, but we are after some ancient history."

"I didn't do Hoffa," Silver cracked. "That's a rumor. Nuthin' to it."

"Cute," Eddie said, his voice hard. "How 'bout Vito Alfano?"

Silver looked stunned. "Vito? What the fuck's Vito gotta do with anything?"

"You do him?"

Silver sounded offended. "No, I didn't do him. I was *supposed* to. And I woulda done a better job, too. Put him where nobody would find him. But, *oh no*, some amateur dink named Mouse copped to it. Got what they paid for. Assholes. Talk to him. He's gotta be outside by now. Never made any sense to me."

Eddie fell silent as Fredo said, "Why did they get Mouse to do it when they had you?"

"Why the hell should I tell you?"

Fredo snapped open a switchblade. "You really want your tongue cut out for *this*? That makes you as stupid as you're sayin' they were. What d'you care?"

Silver accepted that. "Right. Fine. Rumor was the Mouse only stood up for it, like I said. Nobody knows who pulled the job."

Eddie spoke again. "Why pop him at all? What did Vito do? He was connected."

"I know, I know. Knuckles's kid, and a jackass. Got what he deserved, you ask me."

"I didn't. I asked what he did to deserve *killing*."

"Yeah, yeah. He shot Nick Bianchi after fucking his wife."

The cousins exchanged startled looks. "But Bianchi wasn't killed," Fredo said.

By now, Silver was only tolerating them, all earlier reservation evaporated. "I didn't say he was killed," he said testily. "Vito wasn't that good. He just winged him. But even with his pull, he couldn't do that to Bianchi and live. Nick was Al Zucco's golden boy. Vito didn't have a chance, and Knuckles knew it—kid or no kid. End of story."

"Except for the part about who killed Vito after you'd been contracted."

Silver rolled his eyes. "God, you guys. Put it together. It ain't that hard. If the bosses got the Mouse to fess up instead of letting the cops run around askin' questions, that means they were protecting one of their own. Who's the offended party? If I was you, I'd look to whose wife wandered and who then picked up a piece of lead. That would be one seriously pissed-off guy."

Silver looked around, as if for a dropped pen. "Where's my gun?"

Instead of laughing at his poise, Fredo produced the automatic, dropped the magazine, cleared the chamber, and handed it over, at the same time opening the van door. He sent the magazine skipping across the snow-slick pavement outside.

As Silver straightened and began climbing out, Eddie asked him, "Where's Bianchi now?"

"Don't know. Don't care," was the response. "Ask the people he hung with."

Silver faced them as he readjusted his coat and hat. "Next time you wanna talk, call me. This was bullshit, and you two bozos have watched *The Sopranos* too many times. Just so you know."

Fredo replied by sliding the door closed.

Sally looked around uncomfortably. She'd been in gyms, weight rooms, and workout spaces of all varieties. She maintained a membership at a place on the edge of town to stay fit. But this was beyond anything she'd ever set eyes on. Located on the top floor of the mill, it was mirrored, high-ceilinged, sun-filled, and jammed with minimally used, premium-level equipment, both aerobic and strength oriented. It even smelled expensive, unlike what she was used to, eschewing the normal tang of sweat and/or disinfectant for an odor akin to a sun-dappled field. She had no idea how they did that.

She wasn't here to exercise. She was hired help, after all, reduced to standing by the door and watching her client, Michelle Lyon, repeatedly grunt against a leg-strengthening platform far across the glittering room.

"Be right with you," Lyon panted, adding a weak wave of her hand.

Sally nodded back without comment, completing her visual inventory. Not surprisingly to her skeptical eye, and not unlike the grotto-like pool in the basement, which she'd visited on the sly earlier, this room was essentially unused. She imagined they both stayed that way most of the time.

She took advantage of Michelle's distraction to study her. Sally's clients ran the gamut. Mostly, they were people charged by the state and represented by the public defender. Down and out, dazed by the requirements of daily living, they were often poorly educated, fond of distracting illegal substances, and prone to acting on impulse. As a result, the legal system had found it convenient to label them losers and ascribe to them a route through the courts almost everyone had memorized and so followed without much thought.

That's where Sally most often came in. For the rare defendant with either adequate means or an unusually hopeful public defender, she was engaged at minimal, state-sanctioned pay to dig into the accused's background and find some mitigating circumstances that might persuade a judge to lighten the sentence.

The funny thing was, Sally preferred these cases over working for the likes of Michelle Lyon, perhaps precisely because of the flashy room they were now in. So-called mitigation cases tended to deal with basic life choices: health, happiness, and an ability to make ends meet under challenging circumstances. It usually wasn't too difficult for Sally to uncover a rationale behind her clients' poor decisions—a recent illness, abuse by another—and impress the judge accordingly.

The Michelles of this world were something else. They paid full freight, and accounted for Sally's end-of-year profit margin, but keeping them company often left her breathing an atmosphere tainted with duplicity, hypocrisy, and entitlement.

At last, with an accompanying metallic crash, Michelle released the platform under her feet, blew out a puff of air, and stood, patting her neck and face with a towel.

"Phew," she let out, gathering a water bottle, checking the wall clock, and moving toward Sally, running the silent gauntlet of skeleton-like, shiny exercise equipment. "I needed that. Good to blow off steam, now and then."

"You do this often?" Sally asked politely, not caring.

"Often enough," was the reply, dismissive and defensive. "This and the pool are real perks of the place, although I won't deny that Debbie gets more out of the pool than I do."

"She get along with the Russell child, Mark?" Sally asked. "They're the only kids here, aren't they?"

Michelle looked disapproving. "He's older. Debbie invites her friends over from school. She's pretty popular, calling a place like this home."

Right, Sally thought. "How's Mark taking the death of his father?" she asked.

There, at least Michelle showed her own special brand of honesty. "I haven't the slightest idea. What have you found out about our little problem?"

She was wearing tights below a tank top, and now added a light sweatshirt she removed from a hook near the exit.

Sally took the cue and held open the door so they could step into the vaulting, empty hallway.

"Alex Lloyd was your culprit. I dropped by her place and collected whatever she had left of what she stole. I left it in a box on your office floor."

"She confessed?"

"She did."

Michelle showed no interest in the reasons behind Alex's actions. So much for mitigation. "Fine. I'll call the SA and have her thrown in jail."

"You might want to reconsider," Sally recommended.

Michelle had been aiming for the top of the broad staircase heading down. She now stopped in mid-stride. "Why?"

"She was properly embarrassed and apologetic," Sally lied, "and accepted that she'd done wrong. Speaking as someone who's been around such folks a fair deal, I think you'd make more mileage not pressing charges than making a big deal out of this."

Michelle all but sneered at her. "Good thing you're a better detective than a businesswoman. I could care less about coddling the disadvantaged. You do the crime, you should do the time. Make sure to send your bill to the business and not me personally."

She turned to head off again, before Sally stopped her with, "Unfortunately for you, there's more at stake here than your conscience."

Sally's tone caused Michelle to frown. "What the fuck's that mean?"

"Alex told me of some manufacturing improprieties she discovered while working for you."

Michelle's face turned redder than when she'd been working out. "That fucking cow. She blackmailing me?"

Sally could speak directly to that, even while omitting that she'd sent Lloyd to see Joe. "I don't think so."

Michelle whirled on her heel and almost ran in fury for the top of the staircase. "I will throw the book at her, and you better watch your back, too, in case you had anything to do with this."

She glanced over her shoulder to add, "And forget about that bill. It'll be a long time in hell before I pay you a goddamn dime."

Then, as if the victim of some inadvertent splice in a Buster Keaton movie, instead of charging downstairs as expected, she dove as if from the edge of a swimming pool, headlong down the stairs.

Sally watched in frozen horror as she landed eight feet down onto her forehead with a resounding snap, curled up like a gymnast, and proceeded the rest of the way as a clumsy, limb-flapping human ball, to lie silently, motionless, and dreadfully inert at the bottom.

"Damn," Sally whispered.

Out of protocol, they were dressed in white Tyvek, but by now, they knew that unlike the Gene Russell scene, this one was going to be quick and narrowly focused.

"No need for the CSST?" Lester asked, to confirm.

"Not the way I'm reading it," Sam told him, looking up from her crouch at the top of the stairs.

Joe had arrived late and was pulling on his coveralls as he approached her from out of the elevator. "What've we got?"

Sam pointed to where Lester was standing with the corpse. "Michelle Lyon. DOA. Witnessed by none other than Sally Kravitz, who described Michelle's takeoff as a full-blown swan dive." Sam shifted over to what she'd been scrutinizing. "Due to this," she continued, gently holding up a near-invisible broken strand of fishing filament, two feet in length. It was threaded through an eye screw mounted into the newel, three inches off the floor.

Sam swiveled on her heels and pointed to the opposite post. "There's a matching one over there."

"A trip wire?" Joe asked. "Sally saw the whole thing?"

"Right. She was briefing Michelle about Alex Lloyd. According to Sally, Michelle was pretty worked up because Sally had just broken the news that Alex knew about Food Flourish counterfeiting their products. Michelle's last words were an accusation that

Sally had better not be in collusion with Lloyd in some blackmail scheme."

"Wow," Joe said. "Nice reaction. Shows how Michelle's brain worked."

"Not only," Sam agreed. "She also said it would be a long time in hell before Sally ever got a check for her work."

Joe couldn't resist a smile. "We sure Sally didn't push her?"

"I think we're good there," Willy said, having appeared without a noise from the gym behind them.

Joe gave him a level stare. "I wish you'd stop sneaking around like that."

"You're just hard of hearing, boss. Happens with older folks."

Joe paid no attention. "Sally's in the clear?"

"Yup. Good thing she was here, in fact."

Willy gestured toward the top step. "This rig's designed to make it look like an accident."

"As with Gene," Joe said.

"With a couple of variations, yeah."

Joe nodded, interpreting, "One being that in order for this one to work, the killer has to be nearby to take the wire back down. Have we accounted for everyone in the building?"

Lester answered from below. "Building's sealed, and a floor-to-floor canvass's being conducted right now, with help from the PD."

Joe looked doubtful as he glanced about.

Willy read the body language. "What?"

"I'm just thinking about another wrinkle. The wire reminds me of an Agatha Christie plot. But what's the percentage of people dying from falling downstairs?"

Willy saw his point. "Sally said Michelle was steamed enough that she was traveling at full speed, which only means that otherwise, she might've broken a leg or something. What was the point of this if it wasn't to kill her?"

Sam had a suggestion. "Making it look like an accident was more important than whether it succeeded? Is that too weird?"

"Not if you add in Gene," Joe said. "All that fussing around to turn his death into a slip-and-fall."

"Plus, it implies," Willy added, "that whoever rigged this isn't in a hurry. If you don't first succeed, try, try again?"

Sam paused before commenting, "That's cold."

"But it suggests the same person being responsible for both deaths," Joe said. "Like a tell. If the proposal is that this setup was designed to vanish right after, how often did Michelle work out up here? Was it a regular thing? Same day, same time?"

"Yes to all that," Lester answered, climbing the stairs to join them. "I've been texting with the canvassing team. That's one commonality they've already logged. She was a creature of habit. Three times a week, she had her routine. Same time, always alone."

"Perfect setup, then," Joe said.

"Except," Willy reminded him, "it does nothing for us. We're already working on the theory nobody's sneaking in here from outside and knocking off residents. It's some member of this messed-up family. The missing piece is why. We find that out, we find who to hold accountable."

Joe wasn't so sure. "Unless," he said, "It's a more generalized fallout. The king is dead, so now everyone's running rampant."

CHAPTER TWELVE

"What's going on, Rachel?" Stan Katz asked her.

"A shitload," his reporter stated. "I've got so much smoke coming at me, I *know* there're at least three fires under it."

Her boss, a *Reformer* reporter before becoming its editor in chief, gave her a wizened, almost tired expression. "Nice imagery. What's it mean? And I hope it has something to do with Michelle Lyon."

Rachel scratched her forehead. "Sort of. Hard to know where to start. Let me ask you, have you heard anything about Gene Russell's death?"

"Like what?"

"That it might not be an accident?"

"The cops're keeping it open. That makes me suspicious. Michelle Lyon supposedly taking a swan dive downstairs only ramps that up. Why?"

"Because I did speak with your pal Betsy Russell, and she made no bones about saying Nathan Lyon was probably murdered and deservedly so. Every instinct I have is screaming that we're looking at three homicides until proven otherwise."

"I have called over to the VBI office," Katz told her. "Not surprisingly, they're being very coy. Are those the fires you mentioned?"

"Yes and no. Betsy got hyperemotional talking about how Nathan had ruined all of their lives. She let slip that Gene, her husband, and their daughter, Penny Trick, had each somehow or another been manipulated or corrupted by the old man. She made him sound like the devil incarnate."

"I heard he wasn't a nice guy."

"Did he come from around here?"

"No, but I don't know from where. If what you're saying is true about his death, though, why haven't we heard about it till now?"

"That's what I'd like to find out."

They were in Stan's glassed-in corner office, with a view of a couple of reporters working at their computers beyond. Katz shifted in his seat before saying, "Oh, oh, here it comes."

But he looked amused, which she took as encouragement. "I want to dig deeper into him," she therefore said.

"Nathan Lyon?"

"Yes. Michelle is unbaked news right now. Her body may not've even reached the ME's office yet. Gene's has got more to work with, admittedly, but *nobody* is officially talking about Nathan, and I think—based on what little Betsy let spill—that he's a major influence on all this."

"You think his death led to the others?"

"Only because he was a micromanager and I have no proof one way or the other." She hunched forward in her seat with enthusiasm. "You have *got* to admit, Stan, we wouldn't be doing our jobs if I didn't chase some of this down."

He offered no opposition, enjoying what he was seeing. This energy was precisely why he'd hired her. "What's your plan?"

"I want to try keeping as many plates spinning as I can," she said. "But I'd like to start with Nathan. At least find out where he came from and how he made his money. That might involve some traveling, though."

He nodded. "Understood. You discover he hailed from California, that'll change my enthusiasm."

"I know, I know."

"But within reason," he continued, "go for it. One favor."

She sensed what was coming and already had no problem with it. "Sure."

"I still want you available to shoot Rotary luncheons and the rest. I know there'll be conflicts. I'm just asking you to keep them at a minimum. We ain't *The Globe* and you ain't *Spotlight*."

She laughed, very happy, her mind already building up speed. "No, no. I understand. That's what I meant by the spinning plates. I'll make it all work. I know the budget's crap. I'll make it worth your while."

He was already waving that away. "Yeah, yeah. Got it."

Rachel left his fishbowl office, crossed to her desk, checked for any texts or emails, and then stepped outside the building, where a gentle snow shower of no significance was drifting out of a sunny blue sky, creating a sparkling rainbow drizzle.

She dialed Sally.

"Talk to me," was her greeting.

"Rod Steiger," Rachel reacted. *"In the Heat of the Night."*

It was a running movie trivia game they sometimes sprang on each other.

"Excellent," Sally congratulated her. "What d'ya got?"

"The thumbs-up from Katz for a field trip. There is absolutely, positively no reason for you to say yes, except that it might be fun and I'd love the company. Plus, no telling where or even if I'll be going."

It was far from a rational pitch, but Rachel knew her audience. "What do you need to decide?" Sally asked.

This, of course, was only one reason she had Sally on the phone. She knew she could count on her support and input. But Sally had also been working a case inside the mill, which meant she might have consulted with Dan Kravitz, whose omniscient knowledge of people's backgrounds Rachel knew about.

"I need to discover where Nathan Lyon came from."

She could imagine Sally's pleased expression as she said, "Easy. Rhode Island. And his name was originally Nick Bianchi. And between you and me, while there's no money in it for me, I have my own reasons for wanting to keep you company."

For Rachel, things couldn't get much better. "When can we meet to work out details?"

Moments later, back inside, she returned to Katz's office and opened his door, leaning in.

"Providence, Rhode Island. Where Lyon's from."

Without comment, Katz rummaged among the piles on his desk and came up with a Rolodex, which Rachel didn't know were being made anymore.

He extracted a single card and held it up. "Ron Powers. Worked Rhode Island newspapers and radio all his life. Freelance now. If it's been there, he's done that. The Mob even tried to rub him out once, decades ago. He's the real deal. Copy that and give it back. I'll let him know you might come knocking."

Joe used a marker to write three names on the office whiteboard, reading aloud as he did, "Nathan, Gene, Michelle."

The rest of the squad was in attendance, watching and waiting. They had been a team long enough to have witnessed life changes in one another—deaths of loved ones, the growth and evolution of children, and times of professional crisis, including some near-overwhelming investigations.

In the process, just as Sam and Willy had disliked each other upon meeting, only to have a child together years later, each one of these people had been forced to take the measure of the others. Their mutual trust and reliance had been forged by such exposures and made of the team a unit as integrated as a flock of birds, instinctively weaving and turning as a whole, free of the distracting doubts or prejudice that often plagued less experienced groups.

Rarely before, however, had they been confronted with such a case—three, for that matter—as compacted and intertwined as the root ball of a dying plant, where even freeing it from its pot looked unlikely to improve its fate.

Joe turned to face them. "First challenge: One case or three?"

"One killer or three?" Sam quickly countered.

"Don't know. One doesn't necessarily cancel the other."

"Who's high on our suspect list?" Lester asked.

"Everybody," Willy offered, "except the little kids."

Joe tapped on the board. "One by one, then. Nathan. Who do we like for him, keeping in mind that it was known he was already a dying man?"

"Penny's an obvious candidate, except that Rob says the old man had stopped abusing her long before he croaked," Willy said.

"Gene?" Lester suggested. "So he could line his pockets sooner?"

No one seemed enthused by that. Joe spoke to their reservation, "So far, Gene's looking like the one good apple of the bunch. Plus, his business was a success."

"Mike?" Sam put forth. "If he knew the wording of the trust, he might've been pissed at being shortchanged, and it sounds like his pretense of a business is sucking air."

"If nothing else," Willy added supportively, "killing Gene would make him feel better. No extra cash in it, but he could gloat in silence. That sounds like something in the Nathan Lyon tradition."

He stopped for a moment, but they knew him well enough to recognize he wasn't done.

Sure enough, he tacked on, as if at random, "Dead man's shoes."

"Meaning . . . ?" Joe asked leadingly.

"It was something Rob said," Willy explained. "We were talking about how Gene had been offered something through the trust that he didn't actually want."

"More cash," Sam suggested.

"Right. But Rob's mentioning of a dead man's shoes—call it instead an inherited promotion—struck me as something applying to a lot more people than Gene, who didn't even appreciate it."

Lester picked up on that. "You mean like power, or a higher ranking in the trust, or anything dealing with a shift of position, real or made-up. Not just cash, but upward mobility."

"This bunch does have a different take on things than most," Willy suggested.

Of the four of them, Lester was the closest to a straight shooter. He therefore brought a couple of smiles when he aired the most convoluted option so far. "How 'bout Michelle for both guys, who then was killed as a result?"

Joe took the idea in stride. "There's nothing saying a double whammy couldn't be in play, even if it leaves wide open who took her out and why."

"It's her print on the rolling pin," Sam echoed. "Conversely, someone like Peggy Lyon could've pulled a fast one. As Gene's wife, her prints are all over that pottery. She might've gotten Michelle to handle a pin and then planted it."

"We haven't discussed Peggy much," Joe observed. "Sam, you did the initial interview."

"And a follow-up yesterday," Sam agreed. "She's either smart as a fox or dumb as a post. Each time, it was all I could do not to check my watch and tell her I had to go. She couldn't decide between crying or acting catatonic. Completely useless."

"Whatever she is, she's very rich now," Lester reminded everyone. "What does your gut tell you?"

Sam hitched a shoulder. "She pisses me off, but I don't see her as a doer. You'd have to convince me otherwise."

In the brief pause following, Joe brought them back to the first name on the board, tapping on it with his marker. "Stepping back from mastermind serial killers for the moment, I don't want us to lose what I think is a key point about Nathan's death: As I said, he was dying when he was murdered. I think that's important."

"Because . . . ?" Willy asked.

"Because it suggests that whoever did him in was running out of time or wasn't aware of that small detail."

"Which everybody we've talked to seems to have known," Lester said.

Joe looked at him. "Did you talk to his doctor? The one who cooked up the death certificate?"

"Yup. He claimed Alzheimer's is a default diagnosis, or some phrase like that. Anyhow, only an autopsy proves it, and Nathan was both clearly demented and generally in decline—his phrase. He claims that whether a doc signs such a patient out as having a bad ticker, lousy arteries, or something else, it doesn't matter. It's still a natural and nobody cares. He said a lot of docs choose the wording on the death certificate to please the family."

"Ain't that convenient," Willy muttered. "I bet he didn't mention money changing hands, to make his wording even more accommodating."

"Nope," Lester replied. "Funnily, that didn't come up."

"There's an additional factor we haven't addressed," Joe said. "Two of our victims, Gene and Nathan, have roots predating the so-called Lyon family's arrival in Vermont. It's been floated that maybe Nathan-slash-Nick caught a bullet from someone in those days. Could Gene's death be connected to the same bit of history?"

"He was too little and not part of the family back then," Willy argued, "and when he did die, it was long after Nathan went toes up. I don't see it. You kill a bad guy's kid to make the bad guy feel bad; you don't do it after he's dead." He held out his one good hand, its thumb down. "I vote no on that one."

No one argued his position.

"I agree," Joe told them, "but it then begs the question of what did happen before the renamed Lyon clan reached our fair state. It's pretty clear Nick Bianchi was up to no good, which the ancient bullet hole supports. The core of the family came from Rhode Island, as did its money. Why not some of the problems that're dogging their heels now?"

"I smell a field trip for somebody," Sam said.

"I'm thinking the same thing," Joe agreed. "There're too many unanswered questions. Speaking of that, and before we move on to victim number two"—again, he tapped the board under Gene's name—"I'd like us to do a little local historical digging. It's now pretty clear Nathan manipulated Penny Trick, and her father by proxy, by covering up her role in the bicyclist's death. To me, that shows initiative and a spontaneous ability to put a devious plan into action—maybe not something Lyon did entirely on his own, regardless of what the Russells think they know. I'd like one of us to go back to that investigation and take it apart, step by step. Anybody?"

"I'll do it," Willy said without hesitation. "I know goddamn well you don't want me in Little Rhody. I might get recruited by the Outfit."

Joe eyed him. "Thank you, I think. This does not give you permission to bust anyone's chops, okay? Off the bat, we just want to autopsy the case file and do a couple of interviews."

Willy's expression remained unchanged, but Joe knew what he was thinking. One thing Kunkle loved to pounce on was sloppy police work. He therefore added, "But in the unlikely situation that you do find anything fishy, we will obviously pursue it."

"Your wish is my command, boss."

Sammie rolled her eyes.

"And," Joe let them know, "I'll probably be traveling alone this time. The state police down there will assign me a babysitter, so my back'll be covered while our manpower up here will be only minimally weakened."

He glanced at the board before saying, "Moving along. Gene."

"Which brings us back to Michelle in her original role," Lester said, "complete with damning fingerprint."

"But why?" Joe asked. "What's her motive for wanting her brother-in-law dead? I think we shouldn't forget that while Food Flourish may or may not be doing well, we know from the trust that Mike and Michelle personally are hardly paupers."

"Unless we're talking about Willy's idea of inherited promotion again," Lester said. "Then, who knows what the motive is." He added as a question, "What about Gene's laptop, Sam?"

"I gave it a once-over," she replied. "I think Emma's would be more incriminating if she knew how to type. That being said, there is one totally smoking gun I was waiting to reveal when we got to it."

"Oh, oh," Willy said.

Sam ignored him. "Gene had a diary of sorts, on top of emails and the rest. It was mostly spiritual mumbo jumbo, reflections on working toward a more Zen-like life. Crap like that. But then, pretty randomly, tucked into a photo file, he had shots of his sister-in-law making out big-time with some guy not her husband."

"Blackmail?" Lester asked.

Sam answered, "It's got the makings of it. As a result, I checked his emails and found a draft from him to her referring to the shots and suggesting a chat, but no indication he sent it and no response from her."

"Interesting," Joe said. "We've got a guy who's rich, successful, content by all appearances, with no enemies, competitors, or identified rivals. He doesn't drink, gamble, or cruise for hookers. And yet, right in the middle of it, sits this implication that he may want to put the screws to Michelle, for reasons unknown."

Silence greeted that.

"What exactly do we know about Michelle versus Gene?" he prompted them.

"I did ask," Lester said, "during the canvass. I think a couple of us did. She clearly didn't have him on her Christmas card list, but if Sam's right about what she found, there must've been bad blood."

"Mike told me Gene was a little head-in-the-clouds, I think were his words," Sam reported. "In the same breath, he described him as harmless."

"We got a single print of Michelle's in that entire pottery," Joe said. "She never once dropped by to visit?"

"According to Mike," Sam replied, "she had no ax to grind; he just made her impatient. Mike implied she might've been a little pissed that Gene's business did better than theirs."

"More so recently?"

"Supposedly," she said. "And there's something else. Just as those incriminating pictures were sitting there, out of context, along with the email, I think it's curious the rolling pin has the only print of

Michelle's anywhere, and that it's the only print on the pin itself—as if it had been wiped prior to her touching it. Kind of unusual on a tool so common that they had three of them."

In the pause following, Joe looked around. "Clearly that itch needs more scratching. And let's consider another angle," he suggested. "Why was Gene the favorite in his father's eye?"

"I'll raise you," Willy countered. "What's the crazy story about his birth? Monica tells you his father was a ship in the night, then it was Nathan, but he didn't know it, then she gives birth offstage with nobody the wiser. And finally, Nathan does find out, and moves everybody, lock, stock, and barrel, so he can connect with a kid he never knew and who never gives him the time of day afterward. I know this family is like a jigsaw puzzle from four different boxes, but Gene's genealogy rivals Jesus Christ's for obscurity."

"How 'bout an experiment?" Joe suggested. "We're in proud possession of both their corpses. Why not run their DNAs?"

"I love it," Willy replied. "But I'm gonna hate it if they match."

"I know, I know," Joe said to their general amusement.

"Speaking of which," Sam contributed, "wouldn't it be in our interest—given the squirrelly nature of these people—to run genetic profiles on Michelle, too, and for that matter anybody else we can?"

"You think we'll get any cooperation?"

"We might get some," Joe said. "I bet Rob'll be open to it. I doubt he has anything to lose and probably thinks it's good policy to play nice with us. And he may convince a couple of the others, like Monica. If not, we can get more devious. I like the idea. It could give us ammo just when we need it. Let's grab everybody's."

Joe didn't refer to the whiteboard when he said, "That finally brings us to the late, not terribly lamented Michelle. Tell me about her. If we follow the law of averages, we'd have her husband behind bars already, wouldn't we? Especially if he found out about the images on Gene's laptop."

"Alibi," Willy countered shortly. "He was downstairs in the shop for hours beforehand, surrounded by employees. Sally told us she used the stairs to make her report to Michelle in the gym. She would've noticed the trip wire had it been there then."

"That alibi makes Mike the exception," Lester mentioned. "The building-wide canvass revealed how little the residents hang out together. Monica, Rob, Peggy, and Penny Trick were all on their own. Kimona Alin was seen around, along with most other staffers, and Ned Russell was on a jobsite."

Nathan/Nick

Killers?

Penny – revenge for past abuse

Gene – to gain faster access to financial pie

Mike – from anger over preference to Gene

An unknown Rhode Island past associate

Question: It was known he was probably a dying man already

Gene

Killers?

Mike – envy from being usurped

Peggy – out of domestic unhappiness & access to cash

Michelle – Gene had photos of her/her prints on weapon

Consider the unknowns concerning his birth

Question: He was universally liked and known to be kind

Michelle

Killers?

Mike - out of domestic unhappiness, perhaps using a proxy

Unknown lover

Related to crooked business

Same person who framed her for Gene's death

Assignments: Travel to R.I. for Nathan/Nick background

Quietly (legally) collect everyone's DNA

Reopen the years-old bicyclist death case

"Give me what you learned about Michelle," Joe asked. "Did she and her hubby get along?"

The three cops had all participated in the canvass or read the resulting information. They now exchanged glances to see who would go first.

"My impression," Lester began, "was neither here nor there. The Food Flourish employees didn't seem to take much notice of them. They weren't warm and cuddly as a couple, or with their staff, but they didn't dogfight, either."

No one argued with that, leading Joe to move on. "What about what we learned through Sally Kravitz, about their adulterating the product? Anyone back up what Alex Lloyd told us?"

Sam answered, "I found a couple of employees who knew about the counterfeiting. The rest seemed clueless."

"And Mike?"

"Hard to tell, what with everything else we've hit him with," Lester reported. "He did look genuinely surprised, could be because he's innocent, which I doubt, or because he didn't see us coming at him with fraud on top of our suspicions that he may've killed his wife."

"Speaking of that," Sam added, "I think Mike Lyon's about to enter a world of hurt. I called Tausha Greenblott about what Food Flourish is up to, and she's coordinating the AG's office, the health department, and the rest of them to consider charges. Between you and me, if it's confirmed, I doubt he'll see jail time. This is Vermont, and he's a first-time offender and a recent widower. But from what Tausha was telling me, Food Flourish will at least be forced to close down."

"During the canvass, did anyone know about Alex Lloyd spilling her guts to us?" Joe asked. "I'm wondering if somebody knew the company secret was out before we came knocking to ask about Michelle's death."

No one responded.

"Okay," he continued. "Was their skullduggery another detail Gene was holding over Michelle?"

"We don't know what we don't know," Willy reflected. "He might've been."

"And what about the man in those pictures with Michelle?" Joe asked. "We know who he is?"

"Not enough to go on," Sam reported.

"It's not gonna matter if they do throw the book at Mike," Willy said a little after the fact.

"Meaning?"

Willy shrugged. "Only what Sam said. He'll be hiring a bunch of lawyers and paying a small fortune in fines, but especially with Michelle dead, according to the trust, he'll still be sitting pretty. Then it'll be off to the next adventure."

Joe mulled that over before proposing, "It's a perfect setup, then, isn't it? Make sure you're alibied at the time of your target's death, which you've meanwhile orchestrated using a hired proxy."

"It's not a huge reach," Willy conceded, who often dismissed such fancies as Hollywood tripe. "There're enough low-paid grunts working in the mill, including those coming and going for whatever reasons, that he could've done that. And let's not forget the man's family heritage. As apples go, he may've fallen close to the tree."

Joe nodded as he said, "Fair enough. So Mike's either innocent or he did it by remote control. And let's not forget that because of Sally's climbing those stairs, the wire had to have been put in place just a few minutes before Michelle got tangled up in it. Are we comfortable that we know who was in the building after we locked it down? What was that? Five minutes after Sally called 911?"

"We are," Lester said, glancing at his screen. "She also had the presence of mind to keep an eye out the window overlooking the parking lot, to see if anyone left before we got there. If we're right that the killer set the trap, intending to remove it right afterward— that person most likely just faded away, rather than make a run for it. That means we interviewed them as part of the canvass."

"You know," Willy interjected, "there's something else about this that's bugged me from the start. Boss, when you first met Kimona Alin, she had a bunch of CCTV terminals. But when we searched the penthouse as part of our limited warrant, we didn't find any recording equipment. In fact, we didn't find any additional monitors. Almost as if, after the old man died, the system had either been partially taken down, or so well disguised, we couldn't locate it."

"What're you saying?" Sam asked.

He gave her a lopsided smile. "It doesn't make sense, it's a question without an answer. I just wanted it out there, so nobody forgot."

"All right," Joe said, adding it to the whiteboard and summing up. "Then assignments are pretty clear, if tough to crack. While I'm down south hoping to unlock Nathan's past, you all do what you can to interview, check backgrounds, get financial insights, collect DNA samples, and find anything else you can think of that'll help from this end." He pointed to Willy. "Including any hidden or missing recording equipment."

CHAPTER THIRTEEN

Rhode Island, the smallest state by land size but second-most densely populated in the country—next to, ironically to Mob followers, New Jersey—has always been attitudinal. The first of the colonies to tell King George to pound sand, and the last to reluctantly join the U.S., it was founded on principles of religious freedom, separation of church and state, and fair dealings with Native Americans. A hotbed of abolitionism, the Ocean State was also the first to respond to Lincoln's call for troops during the Civil War.

Imagine, in this context, how Rhode Island's glaring association with organized crime goes over in the eyes of the average Swamp Yankee, who may unhappily suspect that this darker reputation is due to more than simple bad luck. He or she must consider that another, quirkier characteristic of Rhode Island, perhaps born of its iconoclastic roots, has been a notable fondness among its leadership—political and business—to flout the rules of law.

Maybe it was inevitable that organized crime found root in such soil and just as inevitable that the media eventually turned Mafia coverage into a mainstay.

Most of that, thankfully, is now a thing of the past. The sheer energy of the state, its massive investment in health care, education, and tourism, and its multicultural identity as a can-do place, have transformed Rhode Island. The "bad stuff" lingers, but it's far from the driving force it once was.

Joe pulled off the interstate near North Scituate, at a small restaurant overlooking the Oak Swamp Reservoir, not four miles from the Rhode Island State Police headquarters complex. Miranda Alexander, his assigned liaison, had suggested it in order to, in her words, "get some distance from the flagpole," especially for their first meeting. The implication of two peers wishing to get to work with a minimum of introductory protocol struck Joe as a hopeful sign.

As did his first sighting of her upon entering the place. A tall, short-haired, athletically built woman dressed in slacks and a jacket approached as his eyes were adjusting to the dim lighting of the restaurant. She extended her hand for a firm handshake. "Joe?"

He nodded with instant pleasure, thinking how this woman's style reminded him of Sammie's in so many ways. "Yes. Miranda?"

Instead of answering, she turned and led him deeper into the room, explaining, "I know the owner, so we've got more like an office than a private table. I thought that might suit you better. Good drive?"

"Very," he replied. "It's nice to be heading in a direction where the snow gets thinner."

"You not a winter guy?"

"Actually, I am," he acknowledged. "But we had a fair amount of snow the last couple of days, so it's nice for a change."

"Yeah," she said, ushering him through a wide doorway into a small room with a single table laid out for two, at the base of a large picture window overlooking the partially ice-covered water. "We even have a ski mountain down here, if you're not expecting too much. Yawgoo Valley. I have no clue where the name comes from. I like this weather better than the summer heat, but I can't complain about either extreme, given places like Florida. That's definitely not for me. Sit, please."

They settled down across from each other, and Miranda continued, "It is lunchtime, but we don't have to indulge. Your choice. I do recommend the so-called Rhode Island clam chowder, if you like that sort of thing. I'm betting it won't be like anything you've ever had, and it's supergood."

"Sure," he said. "I love chowder."

"Also, you like your coffee sweet?" she asked. "Most cops I know hate it that way."

He laughed. "Yes, I do. You must have spies up north. Nobody can stand the way I make coffee."

"Then I'll suggest another local oddity, a coffee milk." She added a caveat, "But trust me, if you hate it after the first sip, *please* order something else. I have no feelings when it comes to stuff like that. To each her own—his own."

"Got ya," he answered. "It sounds great."

Somehow, presumably summoned by Miranda, a waiter arrived and took their orders, closing a curtain across the doorway as he left.

"Wow," she then said, taking him in fully. "I gotta say, I liked what you sent me to prepare for this. What a trip down memory lane. I work in the intel unit, as you know, so I'm no stranger to the ghosts of old mobsters floating around, but this was unusual. I knew very little about some of these particular lunkheads."

"Why's that?" he asked.

"It's like any corporation, really," she said cheerily. "You get all sorts of . . . call them subdivision chiefs. They display the company flag and salute the same hierarchy, and they sure as hell are not encouraged to act independently, but shit happens, you know? These are not MBA grads. As a result, the farther you get away from the glitzy makers and shakers—the bosses that hit the headlines all the time, at least back in the day—the more you start finding people almost running their own side operations. It's pretty crazy. I think partly why they got away with it for so long was that law enforcement kept thinking of the Mob as a business model. You know, capo, consigliere, lieutenants, et cetera, like in the movies. That was there, too, of course, but it missed all the smaller details, and you know what they say about details and the devil."

"And Nick Bianchi—who we're calling Nathan Lyon—he fit in there?"

"Far in the outfield, yeah. Protected by a man named Al Zucco, who in all fairness didn't pay him much attention, given that Bianchi wasn't even Family and Zucco had loan-sharking, money laundering, prostitution, gambling, and lots of other concerns to distract him. In the report you sent me, your source got most things right about Nick being a restaurateur's rug rat who got adopted because of his winning ways. Nick had the right ethnicity to slip under the tent flaps after he grew up, and he put that nostalgia and goodwill to work for him."

Their drinks arrived, and Joe gingerly sampled his very first coffee milk—which resembled a pale mocha—finding it as appealing as he knew none of his squad members would.

Miranda had stuck to a Diet Coke. "You like?" she asked, eyebrows raised.

"Very much," he said. "A steady diet of it would kill me, but as a one-off, I'm hooked."

She nodded, clearly pleased. "Outstanding."

"Keep going with who's who," Joe urged.

"Under Zucco came Knuckles Alfano," she said, pausing as the waiter returned with their lunch. To Joe's surprise, his chowder was at once red and more liquid than he'd anticipated. As with the drink, however, he found it very good and gave Miranda a thumbs-up as she kept speaking.

"Alfano's an interesting place to pause," she said, interrupting herself to bite into a club sandwich. "Because he's where the connection begins with your Nick Bianchi." She chewed a bit before finishing, "Knuckles had a kid named Vito, who, not to dance around the issue, was considered pretty much a fuckup by everybody."

She interrupted herself to pull a paper napkin from the metal dispenser at her elbow and begin using it as something to sketch on.

Joe waited, enjoying his soup.

"The problem was," she continued, still writing, "because his dad was a ranking member, where to put him where he wouldn't cause too many problems?"

"And the answer was with Nick?" Joe suggested.

"Correct. Except it clearly didn't work out in the long run, since we found Vito's body in the river years later."

Joe began paying closer attention. "Nick was implicated in that?"

But she veered off course. "Not at all. They caught the guy immediately, a lowbrow named Eddie Moscone, who copped to the deed and only got out of jail less than a year ago."

Joe was disappointed. "No doubt about it?"

"Not that I picked up. Looked straight up and narrow." She slid the finished chart across the table to him.

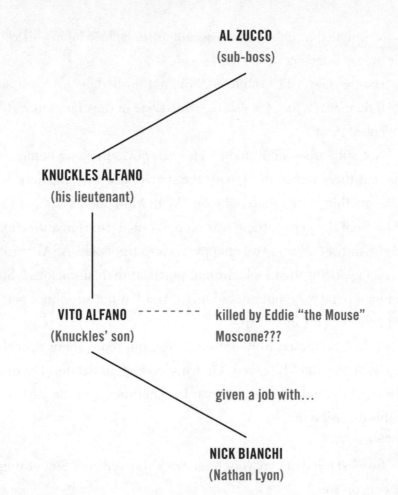

AL ZUCCO
(sub-boss)

KNUCKLES ALFANO
(his lieutenant)

VITO ALFANO ------- killed by Eddie "the Mouse"
(Knuckles' son)   Moscone???

                       given a job with...

NICK BIANCHI
(Nathan Lyon)

"And it had nothing to do with Vito's association with Nick?" he asked, reading.

"Apparently not. When they grilled Moscone about motive, all they got was the usual—'He dissed me,' or something equally original—and that was it. Nobody pressed harder, and everyone went home happy."

"Including Knuckles?"

Miranda put her sandwich on her plate and licked her lips before replying, her voice scornful. "Not a soul raised a finger. It was one of the smoothest homicide cases I've ever reviewed—wrapped up in the blink of an eye."

Joe imitated a slight French accent as he said, "Making all your little gray cells go crazy?"

"Hardly crazy," she countered. "But not thrilled."

"If there was a fix," Joe asked, "which side of the equation would you look at most?"

"Not ours," she said frankly. "This was obviously long before my time, but there was nothing with the state police investigation that looked anything other than righteous. With Moscone standing up for the hit from the get-go, there was no pull-out-all-stops investigation, and the district attorney was happy to close the books ASAP. From my vantage point, that looked more practical than suspicious." She held up a hand for emphasis, adding, "And I'm not shy about going after bent cops if I smell 'em."

Joe had no reason to doubt her. "Nothing more about it in the decades following?" he asked, knowing how often details attending slam dunks could surface afterward, sometimes even as part of a deathbed confession.

"Nope."

"So what is it that's got your brain working overtime? Something's chewing on you."

She tilted her head. "You just get a feel for these after a while. I'm no old dog who remembers when you had to shoot a gun in the air to get backup, but I have spent years digging through past files. Over time, you learn a pattern about how things work. People are creatures of habit. They do things the same way."

"And this one doesn't quite fit."

"No," she said meditatively. "It was too good to be true. There wasn't a peep of protest or complaint, not a ripple. Not from anybody. They found the body; they found the killer; he copped immediately; they locked him up. As they say in the movies, 'Badabing-

badaboom.' Usually—I'd almost say every time—somebody puts
up a fuss."

"But not here."

"Nope."

"Which tells you what?"

She spread her hands wide. "That's it, isn't it? It tells me squat.
It tells me you might be a nice man and a straight shooter, and I'm
sure you're down here for good reason, but all you've done for me is
ruin my sleep."

Joe sat back in his chair, smiling, his lunch finished. Miranda
Alexander was coming across as a kindred spirit. "The way we see
things right now," he explained, "is that we're facing three unexplained
homicides: Nick Bianchi, one of his sons, and a daughter-in-law. All
committed under the same roof at different times, using different
methods, and maybe by different people."

"And you're hoping the Rhode Island connection and a few select
interviews might help."

"I am. As interesting as Vito's story is, were you able to find out
about Nick's business dealings? What was Vito hired to do, for example?"

But there, she shook her head. "Your inquiry was Nathan Lyon,
alias Nick Bianchi. From there, I found Vito Alfano being killed by
Eddie 'the Mouse' Moscone while Vito worked for your boy Nick.
My boss green-lighted my helping you in order to find the rest of it,
hopefully"—here again, she emphasized—"for the benefit and edifi-
cation of both our agencies. I'm assuming you're parked outside?"

"I am."

"I'll lead you to your motel, then. After that, we can use my vehicle to start poking our noses in where people probably won't want
to see 'em. That work for you?"

They rose and moved toward the curtain and the cash register by the door, as Joe asked her, "The Mouse? Really? The Boston Mob comes up with the Rifleman, and you got the Mouse?"

She gave him a stern look. "Don't start."

Detective Sergeant Diane Lints had been the initial state police detective called to the old bicycle death that Willy was reexamining. It wasn't the first time he—or for that matter many cops—had taken another look at a closed case. It was a given among police officers that when they concluded an investigation, they might be summoned to explain their findings—sometimes long after the fact—and that the scrutiny might come from one of their peers, a lawyer, or a reporter.

Awareness of such transparency did not mean the receiving party had to enjoy it, however. Usually, especially when they were the ones under the magnifying glass, they did not.

Lints was therefore cool when she entered the Westminster barracks lobby to collect Willy and lead him to a conference room upstairs, commenting only upon greeting, "So you're the one missing an arm."

"Not missing. I still got it," Willy said cheerfully. "And it's surprisingly handy in throwing people off. You can't beat it undercover."

That did make her pause, cracking her severity enough to at least soften her expression. "That a recommendation?"

"Oh, shit, no," he said. "I'd much prefer to throw snowballs at my kid with both hands."

It was purposefully sentimental, but Willy, for all his edginess, was keenly sensitive to the vagaries of being human. He didn't fault Lints for a wariness bordering on hostility.

And it worked. As they approached the room, she cast him a look and said, "That's got to be a bummer."

"It's okay," he replied. "She just gets twice as many shots in, especially when the snow's not sticky."

Lints indicated a chair at the table dominating the room, choosing one herself near the window, so he had to squint against the light as he addressed her. Old trick.

He pursued his disarmament campaign. "I'm in a jam," he began. "That bicyclist case I mentioned in my email? I just got a tip it might've been more than an accident."

"Like what?" she asked.

"A negligent homicide," he replied. "With a catch."

He could almost see her bracing herself. His hope, however, was that he could breeze by her misgivings and engage her curiosity and help. In order to do this, however, he opted to tease out what he'd learned bit by bit.

"Yeah?" she said cautiously.

"Extra players have surfaced no one knew anything about. You might've been manipulated to draw a conclusion that left them out of the picture. I'd like your help fixing that. It plays to one of the cornerstones of the VBI charter," he added as if out of the blue.

She frowned. "What's that?"

"Whenever possible, support the local-most agency, help them with resources and manpower if needed, and then fade away if we can. Especially," he added with emphasis, "in a situation like this, where you weren't given all the facts to begin with."

It had lightened her mood somewhat. If not mollified, she at least was looking less angry. "Agent Kunkle . . . ," she began.

He cut her off quietly. "Willy. Please."

"Okay. Anyhow, what can I tell you? A few years ago, I was called to an accidental death and played it by the numbers. The ME was summoned, the SA was consulted, all as usual. I ordered up a canvass for possible witnesses. I returned to the scene at about the same time of day when the accident supposedly happened so I could check for regular commuters or delivery trucks as witnesses. I had accident reconstruction do their magic with their computers and 3D gizmos. I sent the bike to the crime lab to check for anything out of order. All for nothing. The victim just lost control, went over the guardrail, and killed himself going down the embankment into the water."

"Which is *exactly* what you were supposed to think," Willy said with a burst of manufactured enthusiasm, lightly tapping the table-top with his hand and feeling like a game show host egging on his audience. "The sons of bitches set you up. That's what I want to put right. With your help," he repeated pointedly.

Her primary emotion had turned to confusion. "How? I don't know what I don't know. What more was I supposed to do?"

"*Nothing*," he said happily, adding, "It was a classic sleight of hand. Move a couple of things, remove a couple more, and bingo: You get an entirely different picture than what happened."

"So what did happen?" she asked.

"For starters," he said, "your bicyclist was helped to his death by a drunk driver."

"Bullshit."

"I got witnesses and a confession," he told her, somewhat shading the truth, "or the closest things to 'em. But that's not the best part. I've got proof of a cover-up. Can I call you Diane?"

The abruptness raised an eyebrow. "Sure."

"Diane," he resumed, "you're going to have some of the most fun you've had in a while. Trust me."

"We sure aren't in Kansas anymore," Sally said, looking around as Rachel drove. It was an unexpected contrast that Sally, the older and more sophisticated of the two, was more the hayseed than her companion. Rachel was a city kid, even if that city had been Burlington.

Nevertheless, Vermont's largest metroplex contained almost a third of the state's population, its widest cultural diversity, its biggest businesses, and most of its political clout.

But none of that prepared either of them for Rhode Island. Merely dropping in out of Massachusetts into the interstate spaghetti bowl of downtown Providence, dominated by glittering, glass-clad skyscrapers, left them agape at the sheer press of humanity.

Thankfully, their directions carried them right through the worst of it, over the Washington Bridge and into East Providence, then south along the East Shore Expressway to wind up in Barrington, and from there the more familiar-looking residential streets of Bristol. Nevertheless, Hope Street remained crowded, if also lined with trees, sidewalks, suburban-style family homes, and small shopping plazas, including one that Sally pointed out.

"There," she said. "To the left. Seabra Foods, like your guy said. Who in God's name came up with that name?"

Rachel's "guy" was Ron Powers, who had given them directions to his house. The next street to the right was Fales, opposite the quaintly named Defiance Hose Company #1. Rachel rounded a small pile of dirty, plowed snow and found herself abruptly in less affluent territory. Still family dwellings, but now largely single level, with fewer trees and a faintly forgotten feel.

It wasn't as cold as in Vermont. The surrounding seawater saw to that. But chilly enough to sustain a layer of snow overlaying an endless row of adjoining front yards stretching before the cookie-cutter homes like a no-man's-land.

"Whoa," Sally said quietly. "Don't drive by it."

Jolted from her reverie, Rachel stopped the car and took in a benign, even inviting red house with an attached garage and two dormer windows.

She pulled into the driveway. "Sorry. Daydreaming."

"I get it," Sally said. "All this flatness puts me to sleep, too."

The two Vermonters got out of the car into an overhead dome of pale blue sky, feeling like aliens in a foreign country. As they took in their surroundings, the garage door noisily opened, revealing a smiling woman in a wheelchair. She gestured to them to join her.

"Come on in. I saw you drive up. Ron's on the phone, so I thought I'd do the honors. I'm Grace. How do you do?"

Sally and Rachel accepted the offer, stepping into the empty garage bay next to a small SUV, as their hostess reactivated the door and enclosed them in a shadowy, warm cocoon. As they shook hands and exchanged names, Grace explained, "Radiant floor heating. We splurged with the proceeds of our last book, on the state's changing fishing business. It turned out more popular than we imagined. No idea why, but I love what it did for our creature comforts. Come, follow me. He'll be off soon."

Her two visitors followed Grace into the house, a place at once homey and practical, clearly lived in by two people given to working nonstop. Throughout a living/dining room combination, piles of books and newspapers were parked within easy reach, two muted TV sets were on to separate news channels, vying for attention against several computer monitors. But everything was clean, not cluttered, and smelled nice, too—a detail explained by Grace offering, "You want some muffins? Just made 'em."

With a final burst of laughter, a distant phone conversation they'd been hearing in the background came to an end, followed by footsteps overhead and the clattering of shoes coming downstairs. A broad-shouldered man in a beard and glasses, his thin hair almost snow white, joined them.

"There you are," he announced. "God, you made great time. Traffic must've been cooperative, for once."

Sally and Rachel repeated the greeting enacted in the garage, during which Ron Powers asked, "How's Katz doing? Miserable as always, I'm guessing?"

Rachel hedged her bet by answering, "How far do you two go back?"

"We three," Powers answered with emphasis. "Grace and I and Stan worked together for AP when we were all just cutting our teeth, God . . . How many years ago?"

"Thirty-seven," Grace answered. "And he was impossible then. It was great for us, though."

"It was," Ron jumped in. "He'd piss people off, and they'd come to us to unload."

"Worked like a charm," Grace finished.

"But," Ron continued, "you two obviously understand the call of the wild. Stan hankered for the Green Mountain State, and the rest is history. I hope he's still happy up there?"

"I think so," Rachel told them. "He retired a while ago, but they lured him back, so I guess he missed it. Have you two always worked together?"

"Yup," Ron said, touching Grace's shoulder fondly. "You get one of us, you get both. It's just always worked out that way."

"And then we went freelance," she said. "About fifteen years ago. We like that a lot better."

"Well," Ron added, "the internet's helped hugely. Just when the papers were starting to fold, we took advantage of this whole new outlet." He gestured toward the multiple computer monitors.

"Now we have more than we can handle," Grace said. "Gives us the luxury of choice, which used to be almost unheard of."

As they'd been chatting, Grace had wheeled into the nearby kitchen and poured coffees all around. Now she asked, "Cream or sugar, anyone?"

Later, they settled around the table in the room's center, also nibbling on fresh muffins, where Ron finally broached the subject of their visit. "So, Nick Bianchi. I have to admit, when you sent us that inquiry, Rachel, we were surprised."

"And a little tickled," Grace added.

"Yeah. Usually, it's Mob, Mob, Mob."

"Or endless crooked politicians."

"This was refreshing," he went on. "I'll grant you that he played with the Outfit, but he was basically an old-fashioned bad guy with no secret rituals or laws of omertà."

"Well," Grace edited, "let's call him a novitiate."

"Granted," Ron agreed. "And there's a small downside there, too."

"Oh?" Rachel asked.

"Well, with all the attention the bigwig dons receive, we news-hounds are paid to keep plowing the same old fields. Gotta pay the bills, after all."

"Which means," Grace said, "that smaller operators like your friend Nick didn't have the files on them we like."

Ron rose at this point, crossed the room, and lifted an envelope from a side counter. "We did manage to scrape something together, though, and I think I found someone you'll want to speak with."

He placed the envelope before the two friends. Sally and Rachel poured out its contents and began sifting through them as the conversation continued.

"If you'd like the CliffsNotes version," Grace said, "that basically says young Nick was a social climber, using Mob connections he'd made at his father's knee to later establish a food supply business of dubious legitimacy."

"His dad ran Bianchi's," Ron explained, "which was a hugely popular eatery among upper-crust mobsters."

"The choice pieces of our research," Grace went on, "are those small clippings at the back. Basically gossip." She indicated a small bundle of articles. "The business angle is common knowledge, pretty boring, not very revealing, and—because Nick was a nobody compared to the criminal glitterati—very spotty. *But*," she said, her expression bright, "those little suckers can be very handy."

Ron couldn't control himself, reaching out and picking one up. "This one's perfect. 'Local up-and-coming businessman Nick Bianchi with a mysterious new woman on his arm.' Back in the day, that would've been the kind of thing to get us chasing down the woman for some background."

"*If*," Grace emphasized, "we'd ever given a damn, which we rarely did."

"That being said," Ron chipped in, "we found an old woman who used to be his secretary, and she's who I'm thinking you ought to see first."

CHAPTER FOURTEEN

- - - - - - - - - - - - - - - - - - -

Willy looked up and down the highway. "It didn't happen this time of year, did it?"

Diane Lints shook her head, adapting to being treated as a partner. She was also curious about what he had to say. "It was summer, we think just before sunset, based on his riding habits."

"Still," Willy spoke softly. "It's not like the scene's hardware has changed any."

He was referring to the guardrail, the rocks beyond, and the precipitous plunge into the gray, rushing water below. The road, a broad, smooth, flat piece of macadam curving slightly to the inside, was free of visual obstructions and had a generous and well-marked breakdown lane.

"Run me through the logic of the accident reconstruction folks," he requested.

Diane pointed out the area's features as she spoke. "They said he was coming from the south, probably at a good clip."

"Like what?"

She didn't mind the interruption. "Maybe twenty-five? Something close to that. They always throw in a decimal, I think to show off. He was wearing a helmet, fingerless gloves, riding shorts, the whole getup. Anyhow, well equipped, and by the wear on his equipment, a veteran rider. This was borne out later during interviews with friends and family. That's also how we estimated the time of day it happened."

"Married?"

"Nope. A longtime girlfriend who sometimes rode with him, but she was away on a job somewhere, which was confirmed. She and his folks said he was not a risk-taker, but did like speed. The girlfriend always suspected he preferred riding alone so he could open up more."

"When was he found?"

"After dark," she explained. "It took a while for people to miss him, since there was nobody at home waiting for him. By the time word got to us and we retraced his route, it was late."

"No alarms went off in your head throughout?" Willy asked, straddling the guardrail and studying the rocks beyond.

"Not one."

"Okay. What did the techies think happened?"

"Pretty straightforward," she replied. "We sealed the area off until sunrise, so they could see better, so it was done by the numbers. The short story is that the road curves inwards here, and he didn't. I did push them for more, but they argued there was nothing to indicate otherwise—no skid marks, paint transfer, witnesses—and that a single stone could've been enough to twist his front wheel and launch him over the railing."

Willy's expression made clear what he thought of that. "There was transfer on the guardrail at least?"

"Yup." She squatted down and pointed. "You can't tell anything now, years later, but we matched the paint scrapings, part of his broken sunglasses. He lost a shoe here, too. There was some blood along the top of the rail that matched his DNA and injuries."

Willy moved to the rocks outside the barrier. "How 'bout over here? They say he cleared it airborne, or did he bounce?"

"Bounced. Right about where your right foot is, they found more blood. They think he landed, rolled, and the momentum took him the rest of the way."

Willy reiterated. "He's flyin' along, hits the guardrail, cuts himself along its top, lands on the rocks, keeps rolling, falls down the embankment, bounces a couple of more times where it flattens at the bottom, and finally hits the water facedown, dead. That about right?"

"Exactly, if you combine the autopsy results with the accident reconstruction and crime lab report."

Willy kept moving around, running the risk of slipping on the icy rocks. "All that math and science," he said largely to himself.

Diane had joined him, watching him resurrect what had happened. "It's what we present in court, if it gets that far." She said, "And there was not one shred of evidence of a car being involved."

"No, I get it," he replied, distracted. "But all that number crunching can fog up what's in front of us sometimes."

She tried following where he was going. "What do you mean?"

He was almost halfway down the embankment by now, and looked up at her. "Well, I follow what the science is trying to say—this rate, that equation, the other angle of projection. But just standing here, going through the motions, seeing where this happened, my instincts are telling me something slightly different."

"The drunk driver," she filled in.

Willy pointed down to the water. "Yeah. I don't think our bicyclist could've ended up in the drink on his own. The driver didn't actually hit him, from what we heard. She just forced him off at speed. That explains the lack of transfer or skid marks. But it also means he got no extra propulsion from a vehicle, and that his trajectory was possibly even slowed by last-second braking, contact with the rail, and finally smacking onto the rocks. I'm playing with the notion he only got halfway down and needed help reaching the bottom."

"Why bother?" she argued. "He didn't die by drowning. Why pitch him to the bottom if he didn't need to go there? Why not leave well enough alone?"

"On the face of it," Willy told her, "I'd guess three reasons: One is it looks more dramatic. Second is the killers had to convince the driver he'd gotten her out of a tough spot and that she owed him. Third is the actual landing didn't kill him—the poor slob needed finishing off, but it needed not to look that way to you folks."

"All that, even though we never knew there was a car in the first place," Diane commented. "Jesus."

"Right," Willy agreed, still studying his environs, his mind filling with alternate possibilities. "Among a bunch of other things nobody knew at the time."

"Like what?"

He smiled. "Don't know yet. That's where we gotta do some digging. But coming here has been an eye-opener, so thanks. You interested in keeping me company? I'll clear it with your lieutenant. The way I'm thinking, it'll sure as hell be worth your while."

Diane was again caught off balance. Her misgivings from the start had been that the VBI would steal her case, tossing her under the proverbial bus in the process. Being made part of the investigation hadn't been in the cards.

Her suspicions now all but evaporated, she told him, "I'm game if you are."

"Neat," he said, wondering if he was laying on the good cheer a little thick. He wanted her cooperation, but felt like he was cloning Lester Spinney.

He had no idea how the skinny guy kept it up all the time.

Miranda Alexander drove a nondescript, three-year-old, four-door Chrysler, which she explained had been acquired through federal forfeiture. Despite its plain looks, however, as soon as they set off from Joe's motel in Johnston, he could tell the car had been customized for speed and that Miranda was not immune to those hidden charms.

As with so many ex–road troopers, she was a natural behind the wheel and inclined to add a few numbers to the posted speed limits.

Not that she often got the chance. Their destination was East Providence, directly opposite their starting point, and right through the heart of downtown Providence.

It was a change for Joe. He had traveled more than most cops he knew, to Chicago, San Francisco, New York, and Montreal, among others. Nevertheless, he was country born and bred, his eyes as trained to mountains, trees, and rural expanses as a sailor's were to sky, rough weather, and islands against a featureless horizon. A change of surroundings was therefore hardly astonishing, but remained a rare enjoyment.

"You been down here before?" Miranda asked as she negotiated their way east.

"I was trying to remember," Joe replied, taking in the architectural jumble of poor and rich, tall and flat, streamlined and antique—all of it packed together like an Olympian-god-slash-hoarder's storage yard. "I don't guess I have."

"Exeter's my hometown," she said. "Slightly south of the city. Little Rhody's only got about a thousand square miles of land, and the highest elevation is barely eight hundred feet, but we make the most of it." She jerked a thumb over her shoulder. "Forty-five minutes west of here, you'd almost swear you were back in Vermont, minus the tall mountains. And as for the ocean . . ." She didn't bother finishing the sentence.

She did, however, tack on, "And, of course, we have more dirt-bags than you can wave a stick at."

Joe's own reservation with the place had little to do with that part. He was paid, after all, to seek out similarly shady characters in Vermont. It was more Rhode Island's pure, relentless, unmitigated crush of humanity that got to him. Everywhere he looked, from individuals to the things they inhabited—cars, trucks, buses, houses, factories, malls, skyscrapers—there was a teeming, roiling, constantly moving blur of people. That, beyond all, challenged his imaginative powers and made him slightly claustrophobic. He couldn't for the life of him figure out what they all did, where they were all going.

Miranda cut south along Pawtucket Avenue, through the center of East Providence, and eventually pulled into a vast parking lot at the foot of a series of monolithic apartment buildings, making Joe think of a human-sized stack of shoeboxes, each indistinguishable from its neighbor.

Miranda killed the engine, swung out, and told him as she locked the doors, "We're about to meet Frank Uboldi. He's the sole surviving cousin of an enforcer named Manny De Luca, who used to work for Al Zucco. You still have that napkin I drew on? Zucco was above Knuckles Alfano in the pecking order, and Knuckles was your boy Vito Alfano's old man. The same Vito Alfano," she couldn't resist adding with a grin as they approached the building block, "who worked in Nick Bianchi's outfit. And yes, there will be a test at the end of the day."

They reached the building's front door, and she led him into a lobby with a bank of hundreds of small mailboxes mounted to the side wall. As she sought out the one she was after, she continued speaking, squinting at the wall, "In a predictable world, we would've thought De Luca either pulled the trigger on Vito, or ordered it done. That's why the sudden appearance of the Mouse as the shooter made no sense. And also why I'm hoping Uboldi has something to tell us. Ah," she interrupted herself. "Here we go."

She stabbed the button before her and waited a minute.

"Yeah?"

"Hey, Frank," she said in a friendly voice. "Miranda Alexander, RISP. I got a question for ya."

"Put it in the mail." But they noticed the intercom stayed on.

"Come on, Frank," she countered. "The soaps can't be that good, and it's too early for *Wheel of Fortune*. I got a surprise for you."

He bit. "What?"

"A real Vermonter."

"What the fuck you talkin' about?"

"Let us in and find out. He's real cute. A little old for me. Like you."

Instead of a response, the door's buzzer went off like a grating alarm clock.

Miranda gave Joe the thumbs-up. "Curiosity. Gets 'em every time."

"He's going to talk to you because of your nice manners?" he asked. "What about omertà?"

"Totally overrated," she replied. "It was a thing. Still is, when it counts. But mostly? Nowadays? Especially among the old guys? If it won't get 'em in trouble, they like to talk as much as any geezer."

The apartment building was a sad testament to uninspired urban planning. Floor upon floor of hallway atop hallway, lined with door after door, almost as far as the eye could see. There was no relenting of the monotony through paint color or carpet choice, no relief for the senses with architectural grace notes. It was all mathematically functional—a practical, affordable storage solution for human beings.

Miranda, as always ahead, reached their destination—Joe no longer really knew where they were—and knocked on the door. They heard shuffling beyond, the snapping of two locks, and were met by a short, round man with a round face, wearing dark-rimmed round glasses.

He looked past Miranda to stare at Joe. "You a real Vermonter?"

"I am."

There was a pause. Clearly the man considered slamming the door, but, perhaps thinking of Miranda's comment about the quality of TV, he instead turned on his heel and faded back into the apartment, ordering, "Leave your guns in the fridge."

They entered a short hallway where one door opened onto a tiny kitchen. "No," she replied.

Uboldi took it in stride, continuing into his living room. It, too, was small, smelled like cigarettes, old laundry, and out-of-date food. It wasn't awful, just lived in by someone with no interest in décor, or in replacing worn-out appliances or furniture. It was a geriatric's final place of repose, shy of a state-run old folks' home. The oversized TV was in fact on, and it did have a soap opera playing.

Their host sat heavily on a bedraggled, stained armchair that accepted his shape like a doting mother's lap. Miranda made herself comfortable on a sofa, opening her coat and crossing her legs. Joe chose a hardback chair near the bedroom door.

"Cops sure didn't look like you when I was a player," Uboldi commented, admiring her.

"I'll take that as a compliment," she said.

"Okay," he segued, muting the TV. "Talk."

Joe took over. "Nick Bianchi. Vito Alfano worked for him."

"Them again? Jesus. Old news."

Joe couldn't suppress his surprise. "Someone else has been asking about them?"

"Yeah. Two guys went after a pal of mine named Dan Silver. Wore masks, played like tough guys. Totally missed that he didn't give a fuck. Why would he? He told 'em next time they should just call."

"How do you know this?" Miranda asked.

He tilted his head as if regarding a dim-witted child. "The telephone? I said we were pals. None of us gets much excitement anymore. We talk like old women."

"Silver didn't know who they were?" Miranda asked.

"Not a clue. They were older, too. Wild guess? Dan said they acted like a couple of pond-bottom foot soldiers out to pasture. Playing detective, from how it sounded, reliving the past. Barrel trash."

"Can you explain the detective part?" Joe asked.

"Sure," Uboldi said affably. "They were trying to figure out who did what to who back when Nick Bianchi was in the game and Vito worked for him, when we were all young bucks." He leered at Miranda to add, "And you weren't even born yet."

"What did he tell them?" Joe asked.

"That Vito shot Nick after screwing his woman—double insult. After that, Vito's days were pretty much numbered."

"Because Nick would return the favor later, with better aim?" Miranda suggested.

Uboldi looked incredulous. "Nooo. Not Nick. He wasn't into shooting people. Because of Al Zucco—Nick was Zucco's pet. He wasn't gonna stand for a spoiled snot nose like Knuckles's kid dissing him like that. Vito overplayed his hand. Had to be taken down."

"Knuckles had no say?"

"Rank, baby," Uboldi told her. "Knuckles maybe didn't like it much—blood is blood, after all. But between you and me, everybody knew Vito was an asshole and a useless son. He'd been playing with fire for years by the time he got whacked. Terrible thing, have your own offspring turn out like that. God's way of spitting in your eye. Anyhow, it was bound to happen. Knuckles took it like a man. He knew the score."

Bowing to Miranda's superior knowledge of the local anthropology, Joe kept quiet as she considered Uboldi's version of events.

"Crap," she said conversationally.

Uboldi was accommodating. "What part?"

"All of it. Vito violates Nick's bed and takes a potshot at him for good measure, then Zucco kills Vito in turn? I don't think so. No boss is going to step into a domestic spat like that—none of you guys would be left alive, the way you screw around."

Uboldi gave her a wide grin. "Good for you. Yeah, that was just the bullshit Silver told the two mopes to shut 'em up. Worked, too. Actually, he told 'em Nick did the job, come to think of it."

"So why was Vito really killed?" Joe asked.

"Yeah. Well . . . I guess you can piss off people at your own level and even jump their women, but you better not pull that shit with the folks higher up, and especially not their daughters."

Joe grew hopeful at that. "He crossed a line with a boss's daughter?"

The anger in Uboldi's voice was clear. "You don't break the rules. People think we're a bunch of animals. They give us made-up names—Jackie Nose, Big Tuna, Cadillac Frank—like we're cartoons. Back in the day, though? We were fucking huge. You didn't take a shit without our say-so. The food you ate, the clothes you wore, the cars you drove. We had a say in all of it. And we were successful 'cause of the rules."

He wiped his mouth with the back of his hand and shifted abruptly in his chair.

"What did Vito do wrong?" Joe asked. "Was Nick part of it?"

Uboldi's face had reddened. His eyes were narrow as he shot back, "Fuck Nick Bianchi. Who gave a crap about him? He was a leech, an outsider. Nobody cared who he fucked."

"So what happened?"

Uboldi shook his head. "What the hell I been talkin' about?" He let out a laugh. "All the shit we used to pull—killings, robberies, blackmails, dope, all of it—and Vito gets to the Pearly Gates because of where he parked his pecker. I mean, if you're gonna pull a stunt like that, you better not be stupid. Vito messed with Angie Zucco, the dumb jerk. The boss's kid. That was bad enough. But then he dumped her like she was a one-night stand."

He paused, thinking back. "She was sweet. Small, skinny, eager to grow up. Kids . . . Al and his wife probably shouldn't've smothered her so much. Her mother wanted Angie to be a nun, probably 'cause of Al's business. I seen it before."

"I'm guessing Angie didn't take Vito's rejection well."

Uboldi burst out laughing again, addressing Miranda. "Jesus Christ, you weren't kidding he'd be better than the soaps." He fixed on Joe. "No, Vermont, she didn't take it well. She cut her wrists."

"She died?"

"She didn't live. She ended up in a coma for years. Lost too much blood before they found her. Yeah, she died. Finally."

There was silence following that image. The TV tried to compete, flashing muted pictures of dogs running pell-mell after some food out of a bag. No one in the room paid attention.

Joe sought confirmation. "Al Zucco ordered Vito killed."

"Wouldn't you?"

There was no answer, which encouraged Uboldi to add, "He did, for him and his wife both. But that's not what ended up happening."

"What did?"

"Nobody knows. Al reached out to Manny De Luca, who talked to me about who to use. That's when I suggested Silver. Things were being arranged for the hit. You know—there's a way to do business, 'specially inside the Family. But then Vito was found in the river. End of story."

Miranda asked doubtfully, "The Mouse stood up to take the rap because none of you knew who pulled the trigger?"

"Sure," Uboldi agreed. "Ya gotta give 'em somebody, or it never goes away. Like I said: rules."

"But he didn't do it," Joe confirmed.

"Nobody cared. You don't want people stickin' their nose in. That's what counts. Neat 'n' tidy."

"Can we back up a little?" Joe asked. "What's your take on why Bianchi was told to hire Vito in the first place? Did Vito need care and feeding?"

"He wasn't no good at anything else. Bianchi was on the rise, getting Zucco to open doors by kissing his ass. Vito was the price tag. I heard it was a management job. You know he was probably fucking Nick over."

"They get along, Bianchi and Alfano?" Joe asked. "As far as you knew? They were together for a lot of years."

The old man's reaction was acerbic. "Sure. Ain't that always the case when somebody ends up dead? What the hell do you care, anyhow?"

"Vermont's where he finally died."

"No shit? Killed?"

Joe hesitated, for an instant only. He was a stranger in a strange land, asking for favors. "Yeah."

For the first time, Uboldi turned philosophical. "Huh. Recently?"

"Within the year."

"Shit. He was older'n me. Who got him?"

"Don't know."

"You think somebody from down here?"

Joe ignored the question. "What was he like when he was making his chops?"

"Didn't know him that good," Uboldi said. "A jerk, from what I heard, like Vito, but different—smarter, tougher."

"Did he have a successful career?"

"Far as I know. Never heard nothing different."

"He had a kid early on," Joe said. "Named Rob. You know or hear anything about him, or a young woman named Monica, whom Nick later married?"

Uboldi was already dismissing those questions and for the first time glanced at the TV set. "I told you already, Vermont. Forget Nick Bianchi. He had his time, made his buck. What do I care?"

"I guess you don't, Mr. Uboldi," Joe replied, rising. "Thanks for your time."

"I'm really sorry for your loss, Mr. Lyon."

Mike Lyon looked at Lester as if checking a sincerity meter perched just over his head. He was otherwise making sure his daughter's snow boots properly met the bottoms of her snow pants. It was the only missing detail remaining. Otherwise, the small child was looking like a goose down–clad fire plug, from parka hood to miniature Sorels. Even her mittened hands had difficulty not sticking out to both sides, she was so layered.

They were going out to slide down the hill bordering the mill's parking lot, taking advantage of the fresh snow. As with everything else at the complex, this recreational detail—an outdoor play area, complete with banked sled run—had been built into the overall plan.

"Thank you," Mike replied, rocking back on his heels and surveying his handiwork. He was a short man, the opposite of his half brother, Rob, and built like a wrestler. Lester thought back to when his own daughter, now facing college, routinely took this opportunity to announce that she needed to use the bathroom.

Debbie, it appeared, was made of sterner stuff and merely pulled on her father's hand to get him headed outside faster. Lester liked the child, having seen her dancing down the corridor upon his first visit to the mill. At the time, she'd appeared a friendly, carefree spirit. That still seemed true, despite Lester's increasingly dark view of the environment in which she was being reared.

Mike had been amenable to Lester joining them when the latter had knocked on their apartment door for an interview, and Lester wasn't about to refuse a ready-made relaxed opportunity to see what he could learn, especially given the critical loss this little family had just suffered.

"How's she taking it?" he inquired softly as all three headed outside, Debbie skipping ahead.

"What do they know at this age?" Mike responded grimly. "Some shrink's going to make a fortune down the line, especially once she finds out her mother didn't die of an accident. But now? It's like she's been told the sad ending to one of her books. It's not real."

They exited the building and crossed the lot to the base of the sledding area, where a staircase had been constructed into the hill to reach the top.

"How 'bout you?" Lester asked as they started up, side by side.

Mike's expression darkened. "How d'you think? My wife, Debbie's mother, my business partner." He flipped his gloved hand in the air, in lieu, perhaps, of snapping his fingers. "All gone, like that. Murdered, for Christ's sake. What the hell's that about?"

"I know somebody's already talked to you about this, and I'm sorry to be repeating it," Lester apologized. "But we do it in case there were any small details missed the first time. It's hard to think clearly right after a shock like this."

"No kidding."

"I'm sure you've been losing sleep, wondering yourself," Lester suggested, the rhythmic tramp of their feet marking their progress.

"I can't figure it out," Mike confessed.

"How was the business going?" Lester asked, broaching a subject perhaps even sorer than Michelle's death. "You think any of your current problems tie into what happened to her?"

Mike looked at him bitterly. "You should know. You're all part of the same bunch, coming down on us like a brick shithouse. I'm facing fucking jail time because of what you people are accusing me of."

Lester brushed that aside, if disingenuously. "You know my team has nothing to do with that. We're only interested in what happened to your wife."

"I know, I know," Mike allowed angrily, lowering his voice for Debbie's sake. "It's just, what the hell else is going to go wrong?" He turned to indicate the gigantic building looming across the now valley-like parking area below. "It's like the roof of that place is caving in. First Nathan, then Gene, now Michelle and the business. What in Christ's name is going on?"

"You called your dad by his first name?" Lester asked.

Mike didn't mind the non sequitur. "What's the saying? It takes a father to be a dad? We *all* called him Nathan. You figure it out."

"That's tough," Lester agreed. "Still, I heard he was influential when you and Michelle created your business. He'd done something like it back in Rhode Island, hadn't he?"

"You are digging in deep, aren't you?" the other man said. "Yeah, that was when we were settling in, trying to figure out how to make this goddamn experiment work. You know, normally, you live someplace and you commute to work every day. That's what normal people do. But Nathan . . ." He shook his head. "He was possessed by this family-slash-commune thing or whatever you want to call it."

They reached the top, and Mike switched his attention to Debbie. There were several groomed chutes cut into the slope and a shed with a choice of sleds. Mike and his daughter were going to head down together, but she insisted Lester join them on the run parallel to theirs, chanting, "Race, race," as encouragement. Although a first in Lester's history of unusual interrogations, he selected a small toboggan and, despite not being dressed for outdoor sports, went for a competitive slide downhill, Debbie's excited screams filling the air between them.

At the bottom, with her now calling out, "Again, again," the two men set off to repeat the experience, this time carrying their conveyances as they followed in the young girl's wake.

"How were things between you and your wife?" Lester asked, resuming the conversation.

Mike was not as agreeable this time. "Right. Here it comes. Go after the husband. You know where I was when she fell. You have Christ knows how many witnesses. But, oh no. I still had to have done it. What? You think I paid somebody? That I snuck out somehow and raced up there to push her? I even gave you my DNA. God forbid I'm totally innocent."

"None of which answers the question," Lester pressed him as he caught his breath.

"Damn," Mike said wearily. "Unbelievable. You married?"

"Yes."

"Well, then you know how it is sometimes. You fight, you have disagreements. We were in business together. You think that was all smooth sailing? Of course we hit rough spots. Who doesn't? You don't turn around and kill each other."

"Sometimes you do," Lester countered, "especially if one half of the couple thinks the other is stepping out for fringe benefits."

"In your world, maybe," Mike said dismissively. "We didn't give a crap about stuff like that."

"She cheated on you?"

Mike's response was almost pitying. "Jesus. The euphemisms. She had a large appetite. It was fine with me. I don't indulge myself, and she never rubbed it in, but I knew she saw other men on occasion."

Lester took note of Mike's own euphemism, before returning to Nathan. "Look at it from our perspective," he urged. "Your old man's a controlling oddball, he gets you into a business that you'll admit is pretty unorthodox, you all live like privileged prisoners in his castle, with his trust holding a pair of scissors on your golden parachute cords. And your wife isn't even a part of it until you marry her and bring her in. She must've thought she'd been transported to another planet when you moved in here. It's enough to give anyone whiplash."

For the first time, the emotion in Mike's voice felt born of a darker source than loss or frustration. "She never complained," he half spat out.

"Took to it like a fish to water?" Lester asked.

Mike had mis-stepped with his flash of anger, and now beat a retreat, saying, "Whatever. It wasn't that big a deal."

He then increased his pace, pulling ahead, and joined his daughter at the top.

"Again," she demanded, looking at Lester.

But Mike intervened, kneeling before her and wiping her runny nose with a tissue. "The man has to leave, sweetie. He's super busy."

"I had a great time, though," Lester added. "Thanks for the race."

Debbie began to protest, but Mike was having none of it, hustling her onto the sled between his knees, and pushing off without further comment.

Lester didn't mind. He watched them go, before bending down to retrieve the tissue Mike had dropped onto the snow, carefully placing it into a small evidence envelope from his pocket.

CHAPTER FIFTEEN

"Take a right here," Ron told Rachel from the back seat.

Sally twisted around to face him. "Where are we? I thought you said we were meeting some old secretary."

"I didn't say she was broke," Ron protested. "From what I heard, Nick took good care of her, and I think she married money on top of that."

"No kidding. Of the few houses I can see, the smallest ones look like mansions," Sally said.

"It's Richmond," Ron said, as if in explanation. "Not all the high rollers like to live on the ocean. Left up ahead."

Richmond township included some dozen separate communities, several country clubs, a vast wildlife preserve, and, as Sally had just noted, a large number of tastefully self-effacing, New England–style McMansions. These were of varying dimensions, many of them clustered around the edges of planned development drives and circles with names including "pond," "woods," "sunset," and the like. The sole exception that Rachel noticed, driving by, was the charmingly and oddly named Small Pox Trail. To Sally's point, however, most of the neighborhood was screened from view by the dense forestland they'd been missing since entering Rhode Island, approaching as they had from the north. The trees were a mixture of evergreen and hardwood, to northern eyes curiously short in stature, and thick enough in places to be all but impenetrable. Remarkably, and sadly, there were also copious signs of disease and drought, especially harmful to the oaks.

Nevertheless, the visual impact was in startling contrast to the open vistas they'd left forty minutes earlier, reinforcing the state's claim of having a geography as diverse as its footprint was small.

Ron's directions brought them into a large dead-end traffic circle, with a string of luxurious homes, each screened from its neighbor with sculpted partitions of woodland, and each hanging on the circle's outside edge like a lifeboat clinging to a cruise ship.

"How did you find this woman?" Rachel asked as she cut the engine and they all got out.

"Aha," Ron said, buttoning his coat against the chill. "One of Grace's and my better sources is a clerk of the court whose responsibility is filing company closures, bankruptcies, and the like. Within that paperwork can be asset divestiture. All we had to do was look up Bianchi's old business to discover that an impressive amount of cash had been delivered to Alison Young, decades ago, about the time he moved to Vermont. To me, that speaks of either loyalty and gratitude, or a payoff. Either way, I'm hoping it includes an intimate knowledge of Nick by Alison."

He waved a hand toward the large house, finishing, "I recommend everybody cross their fingers."

The woman who opened the door was small, wiry, white-haired, and with alarmingly bright blue eyes. She was ancient in appearance and surprisingly spry physically. "Yes?"

Rachel made the introductions and explained that she was researching Nick Bianchi, a local Brattleboro celebrity and philanthropist—stretching things a bit—who'd recently died.

It was enough to get them through the door, which, at this point, was the best Rachel could hope for.

Alison Young took them through the house, into a very large living room with a view of a snow-covered backyard of impressive dimensions, even though, here, too, the surrounding trees looked considerably the worse for wear, well beyond the winter's annual denuding.

"Please," she urged them. "Sit where you'd like. Can I get you something to drink? Coffee or tea?" Simultaneously, having seated herself in a wingback chair, she rang a small silver bell and was instantly rewarded with the appearance of a stocky woman in a uniform, who stood expectantly by the door.

"Anyone?" Young repeated.

Ron was the first to answer, raising his hand. "I'd love some coffee. Cold day."

The two women followed suit, and the maid vanished as silently as she'd surfaced.

Sally did her best not to smile at the ritual. In her peculiar past, following her eccentric father's wake, she'd only seen a maid in the movies.

"So, you'd like to know about Nick," Young began.

"If that's all right," Rachel replied. "I feel a little awkward, barging in uninvited like this."

Young set her at ease. "Not at all," she said. "Nick Bianchi made me wealthy beyond anything I could've imagined, for no other reason than I stuck with him from the start. He made a joke of it back then, telling me that Ray Kroc, who turned McDonald's into an empire, had made his secretary a millionaire because she'd agreed to work for stock options only. 'Well,' said Nick, 'I can't give you stock, but I can do the next best thing.' It was an extraordinary gesture. The least I can do now is tell you what I can about him."

She then cautioned, "I warn you, though, that may be less than you think. He was very private, and there was a lot I knew nothing about."

"How extraordinary," Rachel responded. "You must think very highly of him."

Young's eyes widened. "Oh no," she said. "That's what was so surprising about what he did. Nick was a son of a bitch, down to his bones. He lied and cheated whenever he could. That's one reason I don't mind telling you what I know about him."

Dead silence greeted that disclosure.

"Was that too blunt?" she therefore asked.

Sally and Ron burst out laughing as Rachel shook her head. "No, no, Mrs. Young. I'm so sorry. It was just unexpected."

Young smiled then, reassured. "Please call me Alison. The Mrs. Young thing has always made me uncomfortable." She indicated their surroundings. "And don't let any of this fool you. Or my way of speaking. I'm a working-class Warwick girl, born and raised. I just got lucky, and I've been faking it ever since."

Rachel tapped her chest. "Rachel. That's Sally, and he's Ron. No bullshit."

"Excellent."

The coffee arrived on a tray, complete with cream, sugar, artificial sweetener, and—unexpectedly—maple syrup, which Alison added to her cup. Rachel had only seen Joe Gunther do likewise, much to her own horror.

"All right, then," she resumed. "You say you're writing an obituary for Nick. Seems a little unlikely."

Honoring Alison's request for honesty, Rachel risked being more open. "Extremely," she conceded. "It started that way, but there's a rumor he didn't die of natural causes."

Alison chuckled. "Someone got to him after all these years? Amazing."

"It might be worse than that," Rachel told her. "It was almost a year ago and discovered by accident. And just recently, one of his sons and a daughter-in-law have also died under murky circumstances, making us wonder what the heck is going on. We thought looking into his past might help."

Alison absorbed that, taking a long sip of her sweetened coffee. "Well, I can't say I'm very surprised," she said. "I am sorry for the children. But Nick never lived conventionally. There's no particular reason his death should be much different. The son wasn't Rob, was it?"

"No, it wasn't. You knew the family well?" Rachel asked. "I thought maybe you'd been restricted to just company business."

"Goodness, no," Alison protested. "That's how it should have been, and what Nick might have preferred. But he was too disorganized not to have someone like me at his back, sort of an air traffic controller, if you get my meaning."

"I do, I do," Rachel said supportively. "Does that mean you knew Monica, too?"

Alison frowned at the mention. "Oh yes."

"Not too crazy about her?"

"The feeling was mutual. Is she still around?"

"Runs the family, along with Rob."

Alison took another sip before saying, "Really . . . They live together?"

"They share a huge house. The whole family does. It's a converted factory building."

"After all this time. At long last. Rob never married, did he."

It was a statement, causing her three guests to exchange glances.

"No, he didn't," Rachel confirmed. "What're you saying? Did the two of them have a thing?"

Alison looked pleased, and certainly Sally imagined that she was having a good time, not only revisiting old memories, but before a keenly appreciative audience.

"I should say so," she confirmed. "Monica traded Rob in for his father. She had an eye for self-improvement."

Rachel couldn't contain her surprise. "No kidding? How did that sit between father and son?"

"It was odd," the older woman said. "I shouldn't have been surprised, suspecting how much of Nick might be in Rob, but they were such different personalities. Rob retreated at first, understandably. He was only a teenager, after all. But then he turned completely around, almost becoming like a butler or a family advisor—cold, efficient, all knowing, always there. Creepy in someone so young."

"Did you know there were two more sons, Gene and Michael?" Rachel asked.

Alison shook her head. "I wouldn't have. When Nick and Monica left Rhode Island, it was a door slamming shut. That was it, not that I missed them, to be honest. I'd had my fill of that family and its doings."

"Do you know if Monica had another child, back when she was being wooed by Rob and Nick?"

Alison's brow wrinkled. "She was almost a child herself, if a precocious one."

Rachel took that as a negative and followed with, "Did you ever hear the name Nathan Lyon afterward? A postcard or legal document?" Sally asked, "Or anything coming from Brattleboro, Vermont, perhaps from another source?"

"No," she said. "Who's that?"

"Nick's new name after he pulled up stakes here."

"Ah."

"It's becoming pretty clear his doings down here weren't always legal," Rachel suggested.

Alison smiled. "I should say not. That's where I tried to tend to my knitting. There were so many people who went in and out of Nick's office who knew nothing about restaurants or food or the culinary supply chain. They were just hoods. I did my best not to remember faces or names."

"Who was Rob's mother?" Sally asked.

"A young woman named Sarah Lucas," Alison answered without pause.

"What happened to her?" Rachel asked.

After a moment's reflection, Alison replied, "She floated away."

As poetic as that sounded, Rachel wasn't about to take it as a last line. "But she had a child with the man," she reacted empathetically. "She must've been around for a while before doing her floating."

A tiny, almost imperceptible shift seemed to settle onto Alison Young at that statement. She cast a look out the broad window, her coffee forgotten in her hand. When her gaze returned to Rachel, she was slightly less philosophical and more focused. "You're still very young." She turned to Ron, who'd been only attentively listening until then. "You are, too, relative to me, but less so. I bet you've had that moment when you've taken a high school yearbook off the shelf and looked through it?"

"Oh, you bet," he said. "With some thorny end results."

She beamed. "Exactly. All those fresh faces, those comments scribbled in the margins and under the photographs. Well, that's how I'm feeling now, talking about those days, when we were barely in our twenties, horny, hungry, careless, and full of plans. You really do feel like you could live forever and that nothing bad'll stick to you."

Rachel put aside her coffee cup and leaned forward. "Alison, I get the feeling you're sorting out what to tell us. Don't worry about getting it right fresh out of the bag. Just say it and we'll figure it out together."

"You weren't just Nick's employee," Sally suggested.

Alison suppressed a smile, her cheeks flushing. "You're very good. You all are. No, you're right. We were all pretty playful then. This was before Monica or Gene or any of that, of course."

"Does that mean," Rachel asked, "that Sarah and you both sort of . . . intermingled with Nick?"

They all laughed, after which their elderly hostess allowed, "Nick and I had a fling. Everybody was doing it."

"And Sarah?"

"Of course."

Rachel turned serious. "But Sarah got pregnant."

Alison saddened. "That changed everything. It wasn't like we were the only people on an island. This was Providence, Nick was upwardly mobile, the company was, too. I already mentioned all those men coming and going. Well, there were young women, too. Lots of them. Everyone talks about San Francisco and the summer of love, or gay Paree in the movies, or Carnaby Street. But that sense of freedom was everywhere, including stuffy old New England. Providence nowadays is health care, Brown, and RISD, or old mobsters with funny nicknames, but when we were young, it was alive with energy. There were languages and cultures and ethnicities all bumping into each other, making sparks against the traditional old guard—entire neighborhoods changing hands."

She paused to catch her breath, reminding her guests of her age. Ron even made to rise and render comfort, before she stopped him with her hand. "No, no. I'm fine. Thank you. I just got a little carried away." She took a breath before saying, "Poor Sarah was like a stone thrown into a small pond." She then quickly corrected herself. "No. That's not right. I'm not being fair or honest. The stone was Nick, not her. Remember what I said about him? This was the first time he really showed his colors, at least to me. And maybe I saw it because I wasn't the target. But it made me pull back into my job and stop playing around, at least with Nick. Sarah was turned by him from a plaything into a broodmare, completely disposable after Rob was born. He simply threw her away. It was awful and cruel."

Breaking the silence stretching among them, Sally asked, "She had no family? No one to help her?"

Alison was crestfallen. "No. And we—I—was useless when it counted. I could blame the times, or Nick's personality, or my fear of losing my job. But those are all excuses. I was a coward. Sarah had appeared, none of us knew from where. And after she gave up baby Rob to Nick, she vanished."

She'd been staring at the floor and now looked up to take them in. "I watched it happen, just like I did years later when Nick stole Monica from poor Rob."

She was crying now, dabbing her eyes with her napkin. This time, Ron did cross over, kneeling to lay a hand on her thin forearm. "I'm so sorry, Alison. It wasn't our intention to make you feel bad."

She regarded him kindly, patting his hand. "I know. Things like this, going back, you only remember the good times at first. But it wasn't only fun. People act out in ways they can't undo, and others suffer."

Ron looked over his shoulder at Sally and Rachel, but they were already getting to their feet. Each in turn voiced their thanks and re-grets, leaving Alison Young with her memories, her remorse, and her snowbound view of dying trees.

Later, in the car leaving Richmond, Sally broached what had hov-ered behind the entire conversation with Alison like a specter. "Of course," she said, "we shouldn't forget that somebody finally did get to Nick and killed him."

"Alison feeling her oats?" Rachel suggested from behind the wheel.

"No," Sally countered. "But what she told us could be important."

Rachel shot her friend a quick look. The comment revealed one of the dynamics between them that helped cement their friendship—a symbiotic combination of mutual support and competition.

Ron put it into words from the back seat. "Ah. So says the PI to the reporter. Where's the ball going to drop with you two?"

Sally turned toward him. "It's an either-or?"

"Fair enough," he replied. "But you still have to decide, if I understood you just now: Do you tell the police what you learned, and lose your exclusive, or do you withhold evidence in a murder case and piss off the cops to win points with your editor?"

Sally raised an eyebrow, but included Rachel with her inquiry. "Same answer. Why is that an absolute?"

Rachel saw where she was headed. "I could tell Joe as a goodwill gesture—and stay out of trouble—but make it clear it'll be coming out in print anyhow?"

Ron could only be amused. "Holy smokes. We definitely play in different sandlots. I totally get it. Don't think I'm being condescending. If anything, I'm envious. The idea that you could share information with law enforcement and still be free to file it as news is pretty much unheard of down here. We're not so nice with each other. There'd be lawyers lined up at the counter, waving paperwork."

Rachel heard what he was saying. "I wonder if there's a chance of that, even with broad-minded Joe?"

Sally finished the thought. "That telling him about Sarah being Rob's mom and Nick stealing Monica from Rob might move him to slap a muzzle on you? I don't see why. It's helpful to him, but it's nothing that would derail a prosecution if it came out in the paper."

"Plus," Rachel rationalized, "it's got to be good in the brownie points department."

Miranda started the car to get the heater going and said, "Can't hit a homer every time, I guess. I hoped we'd have better luck."

She and Joe were in Cranston, having just left the Adult Correctional Institution where Eddie Moscone had been housed for so many years—site of an enormous and rambling state building complex covering multiple blocks. She could have placed their inquiry by phone or computer, but she'd taken advantage of the ACI's proximity to show the place off. It was in parts almost as decoratively constructed as a college campus, and Joe had been suitably impressed, despite their having collected no forwarding address for Moscone.

"I suppose that's the reward for serving your full sentence," he replied, settling into the passenger seat with his cell phone in hand. "You get to act like any member of the public."

"It's not like we couldn't find him with a little more effort," she said. "People like him don't just disappear."

"Oh, I know. To be honest, though, I'm not sure what it would gain me. After the time and effort he put into keeping quiet—it looks like for a crime he didn't even commit—I have serious doubts he'd be as chatty as Frank Uboldi."

Miranda indicated the phone he was holding. "You need to respond to something there?"

"I got a text just now," he explained. "It's a little nuts. A reporter from home is down here doing research into Bianchi, working a parallel furrow to our own."

"Okay," his companion said neutrally.

"It's hardly *The New York Times*," he went on. "The paper she works for is more likely to run a knotweed invasion on page one, not an investigative piece into mobsters rubbing each other out. I'm guessing her editor has a hand in this somewhere. He's an old-fashioned warhorse."

"To give them their due," Miranda argued, "it can't be every day you country folks rack up the body count you've got now. It's gotta be boosting circulation."

"It will be, probably," Joe agreed. "I don't know that they've started publishing any of her articles yet. Anyhow, she dug up a couple of ancient-history items that might clarify the DNA research my squad's chasing down."

"What did she say?"

Joe peered more closely at his phone and read, "'Am in the Ocean State. Just interviewed Alison Young, Bianchi/Lyon's old secretary. She says Sarah Lucas is Rob's mom, & Bianchi dumped her after taking the baby. Lucas now lost to the wind. Also, teenager Rob was first to move in on Monica. Bianchi stole her from him after.'"

Miranda whistled. "Jesus. What a snake pit." She waited a couple of seconds before asking the obvious, "And why did this person tell you this?"

"She's almost a relative," he explained. "My partner's daughter. Still," he conceded, "it does raise the question." He waggled the phone back and forth, adding, "If you don't mind?"

"You kidding? I have a ringside seat at the circus. Carry on."

He dialed Rachel's number, putting the phone on speaker so Miranda could eavesdrop.

"I thought you might call," Rachel said as a greeting.

"We're not alone," he told her. "I have a colleague with me. Are you Woodward or Bernstein?"

"Ida Tarbell," she countered.

"Point taken," he granted her, "if a sadly obscure one, nowadays.

On that score, why tell me about Sarah Lucas and how Nathan broke Rob's heart when it never would have crossed the real Ida's mind to share that with law enforcement?"

Rachel was clearly feeling feisty. "Because the cops in her days were slimeballs."

"I'm very flattered."

Her response warmed his heart. "You earned it, Joe. I thought it might help."

"It will, and it does," he said. "And I thank you for telling me. And yes, I'll remember it when and if it produces something I think you can run in the paper."

"Deal," she said.

"While we're on it," he asked, "when you were interviewing Young, did the name Vito Alfano come up?"

"No. What would've been the context?"

"As a partner of Nick's or a colleague."

"She said there were a lot of criminal types who came and went, but that was it, although she did admit there were enough of them to make her stick to her knitting, in her words."

"Okay. Thanks. An additional favor?" he asked.

"Sure."

"First and foremost. I can tell you're having a blast. Please, for Christ's sake, do not get into trouble. You are proceeding safely, yeah?"

"Yeah. And I'm not alone," she replied cryptically.

He had no choice but to take her at her word. "Second," he therefore went on, "you mentioned Young as a source. Is that proprietary, or can I have a crack at her, too?"

"No, no. That's why I mentioned her by name. I'll text you her contact info."

"Thanks, Rachel. I would love to hear you were heading back

home today. Your being down here makes me as nervous as a cat on a highway."

"Love you, Joe."

The connection went dead, although not before the promised text came through.

"If her mother's anything like that," Miranda said, "you've got a character on your hands."

He smiled, reading off the phone's screen. "I'm a blessed man."

CHAPTER SIXTEEN

Willy and Diane Lints found Ned Russell in his office at the mill. Notwithstanding the builder's complaints about how and why he'd ended up there, Willy couldn't sympathize much upon crossing the threshold. The place was airy, spacious, light-filled, and handsomely accented by what were clearly Russell's own architectural details. Overall, it was stunning.

Willy didn't hold back. "Damn," he said loudly enough that the owner could hear from his drafting table. "I would hate working in this dump."

"There's more to a place than how it looks," Russell said without pause.

Willy smiled broadly, indicating his companion. "Detective Sergeant Lints, state police. I'm Kunkle—VBI. We were hoping to ask you a couple more questions."

Russell's expression didn't change, but he put down his pencil and rose from his stool, indicating a small grouping of chairs near the window. "Okay," he said without inflection. He didn't shake hands or offer coffee. He barely made eye contact, although Willy and he had never met before.

"What's up?" he asked after they'd settled in.

Willy took the lead. "I know we've been bugging you about Nathan and Gene and your daughter and your arrangement here at the mill. The two of us are going further back in time."

Russell eyed him warily without comment.

"We're following up on what you told my boss, Special Agent Gunther, about how Nathan Lyon blackmailed Penny after she had that encounter with the bicyclist."

The older man frowned and stood again, shouting over his shoulder, "*Betsy!*"

The two cops sat still, nonplussed until a woman appeared from the back of the large room, smiling and smoothing her shirt front with her hands. "Oh," she said, approaching. "We have company."

"Hardly," her husband growled. "Cops. They wanna know about Penny and Lyon again. I'm going out."

With that, he swept a coat off a hook near the door and vanished with a bang.

Betsy Russell didn't seem perturbed, looking around and asking, "He didn't offer you something to drink?"

Willy and Diane got up clumsily, or made to until Betsy ordered them to stay put. Eventually, following an awkward repeat of introductions and a double refusal of coffee, all three of them repeated the tableau that had featured the now dramatically missing Ned.

"I am sorry about that," Betsy said. "I think Ned's had his fill of this. It's a waste of time to him—even if you find what it is you're after, none of it's going to bring Gene back or help Penny."

She crossed her ankles and rested her hands in her lap, the perfect hostess, and said, "Of course, I have no idea what I'll be able to do. You were probably about to ask Ned things I know nothing about."

Willy dismissed that with a gesture. "No, I don't think so, Mrs. Russell—"

"Betsy."

"Betsy. We were just telling him that Detective Sergeant Lints and I were searching for more details about when Penny had her accident with the bicyclist."

Betsy's face opened up. "Oh. I can see what got him going. That's not a happy memory."

"Are you okay talking about it?" Diane asked.

"I'll try my best," she said. "I do think it should all come out. I even spoke to a reporter earlier. I don't think I made her very happy, but I tried to be helpful."

"Rachel Reiling?" Willy asked.

"Yes. That was her name."

"What did she want to know?"

"Nothing about what you're asking. She was more interested in whether Nathan was murdered, which I told her I hoped he was. And she wanted to know about how the money was divvied up. I think I mentioned how Gene had once said he wished he could just give it all away and stick to his pottery, except that it wouldn't be fair to Peggy and Mark."

That seemed to fit everything Willy had heard about Gene. "I'm sorry I never got to meet him," he said, for once being quite genuine.

"He was a lovely person," she said simply.

"Unlike Nathan Lyon," Willy commented, bringing the conversation back where he wanted it. "What can you tell us about Penny's accident?"

Betsy was silent for a moment, thinking back. "Well," she began, "of course at the time, Ned and I had no idea. We were at home. This happened quite late, I think."

"What was the first you heard of it?" Diane asked.

"We got a phone call."

"From Penny?"

"No. It was from Nathan Lyon. Early in the morning. He was very businesslike, very cold."

"He spoke to both of you?"

"Ned answered the phone, but Nathan told him to put me on, too, so I could hear what was being said. It was very straightforward. I remember wondering how anyone could remain that detached, saying the things he did. He told us what Penny had done, how she'd called him for help, how he'd arranged things to make it look like she hadn't been there, and how as a result, he expected us—all of us—to fall into line. He used that phrase. It wasn't a long call. He said he'd see Ned later face-to-face, but this was just so we both knew what was going to happen from now on."

"And his meeting with Ned was later that day?" Willy asked.

"Yes. That's when we found out we were moving the business here." She indicated their surroundings. Her voice lowered as she added, "And that we were going to lose Penny to him."

"How did Ned take that?" Diane asked.

Betsy looked at her wearily. "You mean did he want to kill the bastard? Yes. But he didn't. Ned is a strong and proud man. He is not someone to kill another, no matter what they've done."

"What did Lyon tell you, Betsy?" Willy pressed her. "Did he describe how he'd doctored the crash site?"

"Not specifically," Betsy answered. "He told us to pay attention to any news reports about a bicyclist found in the river, along with the location. I suppose in case we ever compared notes with Penny. She could confirm it was the man she thought she hit."

Willy was suddenly struck by a question. "Mrs. Russell. Sorry— Betsy. Did you and Ned get the idea that Lyon had done all the scene managing himself, moving props and changing evidence and whatever?"

"That's what he implied. He never said 'we' or talked about any-one helping him. Is that what you mean?"

"It is."

Willy and Diane caught each other's eye. Having visited the scene, they knew too well how rugged it was.

"Betsy," he therefore asked, "what kind of shape was Lyon in back then? Was he pretty fit?"

"Fit?" she countered, surprised. "I wouldn't say so. He could walk around, but he was frail. Used an inhaler and always had a cane."

"You never went out to where the accident happened?" Diane wanted to know.

Betsy shook her head. "Why would we?"

Willy pursued what the two cops were wondering. "So you couldn't see Nathan negotiating a steep pile of rocks or carrying anything heavy?"

"Not really," she replied. "He wasn't infirm, but he was slowing down. He was careful climbing a set of stairs."

"Great," Willy said. "That's helpful. Something else: How close was he with anyone else? Monica, for instance, or Mike, or Rob? Or even somebody from outside the family? Somebody he held in confidence, maybe?"

But Betsy was looking blank. "I had very little to do with him, once he moved to Vermont and laid claim to Gene. What he did to poor Ned, how he manipulated Penny . . ." She didn't finish the sentence and brushed her forehead with her fingertips, as if shooing away a butterfly.

Willy nodded to Diane. She responded by glancing at the door.

They rose as one. Betsy didn't take much notice.

"Thank you," Willy said. "We'll leave you be. Sorry to have upset you."

"It's all right," was the quiet response. "We're used to it, being with these people."

"You thinking what I am?" Diane asked as they reached the parking lot, zipping up their coats.

He was. "Old man Lyon was too crippled up to make like a billy goat and alter the crime scene."

Alison Young may not have been a kid anymore, as her drive to Kingston for a monthly doctor's visit reminded her. But she had her pride, valued her independence, and trusted her wits to be, if slightly slower, as sharp as ever. All of which explained why she was driving alone, in the middle of winter, on Rural Route 138 in a two-year-old, fully equipped Range Rover that she'd paid for in cash off the show-room floor.

In fact, she may have been feeling her oats more than usual, given the visit by those reporters. Their questions and her responses had revived memories she hadn't entertained in decades. Despite her closing statement that she'd eventually retreated from the fast lane, that hadn't meant she hadn't thoroughly enjoyed the ride. Growing up in Warwick, daughter of a single mom, rebellious by instinct, and angered by circumstance, Alison had struck out early, by her own admission fated for a fast, short life.

But even a wild girl needed a job, which is where Nick Bianchi had come in, whether recognizing her spirit, responding to his own carnal urges, or just suiting a need. Whatever the stimulus, he'd hired her after bedding her, and—as far as she was concerned—had benefited thereafter from her loyalty, competence, and discretion.

She'd never liked him. She'd made that clear. He was self-centered, unfeeling, and careless of others. Nevertheless, her personality had not only coped with, but molded around his, like a symbiotic para-site, and his response in the end had reflected an unexpected recog-nition of what she'd done to protect him.

What was that quote? "The best of times, the worst of times." But maybe also the most stimulating and unusual of times. That was certainly one thing about Nick. He might have been a monster, but he'd never been dull company, and despite what Alison had seen him do to others, he'd never once mistreated her. It had helped her after-ward, following his departure, to confidently march on to her next life stage, getting married late in life, and finally becoming a silver-haired widow of means, living as she'd never imagined she could so many decades earlier.

Lost as she was in her thoughts, negotiating the flat, gentle, thinly traveled but well-plowed Kingstown Road, she didn't notice the van behind her closing the distance, and was caught by surprise when it abruptly swept past and cut her off, just shy of the Heaton Orchard Road.

Two men wearing masks exited and approached at a run, slow mov-ing and clumsy despite the handguns they carried. One gestured to her passenger door while the other covered her through the windshield.

"Unlock the door."

After she complied, he slid in beside her.

Knowing what reception any comment from her would garner, she silently placed both hands at the top of her steering wheel, in full display. Her unwanted companion, interpreting the body language, gave his colleague the thumbs-up to proceed.

"Follow the van."

In caravan, they turned down the Heaton Orchard Road for a few hundred yards, Alison's brain alive with near panic, but staying silent and outwardly calm, until they reached a rough, flat-packed cutoff in the hard snow to their right, down which the van led the way. Ahead, through the stunted, leafless trees, she saw a ragged gap in the chain-link fence surrounding a vast, otherworldly expanse of hundreds, maybe thousands, of slightly tilted, regimentally aligned solar collectors.

Without hesitation, the van forged ahead into the protective camouflage of the panels, continuing halfway down an aisle before coming to a stop. There, the second masked man walked back and climbed into the rear seat, slamming the door behind him.

"What do you want?" Alison asked at last, having recognized by their movements that her abductors had to be close to her own age.

The man beside her answered, "You used to work for Nick Bianchi."

She took her eyes off the vehicle ahead to stare at him—a gesture she'd promised herself she wasn't going to do, in case they thought she was trying to catalog details for later.

"What?" she stammered, startled that the very memories she'd been entertaining all day were still coming at her.

"You heard me."

"Yes," she answered shortly, hoping to keep her responses succinct.

"What did you do for him?"

"At the end? Personal secretary."

She let her eyes return to the outside, attracted by the near-mesmerizing setting they'd chosen for this conversation. The eerie combination of endless dark, flat panels contrasted with the leglike underpinnings that kept them facing the cold and distant sun high above. They were like an army of alien soldiers, crouched low and poised, awaiting the order to move out and invade.

"Did you know Vito Alfano?"

She kept to her private vow to be brief. It might have been a very long time ago, but she knew this type of person all too well. "Yes."

"How?"

"He worked for Mr. Bianchi."

"You know anything about how he died?"

She hesitated, baffled. From what she'd taken to be a robbery or a kidnapping for ransom, this was heading nowhere she could guess. "He disappeared. Wasn't he murdered?"

"You don't know?"

She stared at him again. "Well, *I* didn't do it. It's what the papers said."

"You don't know who killed him?"

"No. Why should I?"

"You worked for Bianchi," the man insisted. "You *had* to know something."

"How did they get along, Vito and Bianchi?" the man behind her asked in a quieter, almost soothing voice.

She paused before choosing to tell what she knew. This was complicated enough without throwing in lies. "They didn't like each other."

"Why?"

"Different styles? They didn't choose the arrangement."

"Zucco made that happen?" the man in front asked.

She was confused again. "Who?"

"Zucco. He made Bianchi take Vito. Part of the deal, as a favor to Vito's dad."

She pushed back ever so slightly. "You know more than I do."

"You were his right-hand man," he protested.

Her face flushed. "I am not a man, and Mr. Bianchi kept most of his dealings private. I was the front office of the company. I just know that Mr. Bianchi wasn't happy when Mr. Alfano joined us, especially as an executive."

"So what did Vito do?"

"For the company?"

"No. For the president of the United States. Yeah, for the company. You play dumb and it's not gonna matter that you're an old broad."

Alison had a comeback, but held it back, answering, "Mr. Bianchi and he worked those details out. I had no reason to know."

"There must've been talk."

She tried to suppress a sigh, her earlier fear edged out by growing impatience. She even gave thought to the fact that she was going to be late for her doctor's appointment. "There were rumors he was developing projects on his own that threatened what we were doing."

"You know Bianchi's wife?" the man in the rear asked.

She scratched her head. What next? "Monica?"

"Yeah. How did she get along with Vito?"

"*Vito?*" she repeated, startled. "She didn't. I mean, they barely saw each other. What're you asking?"

"They didn't screw around?"

She laughed at the idea. "No."

"How long was Vito part of the business?" asked the quieter one.

"Many years."

"Long time to hate each other."

"That took time. Everyone was busy, and it didn't seem to matter what Alfano did. I don't know about anyone named Zucco, but maybe he's why they were together so long."

"When did Vito shoot Nick?"

Alison twisted in her seat. "What?"

"Vito shot Nick."

"With a gun?"

That left both men speechless.

Alison was stunned, her mind in turmoil, filled with memories she was being forced to rethink.

"He went away for a while," she volunteered, against her own rule. "We were told it was for a stomach problem."

Her side passenger laughed. "You could say that. He never said anything when he got back?"

"No," she said quietly, almost to herself.

"I don't get it about the wife," the man in back murmured.

His friend turned on him. "Will you quit it with that? Who cares? You," he addressed Alison. "Where did Nick go?"

She'd been distracted by the other man's aside, however, wondering if the two of them hadn't gotten things confused. Was it Monica they were asking about, or Sarah, who dated back to the early years she'd been reminiscing about? Relationships, including her own, had been more flexible then.

The front man poked her shoulder. "Hey. Where did Nick go?"

She cleared her head. "Go?"

"Yeah. Come on. He shut down operations and took a powder. Where to?"

Alison remembered what one of the three journalists had said. "Vermont."

"You're shitting me."

"That's what I heard," she said. "Brattleboro, Vermont."

"The whole family?"

"I'm not even sure that's right," she replied. "It's just something I heard."

"We woulda known about that," the more aggressive one said.

"Maybe not," the other commented. He tapped her lightly on the shoulder. "He change his name?"

She pressed her lips together. Nick Bianchi had been a bad man, regardless of her feelings toward him. But who was to say these two weren't worse?

Her hesitation was telling, and the man beside her had reached the end of his patience. He produced a gun from his coat pocket and pointed it at her. "Lady, don't fuck us around now. You're about to get your life back. Don't make me shoot you."

The logic that shooting her would somehow get him what he wanted was clearly lacking. The final result for her, however, was easy to see, reasonable or not.

"Nathan Lyon," she said.

Her two passengers exchanged looks and left the car.

Alison sat at the wheel for a while after the van trundled off, leaving her surrounded by her army of oversized mechanical ants. A familiar buzzing from her purse drew her out of her reverie.

"Hello?" she answered.

"Alison Young?" said the man with a deep, pleasant voice.

"Yes."

"My name is Joe Gunther. I'm a police officer from Vermont. I think you met a couple of friends of mine earlier? Rachel Reiling, from the *Brattleboro Reformer*?"

Alison felt an enormous weight settling on her. "Yes."

"I'm sorry to impose," he said, "but I was hoping you'd be willing to meet with me at your convenience, so I could ask you a few questions related to what you told them. Might that be possible?"

She considered the question, now asked by three different sets of people, and how its effect on her had changed over such a short time, from amusement and nostalgia to things darker, more menacing, and—sadly—perhaps more reflective of a truth she'd willfully ignored for too long.

It was more than she wanted to confront, this late in life. Sitting in her fancy car, with more accessories than she knew how to operate, she'd had enough with disillusionment.

"No," she answered softly, and hung up.

Diane Lints looked around the small single room that housed the VBI's southeastern four-person squad.

Willy caught her expression as he draped his coat across the back of his chair. "You starting to see why some of us think the state police get most of the money?" he asked.

"Jesus," she said. "If this is all you people need, we could find you a corner in the Westminster barracks. We already house the fish cops. That's *way* better than this."

"Nah," he said. "We're kind of stuck on our independence."

"Ooh," she reacted. "Don't wanna be tainted by the Green and the Gold?"

The reference was to the color of their uniforms, a source of great pride.

"Too late now," he retorted. "Most of our ranks are filled with your people—all happy defectors, from what I hear. Something for you to think about."

Diane sat at Sammie's desk, where she enjoyed a view of Lester's, festooned with all his skinny bird artifacts.

"You ever meet Les?" Willy asked.

"Don't think so."

"Tallest, skinniest dude I know. Stork was his handle at the academy. Can't imagine why."

She shook her head in wonder at the array.

"Okay," Willy said, putting his feet up on his desk and leaning back, his one good hand behind his head. "Let's take it apart."

Diane understood immediately. "Bicyclist, minding his own business, riding a route he knows well on a piece of equipment he's ridden for years."

Willy joined in. "Gets forced off the road by Penny Trick, who's drunk, drugged, distracted, or all three."

"Hit and run, or close enough to it. Doesn't touch the brakes, doesn't get out to check, probably doesn't even stop."

"But she does know what happened."

Diane nodded. "Right. Calls her own personal Svengali."

"Which is where it gets tricky," Willy proposed. "'Cause while we know Nathan Lyon transformed the scene, we're not sure he did the dirty work himself."

"A sidekick."

"Right," he agreed. "But who? And how do we prove it?"

Diane opened the briefcase shoulder bag she favored and spread some of its contents onto Willy's desk, beside his feet, which he didn't bother moving.

There were reports, site maps, sketches, photos, the autopsy report, and more.

He dropped his feet then, sat forward, and began pushing the photographs around, almost absentmindedly. "There's gotta be something," he muttered.

"Not much to work with," Diane said. "Helmet, gloves, clothes, the bike itself, whatever specimens of the body the ME kept on file. Anything left at the scene is long gone."

Willy straightened, struck by a sudden thought. "What happened to the helmet?" he asked.

She pawed through the paperwork to locate an inventory. "Went with the body."

"Huh." Willy reached for the phone.

Within seconds, given her office's small staff, Beverly Hillstrom was on the line. "Special Agent Kunkle."

Willy gave Diane a conspiratorial smile. Despite the decades they'd known each other, it remained Beverly's practice to maintain formalities at all times.

It was not a habit he reciprocated.

"Hey, Doc," he said, knowing her dislike of the nickname. "I think I might have your kind of puzzle to solve. You mind if I put you on speaker? I'm with Detective Sergeant Diane Lints."

"Of course not. Detective, how are you?"

"Fine, ma'am. Thank you, ma'am," Diane said to the authoritative voice in the room.

Willy could hear Beverly's amusement as she said, "Relax, Detective. I can't bite you from here."

"Yes, ma'am."

Willy moved on. "You did a case years ago on a purported bicyclist-versus-guardrail, where the poor bastard did an ass-over-teakettle into the river afterward."

Knowing she would ask, he reached for her report and recited the date and case number.

There was a pause while they both heard a keyboard clacking in the background.

"Got it," she reported briefly. "Blunt force trauma. The water seemingly played no role in COD."

"That's the one."

"Are you suspecting foul play?" she asked.

"We are," he said. "The problem being we've got nothing to work with except what you've got up there."

Beverly's voice registered her surprise. "What *we've* got? That wouldn't be much, Special Agent Kunkle."

There was a brief pause on the line, which Willy didn't interrupt. He was gratified when she returned with, "Except for the helmet, of course. We do still have that."

He laughed outright and grinned at Diane. "Outstanding. I was hoping you'd say that. Thank God you don't throw anything away."

She replied, "Not if we get stuck with it because the family or the funeral home or the police don't want it or forgot to retrieve it. We have a cinder block, still wrapped in the chain used to weigh down a body fifteen years ago. You never can tell."

"Big closet," Diane said under her breath.

"Can you do me a favor?" Willy asked the medical examiner.

"You'd like me to send the helmet to the lab," Beverly suggested.

"You got it," he said. "It occurred to us that if you were altering a scene and short on time, the one detail you might overlook is leaving your fingerprints on the helmet when you pose it someplace artistic."

"I completely understand," Beverly told him. "I'll send it out today."

CHAPTER SEVENTEEN

Corey Ryder was sick of always getting the shit end of the stick. He was cool, good with the ladies, knew his way around a car engine, had a lot of friends, and was the go-to guy when it came to scoring what he called "primo H."

But somehow, in front of a crowd of similarly talented Brattleboro twentysomethings, he rarely actually scored the deal, got the girl, or landed the job that would better his prospects and improve his self-regard. He was, in short, a legend in his mind only, which was beginning to chafe.

Tonight, things were about to change. In one dramatic move, he was going to fatten his wallet, improve his prestige, retire his debts, hit the front page of the paper, and be the envy of everyone who'd ignored him in the past.

It was snowing hard, as planned. Fewer cars out, fewer witnesses, but at the end of a long day of commerce, still with money in the till. Already camouflaged by the winter gear people wore this time of year, his ski mask and gloves completely reasonable, Corey entered the gas station like any casual customer, ignoring the clerk in favor of the snack aisle—in fact, checking for customers, camera placement, and other employees. Satisfied that things hadn't changed from when he'd done his research a few hours earlier, he sauntered up to where the clerk was seemingly entering something into a logbook by the cash register.

Tommy Squires had worked here and at other area gas stations for the better part of twenty years. He'd never been a man of ambition. A local boy, graduate of the career center, hardworking, attentive to detail, respectful of others, quick to smile, he'd been advised more than once to aim higher, build some goals, and stretch his imagination.

But Tommy had never seen his lot as needing improvement. He lived contently in a single room above Main Street, enjoyed the long walk to work every day, and found the environment of the gas station to be interesting, entertaining, occasionally challenging, and on a night like tonight, perhaps downright exciting.

He'd been robbed before, several times, both here and elsewhere. Places like this were so popular with shortsighted aspirants to upward mobility, he'd joked with police, they might as well have been called "Stop-'n'-Rob stores."

The guy who'd just entered, for example. Tommy had pegged him earlier, when after selecting a soda, he'd patrolled the room like an interior decorator assessing a new job. The look in their eyes, the nervous body language, and the premature guilt stamped all over their faces—even while buying a Coke, for God's sake—were additional dead giveaways to Tommy that they'd be meeting again soon. He'd even memorized the man's features.

And so here it was, the inevitable moment. Of course, this time the poor bastard had worn a mask, pretending to ward off the cold, as if the camera earlier hadn't captured his shape, height, the same clothing, and everything about him, including his inappropriate and memorable red sneakers.

As soon as he had entered the building, Tommy surreptitiously reached for the silent alarm's inconspicuous remote control and placed it beside the cash register.

"Hi," he said brightly as the masked man approached the counter. "Find everything you were after?"

Corey placed his snack between them and said something.

Tommy furrowed his brow, straining to hear. "I'm sorry, man. I didn't catch that."

"Money. Give me your money."

"Out of the register?"

"I got a gun."

Tommy became serious. No point being stupid. That only got you killed.

"I understand," he said immediately, placing his left hand on the alarm while working the keys with his right. "I'm not being a wiseass here, but do you want the change or just the bills?"

Corey stared at him a moment. "Bills."

"Bills it is. Happy to help. I'm not the owner, and I don't want to be hurt."

Seeing the bills being laid out triggered a thought Corey hadn't considered before. "You got a safe?"

Tommy winced internally. That was always the catch in these situations. "There is a safe, and I'm happy to show it to you, but I have no way of opening it. The boss is the only one with the key. It's a store policy. I'm really sorry."

That seemed to be good enough. Corey nodded and considered the bills before him. "You got a bag?"

"Sure do," Tommy said, hesitating. "I have to reach under here to get it, though. I don't want you thinking I'm up to anything."

"Go ahead."

Tommy produced the paper bag with practiced ease and slipped the money inside, pausing before handing it over to ask, "You want your candy bar?"

His hand in midair, Corey stopped. "Huh?"

Tommy looked at the item questioningly. "The candy bar?"

"Oh. Sure."

Tommy added it and handed the bag over. Ingrown habit kicked in then, probably stimulated by pent-up nerves, as he concluded the interaction, "Have a nice evening."

"You, too."

The Brattleboro officer on patrol, a veteran of many years, his lights off and parked out of sight, watched Corey Ryder leave the gas station, bag in hand, check right and left, and begin walking toward downtown on Canal Street.

"Heading your way, Jack," he said into his cell phone. "Let me know when you see him."

"Roger that."

A minute later, Jack said, "Got him. East side of the street."

In a smooth, undramatic, well-practiced maneuver, the first cruiser snuck up close behind Corey as he walked and only hit its lights twenty feet away from where the other vehicle was tucked down an alley. In the snap of a finger, Corey was rooted in place, boxed in by both cars, spotlit by colorful, pulsating strobes and with two armed police officers screaming at him to lie down on the ground.

Surrounded by darkness and thick, falling snow, the whole scene had the feel of a spontaneous wintertime fireworks display—a sight to delight the eyes.

Corey looked up as the small room's door swung open. Before him stood a man with frightening eyes and a limp left arm, whose hand was tucked into his trousers pocket like an afterthought.

He looked at Corey silently, motionless, those eyes taking him in like a shark's.

"Who're you?" Corey asked.

"That's up to you," Willy said, closing the door, completing the impression that whatever happened here stayed here, regardless of the consequences to Corey.

The young man, already plagued by his hapless self-image, was overwhelmed by despair. It was clear he'd completely overstepped his capabilities with this latest stunt. He now felt like a mouse in a maze, watched by white-coated scientists looming overhead.

"I don't understand."

"You made a statement to the cops who arrested you," Willy said. "You told them sometimes a deal could be made for people like you, who had something to trade. Is that right?"

"Can you make that happen?"

"Answer the question."

The flat, deadly tone of the man's voice made Corey swallow. "I think so," he said.

Willy took three steps into the room, almost looming overhead. "Explain."

"I heard you people were sniffin' around the mill, lookin' for who's causing problems there."

"Causing problems?"

"People dying. You know . . ."

"What do you know about that?"

Corey rubbed his head with one hand, the other being cuffed to the wall. "I'm not sure."

Willy leaned forward, his head hovering ever closer. "You're not sure about what?"

"It might get me in trouble."

"You *are* in trouble."

"Well . . . more trouble."

Willy sat opposite the boy, removed his inert left hand from its pocket, and laid it on the table between them, like a motionless pale pet. Corey's eyes widened as he took in the withered limb, its fingers slightly curled as if dropped from an eagle's talons. He seemed transfixed by the sight.

"I need to make something clear to you," Willy said quietly. "You're at the very top of a slippery slope, like the slide at a playground. Right now, right here, you get to choose how you go down—slowly and carefully, or headfirst and at great speed. Maybe you just drop off and land like a rock. It depends on how much you give us. Everybody down the line—me, the lawyers, the prosecutors, the judges—are each going to ask themselves the same question: 'What did Corey Ryder do to be part of the solution here?'"

Willy moved his seat to get closer, causing Corey to press his back against the wall. He kept staring at the hand on the table.

"If any of us," Willy continued, "at any time during this whole process, gets the feeling you're holding out, not being honest, or trying to be cute . . . Well, I can't speak to what might happen. Do you understand how important it is for you to play straight?"

Corey nodded, his brain numb.

"Right now," Willy resumed, "you don't know what to do. You hope there's a way out—a light you can follow." Willy edged closer still. Their knees were now touching. "I am that light," he said. "The truth you're holding on to is like the battery for that light. Tell me that truth, Corey, and the rest will work itself out. What is it you know about what happened at the mill?"

There was a long silent moment during which neither man moved a muscle.

Until Corey said, barely audibly, addressing the hand, "I put the wire across the top of the stairs, what the lady tripped over."

"Okay," Joe said. "We've got a lot to unpack, the hottest piece being what Willy just dragged in."

"Thanks a bunch," Willy retorted from his desk. "Make me sound like a dog."

Lester threw a piece of his doughnut to him. "Good boy."

The mood in the office was upbeat. Joe didn't fault them feeling pleased about their progress. From the scarcity a few days ago attending three unexplained deaths, they'd made sudden and significant headway.

"Go," he encouraged Willy.

"Aspiring to greater social standing," Kunkle began, "not to mention a little cash, Corey Ryder robbed a gas station last night and got a hundred feet out the door before being grabbed by two of our local finest. Upon realizing what his ill-gotten eighty-six dollars was about to get him, he remembered his latest *Law and Order* reruns and told the arresting officers he had something to trade, pertaining to one of the deaths at the mill. They called me, I went to see him, and to cut to the chase, he told me that having recently worked for Food Flourish as a packer, he'd been paid by Michael Lyon to rig the trip wire that took out Mike's wife. Like we thought, Corey was supposed to remove the evidence, making it look like a terrible accident, except that Sally was there to queer the deal. So instead, Corey crept back downstairs and mingled with the others, unnoticed by all, including us."

"And he'll testify to this?" Sam asked.

Willy answered her indirectly. "Tausha and the SA will have to work out the details, but they're on board to make him feel more like a righteous citizen than an accessory to murder, until he's ratted out Mike on the stand, assuming it goes to trial."

"That's the who," Lester stated. "Do we have the why?"

"Not quite," Joe informed him. "But we do know where to apply the pressure to find it out."

"Sex, money, or both," Willy weighed in. "That's my bet. I never swallowed for a second that Michelle's screwing around was fine and dandy with her hubby."

"Next item," Joe resumed. "We have DNA results coming in. High marks to Lester on this. In very short order, he's been running around like the last man in a circus parade, collecting trash, Kleenexes, legitimate swabs, and familial samples, in order to assemble an almost complete genetic lineup of every resident of that damn building. I think you will soon be impressed with the end product. Lester."

Spinney, looking slightly embarrassed by the buildup, sent his computer screen's contents onto the large, wall-mounted display, where they could see a chart entitled "Mill DNA Family Tree."

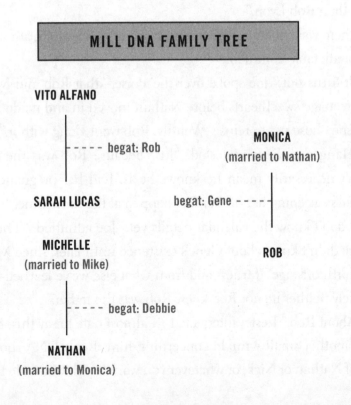

MILL DNA FAMILY TREE

VITO ALFANO

├ ---- begat: Rob

MONICA
(married to Nathan)

SARAH LUCAS   begat: Gene ----

MICHELLE
(married to Mike)

ROB

├ ---- begat: Debbie

NATHAN
(married to Monica)

"Okay," he said. "Picking up where Willy just left off—since things are confusing enough as they are—let's start with the Mike and Michelle Lyon family, beginning with daughter, Debbie. Skipping over the technical mumbo jumbo, which you can read in my coming report, Debbie's mom was indeed the late lamented Michelle, but dad turns out to have been Nathan Lyon, born Nick Bianchi."

"That old goat," Willy said. "I guess she wasn't as discreet with her companions as she led on."

"That's sure as hell something to ask Mike about," Sam mentioned.

"Keep going, Les," Joe said.

"Right. The next rabbit out of the hat goes to another of our suspicious deaths, Gene Russell. We knew he wasn't a Russell by birth, but apparently, he didn't sprout from Nathan Lyon, either. His birth mother was Monica, as we were told, but his father was none other than Rob Lyon."

There was general, incredulous laughter in the room, among several predictable comments.

"It turns out," Joe spoke over the noise, "that Rob and Monica were teenage sweethearts before Nathan moved in and made her an offer she chose not to refuse. Weirdly, Rob went along with it."

"Hang on," Sam protested. "Just because Rob was the father doesn't necessarily mean he knows he is. Did her pregnancy and Nathan's sweeping her off her feet happen at the same time?"

"I don't know the calendar details yet," Joe admitted. "The story is Nick didn't know about Gene's existence until later, since Monica gave birth offstage. If true—and from what else we've learned—then it's likely neither he nor Rob knew Rob was the father."

"About Rob," Lester interjected. "I almost hate to say this, but we have another small wrinkle concerning him. Rob's DNA shows no hint of Nathan or Nick, or whatever you want to call him." He turned to Joe to say, "From what you dug up in Rhode Island, it's likely Rob's mother was Sarah Lucas. As for the father—"

"I'll be a son of a bitch," Willy interrupted, drawing everyone's attention. "It was Vito Alfano. Had to be. I spent half last night catching up on Joe's reports. That would explain why he and Nick hated each other. I kept wondering, 'Why so pissed off?' as I was reading. That would do it, if Vito was not only screwing around with Nick's business, but schtupping his girlfriend, too."

"Just where I was going," Lester resumed with a smile toward Willy. "Vito was a homicide victim, after all, so the Rhode Island ME kept samples. Alfano's DNA confirms him as Rob's dad."

"Damn," Willy said. "What a bunch of horny gerbils. So first, Vito and Sarah begat Rob, cheating Nick; then Rob and Monica begat Gene, lying to Nick; and finally Nick—or Nathan—and Michelle begat Debbie, cheating Mike."

"That's no more than the Medicis or the Caesars or half a dozen other royal families did over the centuries," Joe said. "The catch here is that Vito, Nathan, Gene, and Michelle each died at the hands of others."

Sam finished the thought. "And we need to identify those others."

Joe agreed. "We do, starting with the bird in hand, thanks to poor, miserable Corey Ryder. Maybe his giving us Mike Lyon will be the first falling domino at the head of the line."

"We should be so lucky," Willy predictably said.

CHAPTER EIGHTEEN

"Did I get my money's worth?" Stan Katz asked.

"I think so," Rachel replied. "The plan was to find out more about Nathan Lyon. I've done that in spades. His real name was Nick Bianchi, he was born and made his fortune in Providence, and thanks to you giving me Ron Powers, I've now got a stream of backup documents still coming in that'll support an interesting biography for starters, not to mention a follow-up about the deaths piling up at the mill."

"'How I made my money in the big city'?" Stan asked sarcastically. "'And how it ended up biting me in the ass'?"

She countered, "More like 'How I made a pile playing footsie with the Mob and lost a business associate to the Providence River,' and *then* moving on to current events in our fair city."

There was a knock on Katz's door, and another reporter stuck his head in. "Sorry to interrupt."

"It's okay," their boss said. "What's up?"

The young man pointed to Rachel. "It's for you. A phone call on the landline. Someone called Alison Young? Says you need to know what she's got. Right now."

Rachel looked at Katz, who was visibly pleased. "Start writing it up, Rach. I have no idea who that is, but it sounds like you got something boiling on every burner."

"Too many trees," Eddie complained.

Fredo made no comment, watching for the exit he was after. He'd booked rooms for them in downtown Brattleboro, based solely on the place looking like an older-style hotel, complete with movie theater on the first floor. If they were going to do this, he'd figured, why not shoot for the whole experience? Get a taste for the town that had drawn Nick in, instead of spending the night on some miracle mile that didn't look any different from something outside Providence.

Fredo was feeling near an odyssey's end. Never committed to his cousin's obsession, he'd been responsive concerning its roots. Eddie had been a bizarre version of a true Boy Scout in a corrupt and cynical world. And for that, he'd been mugged, robbed, and betrayed.

Fredo, for more reasons than he wanted to enumerate, had felt bound to support Eddie's quixotic journey.

But at last it was nearing conclusion. By entering Brattleboro, they were crossing a threshold to completion, and, he hoped, a return to sanity and normalcy.

"How do you want to go after Mike Lyon?" Willy asked his boss.

Joe had mulled this over. "So far, despite the body count, we've been able to take our time. Outside our little circle, Nathan is only rumored to be a homicide. Gene and Michelle for the most part are considered accidents. My instinct is to box Mike in, but beforehand, use Corey Ryder as leverage to get warrants for Mike's records, phones, internet usage, whatever we need to find out everything about him."

"And until then?" Sam asked.

"Nathan and Gene?" Joe responded. "The missing link in both

cases is that damned CCTV system. There is no way on God's earth you have something that fancy not hooked up to a recorder."

"You still think it's squirreled away somewhere?" Lester asked.

"I do."

Willy pulled out his phone, responding to a text telling him to check his computer's in-box. "Son of a bitch," he commented.

"What did you get?" Sam inquired.

In place of answering, he sent the screen image to the large monitor. "It's the lab. The prints they lifted off the bike helmet of the poor bastard Penny Trick sideswiped? Guess who they belong to?"

"Wow," Lester commented.

The name on the lab report was Rob Lyon's.

Joe chuckled softly. "Nice work, Mr. Kunkle."

"Credit where it's due," Willy replied. "Diane Lints was a big help."

"So noted." Joe took in his squad. "What I just said about Mike"—he indicated the big screen—"now applies to Rob, too. We've got probable cause for each of them."

He moved to the window and glanced out thoughtfully. "I'll pull in extra agents to put those two under the microscope. Gene and Nathan just got bumped to the back again. I have a hunch that when this dam finally breaks, there'll be a lot floating downstream that'll help us out with them anyhow."

Fredo's choice had been the Latchis Hotel, an art deco building on the corner of Brattleboro's Main and Flat Streets, built just before World War II, and housing everything he'd found appealing during his internet search. The place not only had rooms with windows that opened, but radiators and old fixtures. This in addition to the movie theater, bar, and restaurant he'd already noticed. It was stuffed with murals, terrazzo flooring, fake Greek statues, and smack in the middle of downtown—a source of extra comfort for his nature-averse, grouchy cousin. On that score, Eddie's only remaining complaint was the view of a hulking, snowcapped peak directly across the Connecticut River.

"What's with the mountain?" he growled, looking out.

His mood wasn't improved when they left the hotel later to head for the library at the far end of Main Street. Uphill.

"For Christ's sake," Eddie complained, eyeing the steep sidewalk. "We gotta go up that? Don't they got buses or a cab?"

Fredo tried soothing him. "Apparently not. The clerk said it wasn't worth trying. C'mon, Eddie, it'll do you good. They salted the sidewalks; they're not slippery. We'll take our time."

And so they did. Two old urban ex-hoods, in city shoes and black leather coats and hats, looking like they'd been sent to the wrong TV shoot site.

Eddie's only comment: "Fuckin' freezing."

The town library, surprisingly large, was located near a traffic island housing the district court—a detail not lost on either man. Still, the warmth embracing them upon entering, not to mention the cheerful welcome from the small, energetic, brightly clad librarian at the counter, made the courthouse a triviality. Her name tag identified her as "Starr."

"Hello," she said. "Are you new to town?"

"How'd you know?" Eddie asked, confused.

"Wild guess. Is there anything I can do for you?"

"Yeah," Fredo replied. "You got newspaper files?"

"The *Brattleboro Reformer*? Of course. Come this way and I'll set you up."

In short order, they were sitting side by side in a far corner of the high-ceilinged room, flipping through pages.

"There," Eddie said suddenly. "Just like she said."

Fredo froze the image at the section featuring Nathan Lyon's obituary. They had mentioned his name to Starr, and without hesitation, she'd set them on the right path.

Eddie's shoulders slumped as he stared ahead, barely taking in the words. "The fucker's dead. I don't believe it."

"I warned you," Fredo stated. "Most of us are by now."

"What's it say?"

Fredo knew what he was after. "After a brief illness, surrounded by his family."

"Damn."

Fredo spoke quietly, interpreting as Eddie sat dumbfounded. "Calls him a local philanthropist and businessman, landlord, and investor. Says he bought an abandoned mill and converted it into a single-family home. That it houses not only all his relatives, but several businesses as well."

"Bastard died in bed."

Fredo stopped reading and turned toward him. "Yeah, he did, Eddie, just like we hope to. And he's the last of 'em. Zucco, Vito, Knuckles, all those guys. All dead. We chased 'em down and accounted for every one of them, including Bianchi, or Lyon, who really had nuthin' to do with what happened to you. Dead and buried."

Eddie scowled at him. "How can you say he had nuthin' to do with it? He's at the heart of it. His beef with Alfano, his lying and cheating, his screwing around. I took the fall for him, Fredo. I did his time."

"According to Silver," Fredo argued. "But what's he know? That's just what he thinks. He doesn't know who whacked Vito. Silver told us Vito's pecker got him killed; Neri said it was his sticky fingers; and Moretti had no clue or didn't care. They're all opinions and they all stink. None of this is real anymore, Ed."

But Eddie was shaking his head as if warding off flies. "No, man. That's not how this ends."

Fredo patted his arm. "What more do you want? The man can't be touched anymore."

A fateful turn of phrase, it turned out. Eddie looked up at him suddenly, then at the obit. "Who's he survived by?"

Fredo's heart sank. He rubbed his eyes tiredly as Eddie leaned into the screen to focus on the article's conclusion.

"Wife, Monica Tardy," he read aloud. "That's the bitch I wanna talk to."

"Eddie," Fredo tried again, keeping his voice low. "Give it a rest. What're you gonna get out of it, except being thrown out? It's a palace; they're millionaires. They got security and cops on a direct line. You know how it works. You're just gonna get dropped in the can again."

"The fuck I am." Eddie pushed his chair back and stood up. "We'll stake the place out. It'll be like the old days. They don't know we're coming. It'll be easy."

Fredo rose to his feet, resigned once more. He couldn't turn him down. "Okay, buddy. Let's find out where they live."

The squad had been expanded to over twice its size. In the past, that had meant new temporary quarters, usually in the basement of the same building, but given the nature of the assignments, the extra manpower went into the field as it arrived. By now, special agents were combing through town records, applying for warrants, contacting internet and cell phone carriers, poring over credit card and bank statements, and using some of the resulting data to visit bars, restaurants, parking garages, and shops for any closed-circuit footage and potential eyewitnesses. Much of the legal work was coordinated through Tausha Greenblott in Burlington, who helped everyone gain access to the appropriate judges.

Lester and Sam held the fort at the office, catching calls and texts, creating a comprehensive chart of the hourly activities of Mike Lyon, Rob Lyon, Penny Trick, Monica Tardy, and anyone relevant they'd contacted during the previous several weeks.

It didn't take long for something eye-catching to rise to the surface, even amid a mind-numbing whirlpool of shopping forays, restaurant outings, grocery trips, visits to the hairdresser, and the like.

"Joe?" Sam said, calling her boss's cell. "You near the office?"

"Yeah. Downstairs at the town clerk's."

"You might want to come up for this. I think we found something that'll float your boat."

"I like how *that* sounds," he commented before hanging up.

He was by her desk within five minutes. "What d'ya got?"

In response, she sat back to give him a view of her computer screen. The lighting was none too good, but the sharpness of Brattleboro's downtown garage CCTV footage was surprising, showing Michael Lyon in a passionate embrace with a woman, his hand up under her sweater.

"I think you just found our door opener," Joe said. "Nice work."

The woman was Gene Lyon's widow, Peggy.

That was for starters. Now the unit had specifically Mike and Peggy to pursue, and in the context of an illicit love affair. They refined their research, building full profiles from that single dark recording. The beauty was not only that the process yielded one incriminating piece of evidence after another—invoices, phone bills, hotel receipts, and more footage—but it supplied an overdue boost to a team in need of good news.

In the end, much like the clichéd safecracker polishing his fingertips, preparing to defeat a tricky lock, it finally fell to Joe to sit down with Peggy Lyon for a conversation.

He got the assignment following a squad-wide debate on best approaches. Sam was of the same gender, Willy the scariest option, Lester the good cop. But Joe, they decided, after researching Peggy's past, had the best chance of imposing authority while invoking the young woman's supposedly most cherished relative, her recently dead grandfather. Shamelessly, Joe altered his hairstyle to better match the old man's, and wore his reading glasses to heighten the reference.

He entered the small windowless room where they'd housed Peggy without explanation, and presented a choice of two cardboard cups. He also had a folder tucked under his arm. "If you're a coffee drinker," he began, sitting down opposite her at the small table attached to the wall, "one of those is black and the other has a little cream."

She took the black one, but only to move it near, where it sat ignored. "Why am I here?"

As he replied, he slowly doctored his own coffee with sugar packets from his pocket. The folder lay closed and forgotten by his side.

"Well, first off, you are not under arrest and can leave anytime you want. I wanted us to meet here so we wouldn't be interrupted." He turned on a digital recorder, earlier placed on the table, explaining, "I also wanted to make sure there would be no interruptions or misunderstandings later about what would be said between us today. All my cards are on the table, as I'm hoping yours will be, too."

She let slip a patently false chuckle, accompanied by, "Why wouldn't they be?"

"Well, there's the problem, Peggy. You've probably heard that the police often take an especially close look at the spouse of a murdered person."

She stared at him, now expressing horror. "Murdered person? Gene?"

"Oh yes." Joe pulled out a narrow wooden stirrer and put it to use. "Made to look like an accident. In fact, made to look like an accident disguising a murder implicating someone innocent. That was quite clever. A form of double feint."

"But Gene tripped or something."

"No," Joe said firmly, looking at her over his glasses. "He did not. I think you know that, Peggy, and I think you regret it."

Here he was drawing on Sam's feedback of her two conversations with the woman, during which she'd stated that Peggy had not only appeared inconsolable, but that her sorrow had seemed believable.

"That's not true," Peggy protested.

He took a sip of his coffee. "We'll be getting to what's true soon enough," he said. "There's a progression to these things, and the first step is usually sorting through the denials and smoke screens. It's perfectly natural, and I'm very comfortable to go that way if you like. What you've done, after all, is a terrible thing. You allowed a problem that once had several solutions to become a disaster."

She opened her mouth to speak, but Joe motioned her to stay silent. One style to these interviews was to stop the suspect from getting a word in, building up their frustration and anxiety while painting them ever tighter into a corner. It was also a way to stop them denying anything, which they might otherwise see as a good habit.

"That's a shame, of course. Rash responses to your kind of problem usually go wrong, being based on impulse and impatience. They're also usually arrived at when two people feed off each other's emotions, which is what happened to you." He looked up from his coffee to take her in, as he hoped her grandfather might have done. "When did things start going sour between you and Gene, Peggy?"

Again, he didn't let her answer. "Not that it matters in the end. The heart gets distracted. Gene no longer held the appeal he once did. The reasons get lost. Could've been the pottery becoming like a mistress. That combined with the baby arriving must have been stressful. All your time taken up with little Mark, and Gene either running the business or throwing pots at night, in search of inner peace, or a return to simplicity, or who knows what, right? I mean, here was this handsome, wealthy, smart young man, nice and well mannered, who'd won your heart, suddenly turning into a workaholic philosopher who found more peace of mind in wet clay than in spending time with you."

"You're wrong," she managed, without much conviction. "I loved Gene."

He ignored her, pressing on. "So what would anyone do? Big house, money pouring out of the plumbing, other people milling about. People like Mike, for instance. He's a relative, works and lives in the building, shows empathy for your situation. He's married to Michelle—hardly anyone's choice for nicest person in the room. She even freely admits she regularly cheats on him. You're a good person. I would guess you were the first to show support, maybe after a public blowup between the two of them. Isn't that about right? Something like that."

He kept brushing past her protesting body language, sensitive to her eyes welling up. "I bet you can't even remember who made the first move. It's hard when two people think they're a match. It just sort of happens."

Now, as he spoke, he unobtrusively opened the folder by his hand and extracted the top photograph. This he slid over so she could see the shot of her and Mike kissing in the garage.

"It's heady stuff, new love, illicit love," he continued. "It fills the head and the heart, takes up all your time."

She was staring at the picture, tears running down her face. He wasn't sure she was listening to him. He pulled out a phone bill with one number highlighted two dozen times on a single sheet and placed it on top of the photo.

"The cell phone becomes glued to your hand, so you can make calls or receive them. You don't talk about big things. Sometimes, you don't talk at all. You just listen to each other's breathing. It's being close when you can't physically hold each other."

He added a still from a second video, of the two of them holding hands at a restaurant, in a far corner, where the lighting as usual was bad. But good enough for now.

"There is one common topic that keeps circling around, though," he suggested. "Again and again. Besides the sex, of course." He chuckled. This time, he produced a picture of Michelle with her daughter, Debbie, in the playground at the mill. But Michelle was yelling at her daughter, her features contorted by rage.

"The two of you talked about Gene and Michelle," Joe stated. "A lot. There, I'm thinking Mike did most of it, given Michelle's built-in short fuse. You did love Gene, remembering the early years. I doubt that was true for Mike. He may have worked with Michelle, but he ended up hating her." He touched Michelle's angry features with his fingertip.

Joe slid across another picture, not too graphic, of Gene's pottery studio on the day his body was found. There were cops, official vehicles visible through the windows, police tape strung everywhere.

"And then this," he said simply.

At last, he paused, allowing her to yield to her sobbing, as Sam had told him she would.

"Tell me," he asked her, "about the conversation you and Mike had after this." He tapped the last picture also.

"I felt so guilty," she managed between wiping her eyes and blowing her nose. "Like somehow I was responsible. Gene was a nice man. I didn't want anything bad to happen to him. I was just *lonely*."

"And how did Mike feel?"

She hesitated.

"Sad, but a little relieved, too?" Joe suggested.

She nodded, mopping up a renewed flow of tears.

"I've got to ask you, Peggy, since I just told you how we're treating Gene's death: Did you or Mike have anything to do with what happened to him?"

Her head jerked up, and she stared wide-eyed at him. "Nooooo. I told you. It was so awful. But when you started asking questions, we got so scared."

"*You* got scared, or both of you did?"

Again, either to her credit or because she lacked the guile to be devious, she merely stared at him, speechless.

Joe spared her having to make something up. "I need to know what you and Mike talked about after Gene's death, Peggy. I get it that you were sad and bewildered. But now that Gene was dead, the future began to look very different. Isn't that right?"

Her voice was as soft as a child's. "Yes."

Joe used the old ploy of shifting his chair closer, ramping up the intimacy of the moment, along with a hint of threat. "I suspect Mike's frustrations about Michelle increased. Would that be fair to say?"

She was silent again, sniffling and crying.

"He's in a tough spot," Joe suggested. "He's in love, fate has handed him an astonishing gift with Gene's death. Didn't he say how nice it would be if what had happened to you happened to him, too?"

She nodded again.

"Yes?" he asked for the microphone's sake.

"Yes," she repeated.

"Tell me about that," he requested.

"He said fate had played a hand in our favor, and that maybe putting a little weight on the scale couldn't hurt."

Joe repressed any visceral reaction, keeping his voice calm and steady, despite the urge to respond, "I bet he did."

Instead, he used her own metaphor to extract the truth. "Did you ever think, Peggy, that Mike played a hand in Gene's fate? In any way?"

"No."

"But from what I'm hearing, the same is not true for Michelle."

Again, she nodded.

"Are you saying he caused her death?"

"Yes."

He couldn't be sure the mic had picked that up.

"I'm sorry, Peggy. What?"

Louder. "Yes."

He reached out and touched her hand. She turned it over, her eyes fixed on the tabletop, and squeezed his fingers.

He took that as a good sign. "I'm so sorry you got caught up in this," he said. "Things gained momentum, until you couldn't stop them."

"He made it sound so reasonable," she admitted.

"He talked about the kids," he suggested sympathetically.

She looked up again, as if he were reading her thoughts. "Yes. How they already knew and liked each other. It would be the easiest thing in the world. We wouldn't even have to move. Nothing would really change."

Except Michelle would have been murdered, he thought.

Pursuing that notion, he said, "I get that you two were in love, that Michelle was difficult, and that Gene's death opened the door. But killing the one remaining obstacle seems extreme unless Mike had something extra motivating him—he could've just divorced her."

It was the proverbial shot in the dark, with nothing to lose as a consequence. They had the DNA evidence that Lester had secured, linking Debbie to her true father. But a verbal corroboration was always a plus.

"You were right about her cheating on him," Peggy said.

Joe played it out. "Okay."

Her voice dropped again as she admitted, "Debbie's not really his."

Joe rephrased that for the microphone. "You're saying Mike and his daughter are not genetically related?"

"That's right. Debbie was Nathan's. Mike told me that's how Michelle was always guaranteed a big slice of the pie, even if they were no longer married. That's why he killed her. He hated her for sleeping with his father."

My God, Joe thought. Psychopathy ran in the family.

He threw out a hook for his final damning piece of confirmation. "You mentioned Mike said how he might put a little weight on the scale. Did he give you the details of what he was planning?"

She put her elbows on the table and wearily buried her face in her hands. Joe waited patiently, a stoical angler sensing his reward within reach.

"Yes," she told him, her guilt now overwhelming her cauldron of other emotions.

"Okay. Let's get into that."

CHAPTER NINETEEN

"You see this?"

Fredo handed the newspaper to Eddie, open at the front page, second section. He'd taken it from the counter in the hotel lobby as they were heading out on their evening reconnaissance. Later, parked out of sight and in the darkness near the mill, he'd used a penlight to scan its pages, coming to an abrupt and chilling halt at the article he now proffered to Eddie.

"What?" Eddie took the paper and squinted at it until Fredo lent him the light.

"It's a piece about Nick, or Nathan, as they call him here. It says the medical examiner's office just changed his death certificate to homicide. The reporter mentions Rhode Island, his working with the Outfit, the whole setup over there." He pointed to the hulking building across the street, which they'd been watching for half an hour.

"You're shittin' me," Eddie said, reading. "Talk about a small world."

"More like a crowded one," Fredo said, mostly to himself.

He waited until his cousin had finished before asking, "What do you think?"

"'Bout what? That they got most of it wrong, like usual? They make him sound like a big shot, when hardly nobody knew who he was in the day. Just another bloodsucker."

"Yeah, well, a buck down there and a buck up here are different," Fredo replied. "This is the boonies. I was kinda wondering if that"—he tapped the paper in Eddie's hand—"changes things for us."

Sadly but predictably, Eddie stared at him wide-eyed. "How?"

"All the attention, the cops, the family with their eyes open. Won't be so simple walkin' in there pretending we're from the gas company or somethin'."

"I say we were gonna do that? They don't say the cops know who killed the son of a bitch, do they?"

"No," Fredo reluctantly conceded.

Eddie shook the paper. "Then none of this means shit. They're all still scratching their heads, and we don't care who did him in." He returned his attention to the mill. "We'll go in after dark. The place don't need a can opener to get in. I doubt they even lock up. Says here they all have different apartments inside, so what we *do* need to find is who lives where. I don't wanna knock on twenty doors asking if Monica's there."

Fredo gave up arguing. "Then I guess it's back to more homework tomorrow morning."

It was a squad-wide decision to invite Diane Lints to join Willy in interrogating Rob Lyon, thereby honoring her efforts as the initial investigator.

The three of them met in the same bland, gray room where Willy had worn down Corey Ryder. In this instance, the table had been repositioned to place Diane and Willy on one side and Rob on the other. In a near parody of Joe's performance with Peggy, both detectives had multiple closed folders before them, which experience had taught them were worth their weight in intimidation.

In some circumstances, putting on a show was key to success.

Not, however, that all the contents of those files were fodder. As Willy stated after introducing everyone for the recording and having Rob read and sign his Miranda waiver—always a hurdle every cop worked to make boringly procedural—"You, Mr. Lyon, have turned out to be the keeper of a great many family secrets."

Rob made a dismissive face. "I'd hardly call our financial intricacies that. Not to mention that you people have had ample time to plow through them. I'd say you know more than I do by now."

"Probably more than you're comfortable with," Willy agreed. "Nevertheless, Detective Lints and I were hoping you'd be willing to guide us through some of the murkier corners."

"Have I turned you down yet?" Rob asked.

"No, you've been very helpful."

Willy pulled out a document for reference, not letting Rob see its contents. "Given how you and Ms. Tardy are the only ones who date back to Rhode Island, I'd like to start there, just to keep in the right picture frame. From your perspective, what did Nathan Lyon—or Nick Bianchi in those days—do for a living?"

"He operated a food supply business."

"Was it legit?"

Rob barely reacted, his usual poker face in place. "It was never deemed otherwise by the authorities."

"He was never caught."

"This is your fantasy, Agent Kunkle. You can put whatever spin on it you'd like."

"How would you describe his associates?"

"The people who worked for him?"

"More the ones he worked with. Vito Alfano, his dad, Knuckles Alfano, Al Zucco. People like that."

"They came and went. I had other things on my mind."

"Right. Vito more than came and went, though, didn't he? He worked there."

"I was a kid," Rob protested. "I didn't know about any of that."

"You were eighteen at the end. Older than Nick when he started out."

"Is that a question?"

"It's a suggestion that Nick Bianchi wouldn't have tolerated a snot-nosed teenager around the house, loafing around. What did he have you do?"

Rob smiled. "I was a grunt. You're right. He wanted me to learn the business or how to run a business in general. He didn't seem to care about my inheriting his. So I shadowed the bookkeepers, the warehouse and shipping department, purchasing, the executive suite."

"What did you learn about his arrangements with the Mob?"

Rob's reply was unhesitating. "Nothing. That was off-limits. That's what I meant earlier."

"Did Vito's activities fit in there?"

"I wouldn't know. Vito was the special projects manager. I never found out what that meant. It was an important department, but separate. My reading was that's how Nick honored his obligation to Knuckles and Zucco, while keeping Vito out of his hair."

"No love lost?"

"They hated each other."

"Did Nick kill him?"

"No."

"How can you be sure? Nick's dead. It's not like it matters to him anymore."

Rob reflected on that key point. "Maybe he did."

"Why did you say 'no' first?"

"Because the police caught someone. Put him in jail."

"How about Vito?" Willy asked. "Did he try to kill Nick? Shoot him?"

Rob frowned. His surprise seemed genuine. Given what investigators had been told about Nick's keeping the injury private, Willy found Rob's ignorance credible.

"What do you know?" Rob asked.

"More than you think. Could be more than you do, from how it sounds. What did you think of Vito?"

"I didn't know him enough to say. I was prejudiced against him because of my father, but he never did me any harm."

"Tell me about your mother."

"Nothing to tell. I was told a one-night stand."

"The name Sarah Lucas mean anything to you?"

It wasn't much. At best, the tiniest reaction in a corner of one eye, but it was something.

"No."

Willy glanced at Diane, who pulled two sheets from the folder before her and spread them out.

Willy referred to them. "You know what these are?"

Rob almost reluctantly bent forward to read. "I'm guessing DNA results?"

"Very good. They're proof that Vito Alfano was your father. He was carrying on with Nick's girlfriend, Sarah, and you were the end result."

Rob straightened slowly, his brain obviously teeming but his features frozen. After a long and telling silence, he said, "Doesn't matter. Nick behaved as my father. That's good enough for me."

"Did you like Gene?" Willy asked, seemingly out of the blue.

To Willy's watchful eye, Rob's response was too calculated. "Sure. What's not to like?"

"Who do you think killed him?"

"No one. I only heard you think he was murdered."

"Humor me. Who would want to kill him?"

Again, Willy sensed Rob's brain in overdrive. His hopes were to hit this man with enough questions from so many directions that a crack would break the dam.

"Michelle," Rob finally ventured.

"Why her?" Willy shot back, intrigued by the suggestion.

"They never liked each other. Gene certainly told me so. I guess now we'll never know."

The segue to an obvious follow-up question hung in the air, but instead of asking for more details, Willy tossed out, "Did you like her?"

"No."

"Why not?"

"She was a gold digger. Gene was right."

Willy stored that away. He liked the term for its possibilities. Often in these exchanges, the suspect used a code to stand in for the truth, hoping—like thin ice—it would prove strong enough to support him if he moved fast enough.

But Willy intended to bring him back there after he'd weighted him down with more baggage.

This time, he did opt for the natural follow-up question. "What was it between Gene and Michelle? He seemed like the ultimate laid-back dude."

"That's selling him short. He was a man of principle. A bit of a prude, perhaps. Michelle was everything he held in contempt—a cheat, a crook, a liar, a thief. I think his feelings were obvious enough that she might have killed him."

How convenient, Willy thought. Doubtless, Rob was cutting close to reality, describing Gene's rigid sense of right and wrong, but he'd done so to imbue Gene with a vindictiveness he'd never possessed. It was a subtle tarnishing of the truth.

It did, however, fit those mysterious kiss-and-tell pictures that they'd found on Gene's laptop, along with the vaguely worded email to Michelle—none of which had ever led anywhere, including to Michelle's computer as the recipient. As with her thumbprint on the rolling pin, they seem to have appeared as if by magic.

"So, in your version," Willy continued, "Michelle got sick of Gene one night, wandered down the corridor, and knocked him upside the head?"

"You asked me to hypothesize. I just knew they didn't like each other."

Willy veered off again. "Speaking of love and hate, it must've been pretty heady for you in Rhode Island as a kid. Nathan had the juice, mobsters wandering the hallways, attractive women coming and going. And there you were, the reputed son of the boss."

"I told you. I was a grunt."

"Tell me about Monica."

Rob blinked, caught off guard. "What about her?"

"She was a knockout. Your age, too. You were in love."

Rob sat back and crossed his arms. "Nonsense. She was Nathan's girl."

Willy smiled and pointed at him. "You sure you don't want to curl up into a ball? Talk about body language."

Rob uncrossed his arms. "You're wrong."

"It's okay," Willy reassured him. "Perfectly natural she and you would couple up. How would either of you know the old man favored her, too?"

"They got married," Rob said with too much emphasis. "They had Gene."

Willy pressed him. "That's the fable, anyway. You and Monica are doing your thing, up pops Nick, nature takes its course, and she gets pregnant. Then why all the rigamarole with her pulling a vanishing act and ditching the kid? I heard the cover story about a husband and having to be discreet. Total crap. She was already sleeping with you and Nick, both. Husband be damned. Plus, Nick could do what he liked. The Mob was covering his ass."

"You keep saying Monica and I were an item," Rob almost interrupted. "That's not true. There was no *me* in your fantasy."

"We've been to Little Rhody, Rob," Willy told him. "We've done our spade work. You and Monica aren't make believe. We *know* you were the original item, and we know Nick stole her from you."

Rob was shaking his head. "You're making this up. I'm sorry."

Willy slid another printout over to him. "We're not making *this* up. It's genetic proof Gene was your baby with Monica."

Watching Rob's face brought Willy up short. Not for theatrics or shouted outbursts. The man had spent too many decades under emotional wraps for that. He had, after all, chosen to stay with the woman he'd loved and lost to his so-called father as an unmarried factotum to them both. He'd assumed the mantle of a Jeeves-like butler and manager, choosing proximity to one while loathing the other, instead of walking away and creating a life for himself. In short, he'd sacrificed for the two closest people he'd ever known and who'd fundamentally betrayed him.

All without knowing the truth about Gene.

Willy studied his eyes, his sudden pallor, more remarkably, how the life seemed to drain from his body. Rob appeared to have died right before them.

Suddenly unsure of the ground ahead, Willy still needed to hear more. He hadn't even gotten to what he had against this man.

True to character, he went for the direct approach. "Sucks to be you, Rob. Son of a man who's not your father, brother of another who turns out to be your kid. And there's Monica in the middle of it. Did she know? Did she collude with Nick or Nathan or whatever the hell you call him to keep you in the dark while you acted like their servant?"

Rob stayed silent.

Willy forged ahead, spreading out scene photos of the staged bicycle accident from his file folder. "The famous evening Nathan called you about Penny forcing the bike rider off the road, for instance. Once again, the old man messing with people's lives, only now he's too old to do the heavy lifting himself. So who's he call? Good ol' dependable Rob. And who jumps at the command?"

Moments earlier, he'd have expected Rob to protest, but now he was playing to a catatonic audience.

He therefore went for the grand reveal, no longer sure of what impact it might have. He placed a photograph of the bike helmet before Rob.

"You messed up," he continued. "It was after dark, Nathan's call came out of the blue, it was probably one of the weirdest requests he'd ever asked of you. But you did your best, as usual. Only this time"—he patted the photo—"you forgot to wear gloves. You left your fingerprints behind, and we ended up keeping the helmet. Bummer."

Rob finally moved. He picked up the picture, scanned it as if it were a map, and allowed for a smile.

Willy was unsure what that meant. "Something amusing?"

Rob's voice was unnaturally calm, perhaps another reflection of his years of duplicity. "I was just thinking that I never saw this coming. Not this. It was just another piece of dirty work."

Diane's voice, coming so late in the conversation, was curiously soothing—soft, low, carefully enunciated, and graced by concern. "You didn't know about Gene, did you?"

Rob took her in as if she'd just shimmered into sight. "No."

"Was the bicyclist still alive when you found him?" she asked.

It was a nice move, earning Willy's admiration, touching on Rob's real sense of loss before springboarding to something almost trivial by comparison.

"Yes. Nathan finished him off with a rock. A dead bicyclist was just that; a wounded one would've had a story to tell and deprived Nathan of leverage over Penny. This was a gift to the old bastard. I just did the lifting and tidying up, as always."

"You drove there together that night?"

"Yes. Well, Penny needed someone to drive her home. She was too messed up by then."

"You must've been Nathan's first thought," she reflected.

His tone was reflective. "Indeed."

Willy shifted to better observe his colleague. The gesture encouraged her to continue.

"That's always been how you served them best, Nathan and Monica, the reckless people you loved."

"They're what I had," he confessed, from some inner space only he could see.

"And there was Gene all along," she prompted him. "The product of the love of your life, attributed by his own mother to a man who wasn't even your father. You must be feeling pretty empty right now. Used again by the people you devoted your life to."

Willy was thinking the "love of your life" line a little much, until it yielded Rob's comeback.

"You have no idea."

"Tell me," Diane urged him.

He sighed deeply before beginning, unburdening for the first time ever, she imagined. "Nathan slept with Michelle, too. That's where Debbie came from. She even paid for a DNA test to prove it. Michelle was made of tougher stuff than Penny and the others. She used Debbie to extract money from Nathan, and after he died, from Monica, threatening to go public and ruin the child, the business, and the family. It was a small price to Monica, but I hated Michelle for it. It was one grab too many. I wanted to weave a web like she'd done, and put her where she'd lose everything she craved."

Both cops waited, their show of patience belying the excitement of finally reaching a confession.

Diane yielded first. "What did you do?"

Rob passed his hand across his face. Gone was the semi-automaton, the icy Mr. Fix-It that Penny Trick had assaulted at the bar. Instead, they were faced with a bereft, conflicted, lonely orphan, his shell demolished and his mourning stark.

"I set out to frame her for Gene's murder, getting her to hold the rolling pin, planting photos of her and some boyfriend on Gene's laptop, along with an email from him. You were supposed to peel back layer after layer, and I was going to have clues waiting for you along the way, building the case against her."

He smiled in despair. "But then she died. And now you tell me I killed my own son as well. Talk about the last laugh."

Willy matched his voice to Diane's soothing tone. "Why Gene, of all people?"

Rob was crying by now. "You wouldn't get it, not being part of this family. But smack in the middle of all the egotism—the cheating, lying, and killing—Gene was like an island of decency and modesty. I came to loathe him, for being what I'd been denied. Nathan saw those qualities early on, and made sure to take care of him, maybe as compensation for being such a prick himself. Who knows? But I never could overcome my jealousy. Then, out of the blue, here it was, my opportunity to eliminate the two symbols I despised the most, framing bad apple Michelle for the murder of Saint Gene."

"You not only killed your own son," Diane said, "you killed the heritage you aspired to for yourself."

Willy couldn't resist adding, "Which the love of your life never told you was yours."

Diane had reached her fill. In breach of protocol, she quietly rose and murmured, "I'm done," and left the room.

Willy let a few seconds elapse while he and Rob separately took stock of the havoc clinging to the air around them.

"Tell me something," Willy then said, feeling like a janitor. "Since we're on the subject, did you also happen to kill the man you thought was your father?"

"No. I wouldn't have dared."

"And another thing. We've found a dozen closed-circuit cameras around the mill, but no recorder. It's like that part of the system was thrown out—probably for good reason. You were the building's majordomo. Can you tell me about that?"

Rob slumped in his chair, his face damp, his eyes red. "I'll do you one better," he said tiredly. "I'll show it to you. I keep it tucked away for good measure. It's like a perverted family album."

CHAPTER TWENTY

Eddie reminded Fredo of a hunting dog, or the cartoon version he knew, given how much he'd seen of actual hunting. Despite Eddie's age, weight, and lumbering gait, he was as poised and eager as if straining against a leash.

Fredo reached out with a gloved hand and touched his cousin's shoulder, whispering, "Relax. We got the whole night."

Eddie brushed him off, growling, "Shut up," without looking back.

Fredo didn't fault him. This was it, after all. The Holy Grail, the Fountain of Whatever. For reasons that had long since left Fredo in the dark, Eddie needed to see Monica Tardy face-to-face, and through her confront the ghost of Nick Bianchi. Nick had been the untouchable centerpiece in Eddie's melodrama, the source of his misguided life plan and all its resulting woes. Perhaps, Fredo thought, his cousin just needed to express some of that loss to the one bit actor still living.

And, as he'd reflected since this began, Fredo felt honor-bound to be the story's Sancho Panza, through thick or thin. Thankfully, while he wished they weren't crouching in the darkness outside the rear of the mill, Fredo believed with more faith than before that they were finally on the cusp of dissolving this obsession.

"Okay," Eddie hissed back at him, stepping inside after jimmying the door lock. "We're in."

The good news was it was late enough that they could hear nothing beyond the building's muted thrumming of pumps, fans, ventilators, and inner workings, sounding like a monster's gentle breathing. The unknown factor was that any place this upscale had to have security cameras, none of which were visible.

But it was dim along the corridors, there probably wasn't anyone watching monitors, and by this point, it was unclear whether Fredo or Eddie gave a damn anymore. So much time, energy, and emotional capital had been expended to get this far, that they were behaving like exhausted marathoners, more interested in crossing the line than in gaining any prize.

They avoided the elevators and stealthily worked their way up, one broad staircase at a time, feeling like mice being watched by unseen cats. But old mice, having to pause at each landing to catch their breaths and cool down. Still, the covert nature of their mission helped pump their adrenaline, compensating not only for their poor conditioning, but also perhaps for the niggling absurdity that they were here at all, chasing down ancient ghosts.

At long last, they found themselves on the fifth floor, unashamedly leaning against the railing for a brief rest.

"This it?" Fredo gasped.

"You saw that magazine article about this dump at the library," Eddie whispered back. "What do *you* think?"

Fredo eyed the front door of Monica's apartment. "So, what now?"

It was a fair question. Shy of smashing through a door that might be built of reinforced steel, they were reduced to either ringing the bell or twisting the knob.

This was now all Eddie's show. Fredo was backup only. As a result, Eddie straightened, shook out his coat, muttered, "What the fuck," and walked up to the door.

It swung soundlessly open under his hand. Like the kid Fredo had known so long ago, he flashed a grin over his shoulder and entered.

There was a subtle, delicate, almost imperceptible fragrance in the air, different from the air-scrubbed environment they'd just left. It consisted of gentle hints of perfume, furniture wax and leather, lingering gourmet food, and herbal sachets, all touching their noses with the subtlety of a flower's aroma.

The smell of money, to Fredo.

The room they entered was baronial in size, soaring, spread out, and gently lighted through some of the largest picture windows either man had ever seen. The curtains were open, and the night's full moon poured its monochromatic liquid light across a collection of tables, sofas, and rugs suitable for a museum.

Both men stopped in their tracks, momentarily arrested by the sight.

Eddie, however, was inexorable, and resumed plodding forward like a flat-footed tourist working his way through a palace, Fredo resignedly in tow.

At the room's far end, they discovered a hallway with a kitchen to one side, facing what appeared to be a near endless row of closets. It took them to another door, this one ajar, and finally into a bedroom large enough to house six cars.

Against the distant wall, near another broad window, was an enormous bed. In its middle, seemingly fast asleep, the shape of a human body.

Fredo looked around the room, suddenly and inexplicably uneasy. At the same moment, Eddie changed stride, from soundlessly gliding from room to room, as circumstances dictated, to simply walking up to the foot of the bed, squaring his shoulders, and pulling out a handgun.

"What the hell're—" Fredo blurted out in alarm.

He didn't get to finish. In a flash card–fast series of images, he saw the room flooded with light, the sudden emergence of eight black-clad, screaming men wearing masks and brandishing weapons, and finally, Eddie, his face white and open-mouthed, turning in surprise, swinging his gun toward them.

The rest had the finality of a loose shutter slamming in a high wind. Screams of "Police," "Show your hands," "Get on the ground," all entered Fredo's head as if muffled by miles of distance, dulled by the loudest sound of all, of gunfire reducing Eddie to a pile of clothing on the rug.

It was later. Fredo was back in the living room, with the lights now on, sitting in a hardback chair by the central table. He'd already been searched, cuffed, and Mirandized. People were walking back and forth in a businesslike manner, some dressed in Tyvek and carrying equipment, others not. He rubbed his sore wrists absentmindedly.

Opposite him, also seated, was an older man with kind eyes, looking a little rumpled in a worn jacket and loosened tie, the dawning hour not seeming to trouble him.

"Better?" he asked.

"Yeah," Fredo said. "Thanks."

The man indicated the others milling about, explaining, "Well, you know how it is. Gotta follow procedure till the dust settles, just to document what happened."

"Sure."

"How long you been in town?"

Fredo was surprised into an honest reply. "Two days."

"You like the Latchis?"

"What?"

"Where you were staying. It's kind of the crown jewel of downtown, even if it is a little funky. I've never stayed there, being local. I was wondering how it was."

"Fine. They have a record player in the room."

The man laughed softly and stuck his hand out. "I heard that. Neat. My name's Gunther. Joe Gunther. I kind of run this bunch."

Fredo shook the hand. "Okay."

"I'm sorry about your cousin," Gunther said. "He didn't give us much choice."

"I didn't know," Fredo said.

"About the gun?"

"Or really what we were doing here."

"He paid for Nick Bianchi's killing of Vito. Did he ever meet Nick in person?"

Fredo scowled thoughtfully, astonished by what this man seemed to know. "Maybe once," he admitted.

"But he knew Bianchi was dead. What did he want with the man's widow?"

Fredo glanced in the direction of the bedroom.

Joe commented, "She was never there. We put pillows under the covers."

Fredo said, "He just couldn't let it go. I thought he wanted to talk to her. Maybe ask for money. I didn't even know he *had* a gun. That's never what we were about, in the day."

"Still," Joe reflected. "You didn't stop him from coming here."

The other man shrugged. "He was like a dog with a bone."

"Which you could've prevented. You had that power, Mr. Sindaco."

Fredo froze at Joe's formal tone and the implication of what was coming.

"I did what I could," he answered cautiously.

"Except tell him the truth."

They eyed each other, two men sharing an insight as yet unspoken, fully aware of what was about to come.

On cue, Joe removed a printed video still and placed it on the table beside Fredo, who glanced at it. It was a shadowy image of him bending over the bed of an older man at night, his hands around the other's neck.

"Ring a bell?" Joe asked. "You think your cousin might've liked knowing tonight wasn't the first time you'd been here?"

Joe had long ago given up anticipating people's reactions under stress. Types he thought would be hysterical remained calm; others wigged out for no reason. You could never tell. Fredo Sindaco remained steady, if vividly consumed by grief and regret.

He shook his head. "I tried telling him to let it go. They were all dead, for Christ's sake. It was over. I couldn't believe it when he wanted to go toe-to-toe with the widow. She had nuthin' to do with any of it." He paused. "And then he pulls a gun. Dumb bastard."

He looked up at Joe, genuinely curious. "How'd you know we were coming?"

"You learned where Nick had moved from an old secretary of his. She called a reporter friend of mine who told me. All we had to do was wait." He pointed at the picture. "The whole building is wired for video. Always has been. It was Bianchi who got you in the end, with his need to know and manage everything. He, and later his son, had recordings going back years. You were a marked man from the beginning."

Joe retrieved the incriminating picture.

"As was Nick," he added. "You could strangle him because Monica had been dosing him nightly with bedtime milkshakes laced with Benadryl, to keep him from disturbing her in the middle of the night."

He rotated the print between his fingers. "There is one detail I'd like you to confirm. Why did you kill Bianchi? I only have a theory right now."

"What if you're wrong?" Fredo countered. "You'd be asking me to incriminate myself."

Joe nodded. "That tells me a lot right here. But I'll play along, since we already got you on this." He gestured with the print. "My theory is you stuck with Eddie through all this because of your own guilty conscience. You're the missing link. You're the one who killed Vito Alfano, by order of Nick himself."

Fredo looked disgusted. "Goddamned Nick. All flash and no balls. He let Vito screw his girlfriend, Sarah, and then couldn't settle it man-to-man. He had to contract it out. Yeah, that was me. Off the books. Nick wasn't Family, and I was no hit man. But the money was good, and I figured what the hell. Vito was a jerk. I didn't care. And then everything went haywire. Out of the blue, there's Eddie standing up for what I did. How was I supposed to know Al Zucco got sick of Vito's skimming? Why did he even care after all those years?"

"That's not why Zucco went after him," Joe said, this weight of unbridled hubris and hate finally pulling him down.

Fredo blinked at him a couple of times. "It wasn't?"

"Vito dumped Zucco's daughter after sleeping with her. She cut her wrists. That's why Vito ran out of rope. He'd crossed the line into Zucco's own family."

Fredo's eyes widened. "Eddie always said there was somethin' else. No wonder those guys needed a fall guy. The cops mighta figured that out."

"How did Eddie get involved?"

Fredo was still digesting what Joe had told him. His response was a monotone. "It was family for him, too. He thought it was his chance to take care of Marie, his daughter. But nobody gave a shit. I knew in my gut he'd be screwed after he got out. I even went back to Nick after the Vito contract, said I'd waive my fee if he made sure Eddie was taken care of later. He told me he would, but you know how that turned out. It took me years after he blew town, before I found him. And you're right: I killed him. Son of a bitch."

"All of which you could have told Eddie," Joe repeated.

"Yeah, yeah, yeah. If this, if that. Tonight coulda turned out fine if the dumb bastard hadn't brought a gun. We woulda got nuthin' from the woman and gone home. What the hell was he thinking?"

"I don't know, Mr. Sindaco," Joe told him. "Maybe just once he wanted to do something for himself, instead of being pushed around, even if it was a little crazy."

Fredo sat with his hands in his lap, looking at the floor. "Could be," he conceded. "And why should this be different than the rest of it? There's nuthin' nobodies like us can do. You talk about me being a marked man. No more than Eddie or most people I know. Even Nick Bianchi, when you get down to it. We all make choices; we all gotta live with the consequences."

He studied Joe, exhausted and resigned. "I do know one thing. I will miss him. He was my best friend."

Joe resisted voicing what he thought of people invoking friendship and family, or living with the consequences of their own actions, when they were more than ready to game all three when it suited.

He rose instead without a word, nodded to a nearby officer to remove Fredo, and returned to work.